Chasing Reality

POWER SOURCE

Ted Jonsson

Copyright © 2016 Ted Jonsson

Acknowledgements

I would like to thank all my friends who have encouraged me to write the Chasing Reality series.

Thank you to the prize-winner of the 1000 Kilos promotion, who got to name a character in the book - Scott C. VanDaley.

There is someone in your life that you do all of this for, and that will never change. Thanks, Tiffany. My inspiration, my friend.

A special thanks to *you* for reading my novel.

Chapter 1

South-West England - 2253

Jonathan Prescott paced up and down his ten by twelve office muttering to himself, his rage reaching boiling point. Sitting back at his desk, he grabbed the phone and dialled Chris King, his number two at Prescott Nuclear Fusions.

"This government official, Scott C. VanDaley, is giving me a major headache. He's determined to stop the new plant from being built at Thatchers Rock. Did you manage to arrange that surveillance I asked for?"

"Five live feeds in and around his home and another two in the cave as you requested. I'm just sending you the link," Chris King replied.

"I know he's up to something," Prescott continued, his impatience apparent, "VanDaley and his two daughters seem to visit the cave quite often, there has to be something inside," Prescott opened the link King had just sent to him.

"Anything said in the past three days has been recorded. Not much though, apart from a reference concerning a date in 2003 and their responsibility to guard to cave. But our guy who put in the surveillance couldn't find anything inside."

"There has to be a better way," Prescott snapped. "What about the committee?"

"Our contact there has the information concerning the three current members with dirty laundry who are voting against the plant. I'm dealing with that, but it may not be in time for the next vote," King waited for the explosion.

"Then we must find a way to stop VanDaley which will cause the committee to fall apart," Prescott shouted. "I want this build to commence in six weeks."

"I can't get any dirt on VanDaley, he's squeaky clean. I could start some sort of smear campaign..."

Prescott interrupted, "No, it needs to be a permanent solution. I'll deal with it."

"What are you planning to do?" King asked.

"Best you don't know," Prescott opened his draw, reaching inside for his ten-shot semi-automatic sig-saucer.

"I'll continue to gather dirt on these committee members," King said, deciding it best not to question his boss. Jonathan Prescott had a reputation for getting the job done at any cost, and with so much riding on it, he would stop at nothing to get what he wanted.

Prescott flicked the magazine out and checked it was full, slipping it back in and checking the safety was on, "Okay, do what you have to do to make that happen. I'll call you later," hanging up.

Pocketing the thirty-eight, he headed out of his temporary office in Newtown Village, taking the walkway to the central tower and the monorail to the north car park. He flicked the remote on his key-fob and the door to his solar powered all electric Ferrari GTE two seater sports-car swung open. He climbed inside and placed his thumb on the ID pad, the door swung shut and the instrument panel lit up.

Accelerating away at speed, he headed for Thatchers Rock, knowing what he was attempting to do would change everything - if it worked.

The traffic was light and he arrived there twenty minutes later. Parking the car up the road a bit and out of site, he made his way down to the slippery path, careful not to fall. Stepping onto a ledge, which led to the cave, he made his way to the entrance. Once he was inside, he headed for the rear cavern.

Finding a suitable spot, Prescott waited, knowing Scott VanDaley or one of his daughters were sure to come along real soon. That's when he would make his move.

He didn't have to wait long.

Scott VanDaley rinsed out his mug, placing it on the drainer, "Lucy," he shouted.

"Coming Dad," she replied, flicking off the TV with the remote.

"I'm going to the rock. I may not be back till tomorrow. Emily will be back later I'm sure."

"If she can get her nose out of her new book," Lucy said.

"Publishers want it done by month end," Scott said. "You know your sister, quite the perfectionist."

Lucy gave Scott a hug, "See you later, be careful."

"Always am, princess," he scuffed her head playfully.

Heading out of the big ranch style property onto the main road, Scott walked the half mile to Thatchers Rock. Arriving there that morning in May, he stood at the cliff edge overlooking the south-west coast. The view out to sea was crystal clear and the reflection created by the sun made the water glisten a silvery blue, whilst the waves gently rolled into the small cove below. At the far end of the cove, an unusual rock formation appeared as though it was growing out of the water, and this created a small island before disappearing back into the sea. This had always been a favourite spot for Scott. The view being quite magnificent.

But this was all about to change.

With the Earth's natural resources running low, the ever-unpopular nuclear energy seemed to be the only known way forward to power the country. New nuclear plants had been springing up on the north, west and east coast of England and had quickly been followed by others on the south-east coast.

Now it was the turn of the south-west.

Jonathan Prescott, the nuclear plant owner, was seeking approval to build a new power plant right where Scott stood. The impact on the surrounding beauty would be intolerable, not to mention all homes within a two-mile radius, including Scott's, would be part of a compulsory purchase plan and destroyed to make way for the new plant.

Scott wasn't just a concerned homesteader; he was the local governments planning committee officer and his planning group were mostly against the project to build a nuclear power plant at this spot. He considered himself to be an honest and fair person, but there were underlying factors involved here of a more personal nature. Scott had a massive secret, one which he and his ancestors had kept for two hundred and fifty years.

Down below where Scott stood there was a cave which ran deep into the earth beneath him. It had originally been accessible only by climbing up from the cove below. However, over the years the rock face had changed, creating a ledge of kinds, which meant the cave could now be accessed from the path leading down to the cove.

Inside the cave and well-hidden was his secret, a gift made to his ancestors back in 2003 and one which they had fiercely protected over the years. Scott was now the keeper of the cave and what was hidden inside, and to date, nobody outside of his immediate family had any clue of its existence. In the wrong hands his secret could change everything, not something he wanted to consider.

What was hidden inside the caves was so technically advanced that even in 2253, its existence was still something of a distant dream. Scott respected this and used the technology responsibly.

The technology had been gifted to Scott's Ancestors by visitors supposedly from another universe, with the agreement that it would never be shared with anyone, or there would be consequences. Stories told over the years suggested Scott's ancestors had to carry out certain tasks for the visitors in return for the gift. It had never been passed on exactly what these tasks were though, but Scott had always adhered to their instructions all the same.

Heading down the rough path towards the cove and onto the ledge, Scott entered the cave and lit up his torch, making his way to the back and into a smaller tunnel like entrance. The tunnel was about four feet high and went on for approximately ten feet before it opened out into a large cavern. In the far-right corner of the cavern was a rock which gave the appearance that it was growing out of the ground, to a height of about a foot and a half. Just right of the rock there were several smaller rocks jutting out of the wall. Scott pushed one of these and the large rock rolled over to expose a manhole cover. Twisting the handle in the centre of the cover, there was a slight whoosh as the seal was broken.

Scott was about to climb into the hole and onto the waiting ladder when he heard a noise behind him. Turning quickly, he came face to face with Jonathan Prescott, the nuclear power plant owner.

It was common knowledge that Prescott would stop at nothing to get what he wanted, right now he had his sights set on what was hidden in the cave.

Scott was completely taken by surprise, a moment of panic, "What are you doing here?"

Prescott smiled sadistically, pulling a gun from his pocket, "I've been watching you VanDaley. I knew you were up to something. I've had this cave bugged, and your house. Get down there now," he ordered, pointing to the ladder which led into the cavern below.

Scott made his way down the ladder and into the lower cavern ten feet below. Prescott indicated for him to stand back then followed him down, keeping the gun aimed at Scott with his free hand.

There were two large metal doors leading from the cavern. The secret Scott and his ancestors had protected for so long was behind the second one.

"Open up," Prescott ordered gesturing to the doors.

"What are you going to do?" Scott was trying to figure a way to stall him.

Prescott levelled his gun at Scott, "Just shut up and do as I ask."

Scott opened the second of the large metal doors and they both went inside. The room instantly glowed blue and a large globe of the world appeared around them. A control-station rose from the ground and the door slammed shut behind them.

This was Scott's secret. It was a time-travelling device and it could send you anywhere in the world to any given time or place.

"I want you to enter this date into the control-station, May 20th 2003," Prescott ordered.

Scott paused for a moment. He knew the relevance of the date and wondered how Prescott had managed to procure the information as it was rarely discussed. Of course, if he had been monitoring for some time, it was feasible he'd overheard something.

"You don't know what your messing with Prescott, you're making a big mistake." Scott said, a realisation of what Prescott planned to do.

"Just do it VanDaley," Prescott took a step towards him, aiming his gun at Scott's head.

Scott set the date into the control-station., the day after the Visitors had installed the time-travelling device, which he was now sharing with a very dangerous man.

Scott knew that Prescott would change history by disposing of his ancestors and taking control of the technology and use it for personal gain. A new time-line would be established and Scott and his daughters wouldn't even exist in the new one.

The view around them remained the same, but what the blue-room displayed now was the same space, but in the year 2003.

"Give me one of those wrist-bands," Prescott ordered, referring to several 'watch' like devices which were in a tray beneath the control-station. Scott reluctantly passed one to him and Prescott placed it on his wrist.

"Thank you," he levelled his gun at Scott's head and squeezed the trigger.

With Scott laid dead next to him, Prescott Hinged open the facia of the watch like device, he saw two buttons, one was blue and the other green. He pressed the green button out of instinct and instantly disappeared from the blue-room in 2253 and reappeared in the displayed image.

Next door to the blue-room and behind the other steel door, Emily, Scott's eldest daughter, was at her desk in the apartment working on her latest novel. She'd heard the shot and moments later her computer pinged, indicating the time-travelling device had just been activated.

She knew at once something was wrong. Scott would always come in to the apartment first to write a note in the diary before he went anywhere. She quickly checked the coordinates from the history log on her computer and copied them down, writing a brief note in the diary.

Hurrying to the blue-room, Emily found her dad sprawled beside the control-station. He was clearly dead. Distraught and angry, Emily focussed on the surrounding image, and seeing Prescott, she quickly grabbed a wrist-band. Scott had always said that the secret of the time-travelling device was of the upmost of importance and the technology should be protected first and foremost.

Pressing the green button on her wrist-band, Emily appeared in front of Prescott. It was his turn to be taken by surprise. Prescott went to pull the gun from his pocket as Emily came at him kicking and screaming, causing the gun to crash to the ground. He pushed her off and Emily stumbled into the control-station and fell hard onto the ground. Quickly grabbing for the fallen gun, Emily raised it to shoot, but Prescott was too quick and kicked it out of her hand. There was a loud bang as the gun went off. The bullet hit the underside of the control-station. Emily kicked out again and this time she connected with his leg, which sent him crashing to the ground.

She quickly went to the control-station, clipping on a wrist-band and adjusting the dials with the intention of sending them both away from the cave so as not to cause further damage.

Prescott came at Emily again, dragging her away from the control-station as the surrounding image changed. They both fell to the ground.

At that moment, there was a hissing sound from beneath the control-station where the bullet had hit moments before.

The green buttons on both of their wrist-bands lit up without warning and they both disappeared into the new image.

The blue-room plunged into darkness as the main power shut down and everything went silent again.

Chapter 2

Lucy got showered and changed. Putting on a pair of tight jeans and a blue cotton blouse, she brushed her long brown hair in front of the wall mounted hair dryer, tying it back when it was dry. Pulling on a pair of black trainers, she grabbed her leather jacket, checking herself out in the wall to ceiling mirror, blowing herself a kiss.

Heading out, Lucy grabbed her phone and dialled her six foot two football crazy boyfriend, Joe, "Where are you?"

"I'm at home, was I supposed to meet you?" He asked, yawning.

Lucy was infuriated, "You said you'd take me to Newtown Village, did you forget."

"Look, give me an hour I'll be there, okay."

"Forget it, Joe, I'll get the bus."

"Come on, Lucy, give me a break."

Lucy hung up, shaking her head. Making her way to the bus stop, which was only fifty feet away, she arrived just in time as a single level thirty seater coach glided silently to a halt beside her. Climbing inside, she paid the driver her fare and sat halfway back in one of the big leather seats.

Arriving at the south car-park of Newtown Village some thirty minutes later, she transferred onto the monorail, which took her to the main tower in the centre of the square mile hi-tech village.

Making her way to level 99, where all the food outlets were situated, she went to the third counter on the left and ordered bacon rolls and coffee.

Her phone rang, it was Joe. She rejected the call, shaking her head in annoyance. Opening a text message, she typed - *'I'm done, don't call me again.'*

Pocketing her phone, Lucy headed for the elevator, back down to level fifty, where the retail outlets were. Spending several hours' window shopping, feet aching, Lucy went back up to level 99 and grabbed another coffee.

Taking a seat by the window, she looked out across the village. The view from there was quite something - not that she was taking much notice, her mood still dark. Lucy had met Joe a few months ago, his good looks and muscular body getting her attention. But his mind was not so healthy and Lucy knew she'd made the right decision to end it that day. This wasn't the first time he'd let her down.

Retrieving the phone from her pocket, she dialled Emily, her older sister – no answer. That was no great surprise as Emily would often spend days in the apartment writing her books. Deciding to leave her in peace, she headed home.

Going straight to the stables, she saddled up her favourite horse, a seventeen-hand black stallion called 'Black-Jack'. She needed to clear the cobwebs from her mind, which the horse sensed, breaking into a gallop as soon as they turned into the massive field.

It was a glorious day, clear blue skies with a tinge of red, the temperature in the region of twenty-one decrees. As Black-Jack galloped along, Lucy felt the pressure lift, memories of Joe fading fast.

Taking five foot hedges with ease, the beautiful black stallion glided along effortlessly. Rider and horse in tune with each-other, anticipating one-another's every move.

Returning to the stables a couple of hours later, she unsaddled Black-Jack and brushed him down, fussing him as she did. The horse responded, baring his teeth in what looked like a smile, or was it a grimace? Lucy just laughed, stroking his long face.

"I'm going for a swim," she said out loud, checking to make sure there was food and water for the horse before leaving.

The building opposite housed a large indoor swimming pool, hot tub and steam room. Getting changed into her one-piece, she swam forty lengths of the large pool. Climbing back out, she headed for the hot-tub, grabbed the music remote and cranked up the volume before climbing into the bubbly water, turning it on full for maximum affect.

Laying there in the bubbles, she closed her eyes, a picture of Joe coming to mind, which she quickly dismissed, still happy she'd ended things with him earlier.

After a good soak, she spent half an hour in the steam room, did ten more lengths of the pool, then showered and changed back into her jeans and blue blouse.

Heading back to the house and ordering a Pizza - barbecue chicken along with a side order of garlic bread, it arrived twenty minutes later. She tipped the driver generously, watching as he smiled all the way back to his car, not because of the tip though - Lucy's charms were hard to miss.

Grabbing a beer from the fridge, Lucy was certain Emily wouldn't be back that evening. Going to the lounge and flicked on the TV, she selected a movie to watch.

The following morning Lucy was up quite early. She'd decided to go and see Emily to find out when her dad was returning. Since her mom had died, Emily was more than just a big sister, she was mom too, her rock.

Arriving at the caves, Lucy knew at once something was wrong as the manhole cover in the rear cavern had been left open. She quickly climbed down, closing the manhole cover behind her. She pulled the lever beside the ladder which returned the rock to its original position.

Entering the apartment first, Emily was nowhere to be seen. Lucy checked the computer log history. The last log read; May 20th 2003. She wrote down the coordinates.

The diary was open and Lucy saw the short note from Emily, *'Gone to blue-room, something's wrong. Emily.'* She was quite worried now and quickly went to the blue-room to investigate.

There was no missing her father's lifeless body beside the control-station.

Lucy felt her knees buckle, tears running down her cheeks, "Why would anyone do this," she shouted out loud.

Her father's words echoed inside her head. *'If anything ever happens to any of us, the time-travelling device must be protected at all costs.'*

Lucy quickly went back to the apartment and made a note in the diary before returning to the blue-room. She attached a wrist-band onto her dad's lifeless arm and adjusted the coordinates on the control-station to their home.

"I'll find who did this to you," she said, pressing the green button on Scott's wrist.

Lucy wiped her tears away with a tissue before entering Emily's last used coordinates the computer had logged onto the control-station. The image was that of the blue-room in 2003. It was in total darkness though.

Placing a wrist-band on her arm and pressing the green button, Lucy transferred into the image, turning on the emergency lights in the blue-room, 2003.

Lucy was the technology genius of the family, and now that she had re-focused, Lucy set to work on fixing the problem.

Plugging her laptop computer into the control-station, she ran a diagnostic programme. The programme confirmed a blown circuit board beneath the station.

Removing it, Lucy grabbed a replacement from the stores cupboard back in the apartment, taking it back to the blue-room and clicking it into place. Plugging all the leads back in, she closed the panel.

Back in the apartment, she slid open the power source cover at the rear of the spacious living area and pressed the re-set button. The long round tube came to life straight away, glowing a bright white.

Sitting at the workstation, Lucy copied the coordinates from the log history on the 2003 computer and wrote a note in the diary, not knowing who would read it if she was not able to return.

'Dad has been killed. Found coordinates to Richmond VA, gone to find Emily. Lucy.'

Putting the diary in one of the drawers below the counter, Lucy headed for the blue-room. Entering Emily's last known coordinates, she waited for an image to appear, but none did. In fact, nothing happened.

She checked the coordinates again, they were correct. Puzzled, Lucy checked the time the coordinates had been entered. She remembered that once before when the system had failed, her father, Scott, had adjusted the time forward a minute.

Adjusting the coordinates, an image came into view. It was early hours of the morning for Richmond, Virginia, and still dark, although there was good street lighting.

There was no sign of Emily though.

"What are you doing in America?" Lucy muttered to herself.

Adjusting the image out for a wider view, she looked for clues as to where Emily could have gone, but nothing jumped out at her. She considered that whatever had happened most likely did during the minute which had been lost.

A thorough look up and down the road gave no further clues. There was an Exxon gas station over the way, two cars parked in the pull in by the shop. On the other side, there was a large building with a massive area for parking. There were no cars there though.

Not sure what to do, Lucy considered her next move.

Deciding, she pressed the green button on her wrist-band.

What Lucy didn't know was that she was walking right into a trap.

Chapter 3

Saturday 12th July, 2008 Torquay, Devon.

There was a tap on the door, Jack opened it and Laura breezed past him, "Morning Pop's. Are we having a fry up?"

"Don't they feed you at home?" He joked. She shrugged and grabbed the bacon and eggs from the fridge, giggling.

Laura was Jack's neighbour's ten-year-old daughter. He'd promised to look after her that Sunday as her mom, Marion, had been given a new prescription for a medical issue she'd had for some time, one which the doctors were struggling to label. The new drugs left her feeling tired and short tempered.

Jack had promised Laura he'd take her to the beach, which he knew was going to be packed since it was July and peak-season in Torquay. Once they'd finished their breakfast, they headed off in Jack's Honda CRX. It was a beautiful day and the beach roads were already quite busy, as were the beaches themselves. There wasn't a parking space to be found, which put a scowl on Laura's face.

"What now?" She said, throwing her arms up in the air.

"I know a nice spot further up at Thatchers Rock," Jack offered, trying to keep her calm. "I took Richard there last summer."

Richard was Jack's 18-year-old Son. He lived in London and was studying at University, part time, whilst spending the rest of his time with a marketing company operating in the south-west.

Laura asked, "So what's at Thatchers Rock, it's not some old peoples beach or something, is it?"

Jack shook his head, smiling. "No, nothing like that, well the cove anyway. It's a private beach of sorts and not known by many tourists. It has an unusual rock formation which is a little like a small island growing out of the sea before it disappears again," he pointed to the cliffs jutting out further down the coast line. "The cove also has some caves to explore. Any good?"

"Come on then, let's go," Laura said with renewed excitement.

They arrived there ten minutes later and parked up. As expected, there were few people about so they grabbed the bag of goodies Jack had packed earlier, snacks and drinks. He'd also remembered to pick up a torch, having already considered this as their 'plan-b'. That was Jack, always thinking ahead, something he'd learned from his many years in sales and marketing.

The view from the cliff edge looking out to sea was quite something. The sea looked calm and the water shone a silver blue from the reflection of the sun. The cove below was deserted apart from a couple of fishermen on the rocks.

Laura looked puzzled, "How do we get down there?"

Jack pointed to the path and she took off at great speed. He set off after her, hoping to catch her before a narrow bit at the bottom which could be a bit slippery.

"Careful, Laura," he shouted, but she didn't seem to hear. Jack managed to reach her just as she lost her footing and started to slip. Grabbing her flailing hand, she held on tight, managing to stay upright, just.

Safely in the cove, Laura was off at speed again, exploring the surroundings and jumping onto the rocks which rolled into the sea - hopping from one to another. Jack caught up with her and pointed back to the caves.

A little concerned, Laura said, "It's quite high up?"

"About ten feet I'd say, but there are plenty of rocks jutting out to climb on."

"Come on then, what are we waiting for. Piggy back," she demanded.

Laura jumped on Jack's back and put her hands around his neck, almost strangling him. They made their way towards the cave and he helped her onto the first jutting rock and followed closely behind, helping with her footing whilst they both climbed slowly and carefully. Arriving confidently at the top, Laura held her arms up in triumph.

Jack shone the torch light into the cave entrance. It looked quite deep, curving round to the left and out of sight. They entered carefully and continued along the narrow passage till it opened-up into a larger cavern. In the far corner was a tunnel like entrance. Shining the torch into it, Jack could see it led to another cavern up ahead. Laura raced through whilst he had to crouch down and take it a bit slower. Once they were both out of the tunnel and into the spacious cavern, Jack shone the torch around to see if there might be some more tunnels connecting to other caverns, but there didn't seem to be any.

"That's a bit disappointing," he said.

"Might be a secret door somewhere," Laura joked, looking around her.

"You've been watching too many movies," Jack said, laughing.

Laura pointed towards a large rock in the far corner, "Could be a hatch or something under that?"

"Oh yeh sure, maybe buried treasure too."

"Yeh, probably something you press and it opens."

"And there are fairies at the bottom of my garden," Jack pulled a face at her which had Laura in stitches. She was kicking several rocks to the right of the larger rock when it shifted slightly before falling back with a thud.

They both froze.

"What was that?" Laura said, staying very still.

"Be careful, we don't want to get trapped in here," Jack was a bit worried the cave could fall in.

Laura went back over the area where she'd been kicking and located the small rock which seemed to shift the larger one. Pushing it with her foot again, but gently this time, the large rock moved slightly.

"You push the large rock while I press the small one," Laura suggested.

He did and this time it rolled back exposing a steel manhole cover. It had a twist handle in the centre. They both stared at it in disbelief.

"I guess I really do have fairies at the bottom of my garden." Jack said, still in shock.

Laura was getting a little inpatient, "Yeh, yeh, whatever, come on, open it."

The twist handle was quite tight but he managed to free it eventually. There was a whooshing sound suggesting it was an air, and probably a water seal too. Hinging it open, it revealed a ladder leading down into another cavern below.

Laura quickly climbed down, Jack asked her to be careful but she didn't seem to hear, free-falling the last few rungs of the ladder. He followed her down into the cavern where they found two large steel doors.

"Let's look inside," Laura headed for the far door.

Pulling the handle, the door creaked open. As they entered the room, it lit up and glowed blue. An image of the planet Earth appeared around them and a control-station sprung up from the ground, lighting up.

Jack and Laura stood frozen to the spot as the steel door slammed shut with a heavy clunk.

Laura screamed.

Chapter 4

Jack and Laura were stunned into silence for a moment, in shock. Jack looked around, considering the technology was like a video-conferencing live blue-room, but as for the globe which surrounded them, it looked a lot like google-earth on the internet.

Laura had other ideas though, "I think it's a space ship."

"It's certainly off the planet, whatever it is. More like a video..."

Laura finished his sentence for him, "Conferencing room - yeh maybe."

Jack scratched his head, He was quite sure he hadn't said that out loud.

Laura smiled, "Let's see what these dials do then," she ran her finger around the outer dial as the image of planet Earth moved from left to right. She did the same with the inner dial and the Earth rolled over.

Noticing two lines crossing, one vertical and one horizontal, Jack immediately recognized them as longitude and latitude lines. Just like google-earth, these were used to pinpoint the location you required.

"Google-Earth," Laura had come to the same conclusion, "Cool."

There was another similar dial beside the one Laura had just altered, she repeated the process. The outer dial zoomed in and the inner dial zoomed back out.

Laura was quickly exploring, adjusting the dials until they pinpointed San Antonio in Ibiza, "We went there last year," she said with growing excitement.

Jack had also been there some years before with his son, Richard. As the beach came into view it was like they were there again, it looked so real and it felt like you could just reach out and touch the sand. They were amazed at the speed in which the image had come into view and how sharp it was. The one thing that occurred to them both was that google-earth shows a still picture, a view caught in time. This image was real time, live and in 3D. People were walking about and the waves were gently rolling onto the sand and out again.

"Wish we could go there now," Laura was mesmerised by what she was seeing.

Jack noticed a tray under the control-station which was full of what looked like wrist-bands. There must have been at least a dozen. Laura followed his gaze and picked one of them up and placed it on her wrist.

"It's a watch I think," she hinged open the top. There were no hands though, just two buttons, a blue one and a green one, "I wonder what these do?" she pressed both.

"Careful you don't..." Too late!

Laura disappeared from Jack's side.

Looking up at the image surrounding him, he could see her looking around quite lost. Quickly grabbing a wrist-band and putting it on, he did the same and was beside her moments later.

Laura looked relieve, "What just happened?"

"I do believe we just travelled almost two thousand miles with the press of a button," Jack said, still a little mesmerised.

"And it didn't cost a thing," Laura said laughing.

They both looked around to see if anyone had noticed their appearance from out of nowhere, but nobody was taking any notice.

"This is incredible, I'm blown away," Jack was still in shock.

"I'd love to go for a swim. I've got my costume on under my jeans and tee shirt. Did you bring a towel?"

Jack produced one from the bag, "Of course I did."

They found a good spot and Laura passed him her clothes and wrist-band before running into the water. Jack took off his shoes and socks, rolled up his trousers and followed her, staying close. Laura looked so happy splashing about. The water was warm to the touch and he wished he'd bought his swimming trunks. Unlike the murky water in Torquay, these were crystal clear, it was all quite dreamlike.

After a good swim, Laura dried herself off and they sat on the beach, soaking up the atmosphere and surroundings.

Laura said, "I'm hungry."

Jack opened his bag and produced Laura's favourite pepperoni sausages, crisps and a bottle of fizz. He'd made a sandwich for himself. They would love to have eaten at one of the many beach cafes, but of course they couldn't as they had no local currency.

Checking his watch, Jack notice it was just after two in the afternoon. Not sure when the tide was due to come in back at the cove, he didn't want to risk them being trapped there, suggesting they should make a move.

"Can't we stay a little bit longer, please?" Laura pleaded.

"I'd say yes, but the tide."

"Yeh, I know, come on then, but I want to come back another day."

Jack promised they would and they made their way to a quiet spot out of sight. Laura's costume was dry so she slipped her jeans and tee shirt straight back on and Jack gave her back the wrist-band.

"So which button to get back?"

Jack had pressed both to get there so he wasn't exactly sure, but guessed anyway, "I reckon it's green for go and blue to return."

"Sounds reasonable," Laura pressed her blue button, disappearing immediately. Jack did the same and they found themselves back in the blue-room.

"Wow that was so great," Laura said, a huge smile on her face.

"Incredible," Jack agreed.

"So when can we come back?"

Laura was off the following week to see family back in the midlands, but Jack assured her that they could come back the weekend after she returned.

"You have to make me a promise now," she had a serious look on her face.

"What's that?"

"Promise you won't come back here without me."

Jack considered that for a moment, "If I do, it will only be to gather information and not to use the blue-room, after all, this belongs to someone and I would like to know what's happened to them."

"Good point! But we shouldn't tell anyone about this."

He felt a little uncomfortable keeping secrets about their time together, but at the same time he did appreciate what they'd found was a bit off the planet and probably not something they could share easily, so he agreed, reluctantly.

They made their way back into the cavern and up the ladder, noticing a lever on the way up. Jack guessed it was probably a device to move the rock back into place. They'd left it open, along with the cover, bad move.

"I want to try something," he said as Laura climbed out.

Pulling the cover down, Jack pushed the lever downwards and heard the rock plonk back into place. He pushed the lever back up and heard the rock roll back over. Opening the manhole cover up, a much-relieved Laura was shaking her head, scowling.

"You could have got stuck," she looked worried. Jack climbed up and closed the cover. "What if I couldn't have moved the rock?" She continued to scold him.

Jack pushed his foot against the small rock and the larger one rolled back into place. "You try it again on your own." Laura did and this time she managed it. "Just needed loosening up huh," he said, smiling.

"Okay clever clogs," she laughed, pushing the small rock again.

With the manhole cover now concealed, they made their way to the front of the cave, looking about to make sure nobody was watching before climbing back down into the cove. The tide had started to come in, but they managed to get back onto the path without getting their feet wet.

When they arrived back at the car, Laura gave Jack a hug, something he wasn't used to, "Thanks for a great day out."

"I had fun too," he roughed her hair. They both laughed and got into the car.

Arriving home some twenty minutes later, Laura's mom, Marion, was just returning from the shops with a bag in each hand. She looked exhausted.

"You two are back early."

"We can go out again," Laura quickly responded.

Placing the bags down on the ground with much relief, Marion said, "Look at you, you've quite a tan, did you get to have a swim?"

"Yeh, the water was crystal clear blue and the beach was knee deep in golden sand," Laura winked at Jack. Marion was already walking towards the house and didn't pick up on the pun. Jack grabbed the shopping bags and they both followed.

"We're leaving at nine tomorrow morning so be back by seven to pack your things ready." Looking around at Jack she asked, almost as an afterthought, "If that's okay with you?"

"Yeh, no worries, we'll go and get a MacDonald's in a bit."

Marion nodded and picked up the bags, disappearing into her house. Walking back over to his place, Jack unlocked the door, "I thought you were going to tell your Mom for a minute, although if you change your mind and want to."

"My lips are sealed," she pretended to zip her lips.

Jack was quick to explain that under normal circumstances they shouldn't keep things from her mom, but for the moment anyway, he agreed it best to learnt some more about what they'd stumbled upon.

Jack was a straight and honest guy, which is why he was quietly freaking out about keeping secrets, but the ramifications of this kind of technology falling into the wrong hands was unmentionable. Not only that, it belonged to someone and he wanted to know who, promising himself he would try and get some time off later that week so he could go back and explore.

Laura was looking at him strangely, "Remember you promised not to use the blue-room?"

Jack reassured her he wouldn't and they both sat down for a cup of tea and talked about their day and what they'd found.

"We need to call it something," Laura said. "I know, it's got to be a travel-portal, yeh, we can call it that. And the wrist-bands, they are travel-bands."

"Sounds good."

"Just imagine, we could go anywhere, maybe even Disneyland?"

"Yes maybe," Jack smiled at her excitement. "Let's find out more about it first though."

Laura pulled a face, "Party pooper."

"I promise you I'm not," Jack said, "I just want to keep our feet on the ground."

"Okay. You better get me a quarter pounder with bacon and cheese, chips, a thick shake."

Jack was laughing, "I get the picture, blackmail huh?"

They finished their cups of tea and headed for Macdonald's, where Laura devoured enough for two. She had a huge appetite for such a skinny little thing.

After they'd eaten, they went down to the amusements arcade near the harbour. Laura managed to win two small jackpots on the slots and put all the money back into the two pence roller machines before they headed home.

"Remember your promise?" Laura said as she was getting out of the car

"I do, pinkie promise," Jack offered her his pinkie finger, she hooked hers around his.

"You better," giving him a one-armed hug, "See you on Friday."

"You have a good time."

"I will," Laura waved till she disappeared into her house.

Jack had a big fashion event to organise in Exeter that week, so he decided to rest up for the remainder of the evening and come to terms with what they'd found. The event was due to finish Wednesday, all being well, so he planned to return to Thatchers Rock on Thursday to see if he could figure out the mystery of the abandoned travel-portal, as Laura has christened it.

Chapter 5

Jack somehow managed to keep his mind on work for a few days. It certainly helped that he was surrounded by beautiful women, not to mention his lovely, but married assistant, Leila. His boss, Mark Jones, had agreed to give Jack Thursday off, on the proviso that he completed a full report of the fashion event and have it on his desk first thing Friday. He was sure this would give him the time he needed to get some answers before Laura returned.

Jack was up bright and early Thursday morning, skipping a cooked breakfast in favour of a bowl of cereal. He packed a small back pack with snacks and a thermos of coffee and a torch. Jumping into his Honda CRX, he headed off to Thatchers Rock.

The traffic was light, but then it was only seven thirty, early by Devonian standards. He arrived at the rock and parked, grabbed his back pack and headed down the slippery slope, managing to get to the cove without falling over. He made his way to the rear of the cove, climbing up into the cave.

Checking to make sure nobody was about, Jack headed for the rear cavern where the large rock covered the hatch. Staring at the rocks that jutted out from the wall to his right, he tried to remember which one moved the large rock, managing to locate it on the fourth attempt. The rock rolled back easily and Jack opened the hatch and climbed down, remembering to close the hatch behind him this time, hearing the rock return with a reassuring 'thud'.

Standing in front of the first large steel door, he wondered what he was going to find behind it. For some reason his nerves started to jangle, hesitating a while longer, considering whether he should just leave and come back with Laura at the weekend. Deciding to stay, he pulled down the handle and pushed the heavy door open, not knowing what to expect.

Jack was somewhat surprised at what he found, not because it was mind boggling, but because it wasn't. What he was presented with was a modern, well furnished apartment. There was a work station to the left with a lap-top on the counter, nothing else. There were two large leather sofas in the centre of the room, with a double bed behind them pushed to the rear left of the apartment. On the right, a fully fitted kitchen - cooker, refrigerator, microwave and most important to Jack, a kettle. There were built in cupboards, checking some of them, they were filled with kitchen utensils and various other items you'd expect to see, but nothing weird.

Finding a button on the rear wall, Jack pressed it and a panel slid open. Inside was a tube running from floor to ceiling. It was about two foot in diameter and glowed white. Whatever it was, it didn't make a sound. He took a guess that this may have something to do with the power source. The air smelt clean and it was dry, which suggested some sort of automated air conditional system was operational.

This was unlike any technology he'd come across and he felt it was most likely from the future. That was hard to get his head around though.

Sitting down at the work-station, he pulled out his thermos flask and poured a coffee. As Laura wasn't there to nag him, he lit a cigarette and fired up the computer. At first glance nothing jumped out, although to be fair, Jack didn't have a clue what he was looking for. He was just certain that whoever owned the travel-portal could be in trouble and in need of help.

Checking the drawers next, he found a Diary. Leafing through the pages, there were several entries, but it was the last one that caught his eye. It was dated 21st May 2003 and read - *Dad has been killed. Found coordinates to Richmond VA, gone to find Emily.* It was signed Lucy.

This part of America was known to Jack as he'd been there on a few occasions in the past. Looking at the icons again on the computer screen, he saw a folder labelled history. Double clicking it, there was a list of numbers, which seemed to be coordinates. There were dates and times by each set of numbers along with a brief description of places, he knew this as the last entry was for San Antonio, where he'd gone with Laura that past Sunday. The one before that was dated - 21st May 2003. Jack assumed this had been Lucy's last entry. It was timed at 9.44am.

There was another entry before Lucy's dated - 20th May 2003 and to the same location. This one was timed at 10.20am. Figuring out that something must have gone down on the 20th he considered that Lucy had found out the next day and followed.

The previous log was made up of numbers again, but it was the four digits that jumped out which had previously indicated the year - 2253. Jack sat staring at the numbers for a while longer, still unsure if he was reading it right. But if he was, and it was referring to the year, then this wasn't just a travel-portal, but a time machine too.

Pouring himself another coffee, he lit up a second cigarette. He wasn't getting any further forward, or maybe his mind had accepted more than enough for the moment and had decided to go in circles.

He'd seen as much of the log as he could understand, but Jack was certain that once Laura got a look see, she would make more sense of it, being the computer whiz-kid she was.

Going to the blue-room, it lit up and the control-station rose from the ground. This time when the door slammed, Jack was expecting it. Adjusting the dials to the Midlands and zooming down to where Laura was staying, he spent a few minutes scrolling around trying to locate her. Jack found her playing football with some friends in a nearby park.

Feeling a little like a voyeur, he instantly felt pangs of guilt. Whilst it was tempting to visit, he'd given Laura a promise and he wasn't about to break that promise.

Gathering his things, Jack took one last look around. He couldn't think of anything else he could have done without Laura, so he headed home to do his fashion event report.

Chapter 6

Driving into work Friday morning, Jack's mobile pinged to tell him he had a text, certain it was from Laura to remind him that she was due home later. Laura had texted every day with a running commentary of her week and the friends she'd re-established contact with. Jack was pleased she hadn't referred to the travel-portal though.

Arriving at the office, he checked the text, it read - '*Leaving in a bit, see you later. Miss you. T. x.*' Jack realised he'd missed her too. Somehow she'd got under his skin and become part of his life. It made him start to think about their secret and what damage it could do and how many people would end up getting hurt. It was wrong on so many different levels.

In the office, he clicked on the computer and plugged in his memory stick. Opening the completed fashion event report, one he'd finished the night before, Jack hit print.

Leila, Jack's number two, popped her head around the door. "Coffee?" she flashed a smile, melting his heart as always.

"Love one, can you bind that report for Mark please."

"Sure thing, I'll be back in a jiffy."

Leila came back in with his coffee and grabbed the report from the printer, "Enjoy your day off?"

"Yes I did actually. I had a few things to sort out."

"So you didn't get up to anything exciting with Laura then?" She was fishing.

"No, she's been away this week, back later. All on my lonesome."

"Ah, poor thing, we'll have to find you a girl-friend," her big brown eyes were studying Jack intently. Leila's comments were normally hidden questions, like Jack, she was good at reading body language.

"Got my little match-maker for that," Jack said, referring to Laura, who loved to introduce him to all her mom's single friends.

"Don't go and break her heart," Leila warned him.

Jack rolled my eyes at her, "She's Ten, Leila, what do you take me for?"

"Bring her in, let me suss her out."

"Yes soon. Don't want you leading her astray," laughing. Leila pouted, then leaned down and kissed him lightly on the cheek, her long black hair brushing his face, which by this time was a little red.

They agreed to have lunch together and Jack got on with his work. Mark Jones, Jack's boss, had been on his back a bit lately. He felt sure something was a bit off with him, but let it ride. The company had a few high-profile events due up and he knew Mark was a little apprehensive. Jack had no such fears as he and Leila made a good team, having worked together for five years, they always got the job done.

Just as Jack was going out the door to have lunch, his phone rang, it was Laura.

"Missed me pops?"

"Yeh sure, who is this?"

"Very funny, not. We've just left, be home for tea. Mom said any chance you could cook something?"

"I'll do better than that," Jack said, laughing. "We'll order take out, Chinese okay?"

"That sounds good to me. Where are you?"

"Just off to lunch with Leila."

"Don't eat too much, leave room for later," sounding more like Jack's late Mother.

"Yeh right boss, got to go, later."

They hung up together. Something caused Jack to pause for a moment as he remembered what Leila had said. Was he being paranoid? Should he be concerned about their relationship? He dismissed the idea immediately, considering that they were fine. Laura was a cool kid and had lots of friends, including boys. Jack was quite sure he was in the right box.

That evening, they all sat in Marion's kitchen and had a Chinese feast of roast duck, satay chicken and beef in oyster sauce, pancake rolls, and Chinese chips, which Laura loved.

After their feast, Laura asked if she could stay over at Jack's, "You promised to take me to explore the caves again!" she winked.

Marion said, "If that's okay with you, Jack?"

"Yeh sure, bring your sensible boots."

"I'll get my stuff," she ran up the stairs to her room.

"You don't mind, do you?" Marion asked.

"So long as you're happy," Jack said shrugging, "I'm not the boss here."

"We're cool, Jack, I trust you," she said, picking up the empty containers of food.

Jack picked up the dirty plates, "Thanks - that means a lot, so how are you feeling today? Are the new drugs any good?"

"Too early to tell, just feel tired all the time, no energy."

She did look quite drawn which worried him. "Just relax and play some bingo on the computer, give them a little more time to get into the system. Call if you need anything."

Laura was back down minutes later, "Come on then, can we play monopoly?"

"Why not, haven't beaten you for at least a week."

"You're in for a beating tonight," she pulled a face at him.

Jack pulled one right back at her, "Bring it on."

Back at his place, Laura took her stuff up to the spare room and Jack set up the monopoly board. She returned with a serious look on her face.

"So, did you go back there?"

"Yes, but as I promised, just to look around and find some answers."

"And did you?"

Jack told her about the apartment, finding the diary and what he'd learnt from the computers history log.

"So it's a time-machine too?"

"I'm not sure, but 2253 has to have some relevance."

"So you definitely didn't use the blue-room then?"

He hesitated and she gave him one of those looks, her eyes like daggers, so he admitted he had, "I did see you playing football with your friends."

"When?"

"Oh, must have been about lunchtime on Thursday!"

She smiled, thumping Jack in the arm, "They were my friends from my old school. I just thought, you could spy on me anytime?"

Jack felt a little embarrassed, she was absolutely right, "You're quite safe. I'm not a voyeur."

"You sure?" she was laughing now.

He shook his head and smiled, "I'm quite sure."

"I know, just winding you up," punching him in the arm again.

They decided to go to the blue-room at nine the following morning, and got on with their game of monopoly, which Laura won.

Jack couldn't help but be apprehensive about what they'd find. To Laura, in her innocence, she thought it was a game, but he knew they were entering the unknown with no idea what to expect.

Chapter 7

Saturday 19th July

Jack was making breakfast when Laura padded down the stairs. "Morning, breakfast will be served shortly."

Laura breezed past him, looking to be in a mood, "I don't feel like a fry up."

"What would you like then?" Noticing her sad expression.

"A new life," she said, flopping onto the sofa and looking rejected. Jack knew she was worried about her mom, and with their secret - he guessed that wasn't helping.

"Have I done something wrong?" Jack asked, ready to take her home in an instant if she was unhappy staying with him.

"No, not you. Sorry!"

"Okay, I'll make us a cup of tea," he said putting the kettle on, getting two mugs out ready.

Noticing the tears rolling down her face, Jack went back over and sat beside her. She leaned against him, sobbing.

"If you'd rather stay home with your Mom, I understand," Jack said. "You must be worried about her."

"I just want her to get better," Laura sobbed,

"Well, let's hope the new drugs help, try and stay positive."

After a few minutes, she sat up, wiping away the tears. "Is that fry up still on offer?"

"Sure thing," Jack roughed her head and she shrugged him off, forcing a smile. He completely understood through, knowing this must be quite an emotional ride for her.

After breakfast, Jack filled his back pack with the usual, not forgetting a torch, before heading off to Thatchers Rock. Parking up, they headed across the green to the rough path which led down to the cove below. Laura seemed to be in a slightly better mood, but still a little subdued.

The weather was lousy and the sun was struggling to come through, but at least it had stayed dry. But that didn't matter today.

They made their way into the cave and down to the blue-room, remembering to close the manhole cover and pull the lever down to move the rock back into place. Laura went to the apartment and Jack showed her the history log, leaving Laura to do her '*computer whiz-kid*' thing whilst he sat on one of the sofas and took another look at the diary.

After a few minutes Laura said, "This is weird?"

Jack put down the diary and walked over to the desk to see what she was referring to, "What have you found?"

"Well, it's that date you mentioned, 2253. It comes up quite often. If I'm right, we're going to have to rename this the time-portal."

She wrote down some numbers on a piece of paper, "Let's go to the blue-room, I want to try something."

Jack followed her and watched as she entered the numbers onto the screen. An image surrounded them, but it seemed to be just a reflection of where they were.

"I took the departure coordinates from Lucy's last entry which referred to 2253 and added an hour. Shall we?" Laura passed Jack a wrist-band.

"Okay." He was a little sceptical as they pressed their green buttons together. It seemed like nothing had happened.

Laura said, "I'm pretty sure we're now in 2253. Let's go and see."

Making their way back to the front of the cave, and as they hit daylight, Jack knew Laura was right. It was warm, very warm. The sun was gleaming down onto the water giving it the appearance of a silver sea. The sky was almost crystal clear blue with a slight red haze.

They were about to climb down when Laura pointed, "That's new."

Jack followed her gaze, noticing at once the rock face had changed. There was now a ledge leading to the path.

"Race you to the top," Laura yelled, taking off at her normal warp speed. Jack gave chase.

At the top of the path they walked across the green, seeing at once that everything had changed. There was no sign of the Thatcher Avenue housing estate, just rolling fields. The only property they could see close by was a ranch style home in the distance which looked right out of an American west movie.

They sat down on the grass and just looked about. No cars, no noise at all. Laura asked, "What do you think happened to all the posh houses?"

"Hard to say, maybe there was a war or something?" Jack shrugged.

"Let's take some pictures. Get your digital camera out of the bag."

He checked the bag, trying to remember if he'd packed the camera, guessing Laura must have as he found it, fishing it out and passing it to her.

Laura started clicking away in every direction, "We can compare them when we get back and see how much has changed."

"Shall we explore a bit more?" Jack pointed to the ranch house in the distance.

Laura nodded and pulled him up to his feet, "Come on, Pop's, sure you can make it?"

"I'm not that old, still the good side of forty."

"Oh yeh, you better take it slow then, old man."

"Race you," he said, zipping up the back pack and swinging it over his shoulder.

"You're an old man," Laura shouted, taking off at speed.

Jack had in fact been 400 and 800 metre champion when he'd been in the armed forces, something Laura didn't know. She put up a good show though. Laura had that competitive edge most kids lack, which made her who she was. Jack eased off a little as they got nearer to the ranch and allowed her to draw level. She knew it too.

"Oh you're good. I can see I need to do something about that."

"Longer legs would do it," Jack said, laughing.

Laura gave him one of her dark looks, "They're growing," then smiled and they both laughed.

Arriving at the ranch style property, nobody seemed to be about and the place seemed eerily quiet. Peering through the windows. It was a beautifully laid out single story home. It must have had at least four bedrooms, Lounge area, dining area and a massive kitchen. It was furnished in style, large leather sofas, beautifully finished lightwood furniture, massive wall mounted TV. It stunk of money, a lot of it.

Making their way to the rear of the property, they found stables with six horses. It was right out of an American west movie. On the side of the house was another out-building, exploring this one they found a large indoor swimming-pool, hot-tub, steam room, the whole package.

Laura picked up a large white towel from the lounge chair, "Look," she pointed at the name printed on it, *LUCY*. "This is Lucy and Emily's home."

Jack found another towel on a nearby pile, it had *EMILY* printed on it, holding it up, "I think you're right."

"We have to find out what happened to them?" Laura had a concerned expression.

Jack frowned. They'd come this far and he knew she was right. They'd stumbled upon all this for a reason, maybe Lucy and Emily needed their help, believing everything happens for a reason.

"Let's get back to our time and make a plan," Jack said.

Laura shrieked with joy, "Yes. Come on then, we've got to find Lucy."

Chapter 8

Finding Lucy

Returning to the blue-room in 2008, Laura went to the control-station and started adjusting the numbers.

"Sussed it, the arrows top and bottom adjust the dates."

Suddenly the image zoomed down and they were surrounded by dinosaurs. It looked quite scary, Laura was laughing uncontrollably.

"This is definitely a time-portal and these are travel-bands," she referred to the wrist-bands they were wearing. Excited at a new level, Laura rushed back to the apartment, "Just getting Lucy's last known destination coordinates," she shouted, tugging open the big metal door.

Moments later she was back, "Strange, but Lucy's last coordinates were exactly a minute after the previous ones. Just want to try this," she entered some numbers onto the screen.

Nothing happened though. Laura adjusted the time forward a minute, this time the image zoomed in and they saw a young girl of about sixteen or seventeen standing beside the road. She had long brown hair and was dressed in jeans cut short with an oversized silver belt that sparkled, a blue tee shirt, black trainers and white ankle socks. She looked fashionable and at the same time casual and laid back.

Something caught Jack's eye, "Zoom out a bit please, Laura"

Lucy - or at least who they assumed was her, was standing just past a set of traffic lights. Behind her was an Exxon gas station and on the other side of the road was a Lowe's DIY store. Jack knew exactly where she was. It was dark but the street lighting allowed them to see everything quite clearly.

"I've been there, I can't remember the name of the road, but there are loads of shops and fast food outlets along there, just beyond the Exxon station." Jack said. "There is a bowling alley down there too and a pretty cool mini golf course. I believe the area is called Chesterfield."

Just as he said that a car pulled up beside Lucy, a blue Chevy Impala. A man stepped out and walked over towards her. She looked startled and went to back away. He was talking to her and smiling. Lucy seemed to ease and was nodding. Then they both climbed into the car and drove off.

Laura adjusted the controls and followed their progress as they headed down the road in the direction of Williamsburg. Before long they pulled off the main road and shortly after that they arrived in a small town. The car came to a halt in front of an apartment building which stood over a row of shops.

Lucy and the smartly dressed guy climbed out of the car and walked to the edge of the building and then down an alleyway. Halfway down they turned right into a side door leading into the apartment building.

This is where it got a little tricky. It wasn't quite like playing a computer game where you walk the character through buildings and rooms. This technology took them into the building, but to the top floor.

Laura quickly tried to adjust the dials but could not determine where they'd gone. She replayed the last thirty seconds but still had no success.

Looking at Jack with a worried expression on her face, Laura said, "We have to go and see she's okay?"

Jack shook his head, "Not yet, it's too dangerous. We need to think this through a bit more."

"But she could be in trouble, we need to find out?"

"I agree with you and we will. But first we need to come up with a plan. Also, we need to familiarise ourselves with the surroundings."

Laura scowled at him. Jack went on, "Take a note of the numbers so we can come back to this point."

"So are we going to help Lucy?"

"Yes, Laura, but first we plan."

They spent the next hour scanning the area, noting where things were, buildings, roads, shops, exit routes the whole nine yards.

Laura asked, "What now?"

"If we are going to follow, we have to be prepared. Let's sit down and plan this out thoroughly"

"Okay, but if she's in trouble?"

"I know, I know, but remember, this is a time-portal," Jack said, smiling. "So it's like pausing a game if you like. We decide when to re-start it. And remember, this has already happened five years ago."

"Suppose you're right," Laura said, thumping his arm. "So when are we going there?"

Jack was still thinking of the preparation. He wanted to go alone but he knew Laura wouldn't have a bar of it. So, they needed to be properly prepared. That meant a change of clothes into something more suitable, some American currency, and a map of the area from Google.

Explaining this all to Laura, they decided to come back the following day. Jack remembered he had some loose change at home, but it was only a few dollars, they needed more. He knew a place in town which was open till four though, so they still had time.

Tomorrow was going to be a big day and Jack was scared, not for himself, but for Laura. What was he getting them in to?

Marion was waiting for them when they arrived home and called Jack over, "Have you got any plans for tomorrow?"

"None at present," he lied.

"What about Monday?"

"Just work, I'll be in the office all day, why?"

"I've been invited out for a long weekend, back Monday evening. I was wondering if you wouldn't mind looking after Laura."

He told her it was fine and that he'd take Laura to work with him Monday. In fact, it suited him as it meant they would have more time to find Lucy if they needed it. Jack had already decided he could call in sick Monday if necessary.

Laura grabbed some things from her place and took them up to the spare room. She shouted down to Jack, "Can we go out tonight?"

"Sure, where do you want to go?"

"Can we go to the pictures? Mama Mia is still on I think." Laura was a massive Abba fan and had mentioned before she wanted to see the film.

"Want to grab a bite to eat on the way?" Jack asked.

This got a good response, "Can we go to MacDonald's?"

"Your wish is my command oh great one," Jack replied.

Soon they were filling their stomachs full of burgers and chips, washing the food down with a thick shake each before heading off to the cinema. They sat and watched the film, which Laura enjoyed, joining in with the singing, and much to Jack's surprise, she had a voice of an angel. Even the people sitting beside them thought so too, giving her a silent applause.

Jack enjoyed the break too, but his mind was still wondering. He couldn't help but worry how dangerous this could get. He knew they had to find Lucy but he would not let anything happen to Laura, it was important to keep her safe.

As if she sensed his concerns, Laura turned her head and smiled, taking his hand, "It'll be okay," she said.

"I'm sure you're right," Jack said, scuffing her hair.

He wasn't convinced though.

Chapter 9

Sunday morning arrived and Jack and Laura headed off to the cove early with their plans made. Laura had printed off a map of the area from Google. Jack had five hundred dollars in cash and they'd also filled the back pack with snacks and drinks. They also brought with them a change of clothes. Small towns in America are often very religious and as it was Sunday, Jack thought it respectful to dress smart rather than turn up in jeans and tee shirt.

He left Laura in the apartment to get changed and took the blue-room. He was thinking about the man who'd picked Lucy up. It seemed strange that he'd turned up when he did and stranger still she went with him so easily. After all, in Richmond Virginia, they were eight hours behind the UK. So, this meant that it would have been about twenty-past two in the morning their time. Jack didn't want to take Laura there at that time, but they still had to figure out where the guy had taken Lucy.

Laura came in dressed up to the nines in a white blouse, blue plaid skirt, a light brown suede jacket and brown ankle boots with knee length white socks. She looked the picture of innocence.

"What do you think?" she asked.

"Million dollars, you'll knock them dead," Jack said.

He'd gone for a grey suit and tie, which he normally reserved for hosting events. Laura entered the coordinates to where they'd last seen Lucy, but they still couldn't figure out how to see inside the building and had no luck finding out where Lucy and the guy had gone.

Zooming out a little, Laura pointed at something moving on the other side of the apartment building, quickly zooming back in.

Laura said, "Are you sure we're still in 2003, that looks like a horse and carriage."

Jack looked closer, seeing the driver of the carriage dressed in grey trousers held up with braces, a long dark coat and sporting a beard but no moustache, and he wore a straw hat. There was nobody with him as far as they could see.

"That's an Amish man, they don't use cars as we do, they travel everywhere by horse and carriage," Jack said.

"What's Amish mean?"

Jack explained to Laura that the Amish folk were an independent group of people who lived separately from society in communities which spread throughout America and that they were anti-technology and lived off the land and were self-supporting.

"He looks like that president, Abraham Lincoln," Laura said pulling a face.

"That's a good description. In fact, all the men dress and look very much the same. They're peaceful people though."

"Strange!" Laura continued to pull her funny face.

They continued to scan the area for further movement, but apart from the Amish man, there didn't seem to be anyone else about.

By eight am their time, the town started to come alive so getting themselves ready and attaching their travel-bands, they found a quiet spot in the alleyway, where the driver and Lucy had disappeared. Pressing their green buttons together they arrived just behind a dumpster, out of sight of the main street.

Jack said, "Let's check out the building, knock on a few doors or something."

The side door to the apartment building was open. It led into a wide corridor with doors leading off both sides. Some were numbered but not all, indicating that the unmarked ones were most likely for the shops out front. The place looked run down and had a stale smell. In the centre, there were stairs leading to the next level with two elevators either side. One had an out-of-order sign on it.

"Where do we start?" Laura said just as an old lady appeared at one of the numbered doors. She was skinny, had straggly long grey hair and was bent over holding a cane.

"What are you doing in here?" The old woman drawled, stinking of alcohol.

"We're looking for our friend, a young teenage girl with long brown hair?"

"No one like that here."

With that she hobbled back into her apartment and slammed the door.

"I don't honestly think this is going to get us anywhere," Jack said and Laura agreed. "Let's have a walk around town, maybe ask some shopkeepers."

"Creepy in here anyway," she said, happily heading back to the door.

There were more people on the street, including more horse and carriages with Amish families on board. They guessed there must have been a community close by.

Laura found them quite amusing and started waving to them as they passed. They seemed friendly and polite and waved back cheerily.

Most of the shops were closed, which was to be expected being a Sunday. However, Laura spotted a cafe which looked open. They stepped inside and a middle-aged lady came over to serve them.

"What can I get you all today?"

The name tag on her uniform said Maureen. Jack said, "Thank you, Maureen, two tea's please and a menu would be good."

She pointed over to the menu on the wall, "You English huh?"

"Yes, we're just passing through. We were supposed to meet a friend."

"Uh huh. So, what would you like sweetie?" She asked Laura.

"Can I have some chips please?" Laura very politely asked.

"We don't do chips till lunchtime sweetie, how about a full American fry up?" She nodded.

"Make that two please," Jack added.

"Sure thing hon," Maureen said, heading back to the serving hatch, returning minutes later with their teas.

When she was out of earshot Laura said, "She speaks funny."

"I expect she thinks the same about us," Jack said and they both laughed.

They could see more Amish horse and carriages passing by. Laura was still finding this all quite amusing.

"The ladies all look the same, I don't think I'd want to wear one of those long smock dresses."

"You reckon I could grow a beard like that?" Jack picked up a paper napkin and dangled in from his chin, pulling a face.

"Ooh, no, definitely not. Yuk," Laura grabbed the offending napkin and screwed it up, shaking her head, smiling. "Can't take you anywhere."

Maureen arrived with their second breakfast of the day and two more cups of tea.

"Maureen, you might be able to help?" Jack asked.

She looked defensively back at him, "I'll try hon. Shoot."

"Our friend Lucy, who we were supposed to meet, was probably with an older man. He's about five ten, slim, short black slicked back hair, dark suit, looks a bit like an undertaker?"

"Yeh, I think I know who you mean," she chuckled. "But last time I saw Terry he sure didn't have no lady with him."

"Does he live around here?"

"Just out of town that way," she hooked her thumb to the right. "Just follow the road to the bridge, take a left and you can't miss it."

Jack thanked her and they both got stuck into their food.

Laura said, "This is really good."

"What, better than mine?"

"Mm, well, yours is good, but...."

"Okay, I get it and I agree with you, 'real-good'," Jack mimicked Maureen's American drawl, which had Laura in fits of laughter.

Finishing their breakfast and with stomachs now quite full, they set off for Terry's place, not knowing what they would find.

Just as they were passing the alley where they'd arrived, Jack stopped abruptly, pointing. "Laura, the car, it's gone."

"Was it there when we got here?" She asked.

"Damned If I know, we could go back to the blue-room and check."

Laura shook her head, "We're here now, so we may as well carry on. Could do with walking my breakfast off anyway, I'm stuffed."

"Same here," Jack said as they continued-on their way.

But to what?

Chapter 10

Not at all sure what they would find at Terry's place, Jack was having second thoughts about going there at all, seriously considering abandoning the search and heading home.

Laura gave him a concerned look, "Stop worrying."

"What if he's got a gun or something and comes out waving it at us. This is America?" Jack said shrugging.

"But we must find Lucy," Laura said.

"I agree, but bowling up at Terry's door isn't the way," He looked up the road, the bridge Maureen had mentioned was less than a hundred feet away.

Just then they saw an Amish horse and carriage coming out of the gravel track which led to the property. It turned left onto the road.

Laura pointed at the carriage, "That's the man we saw in the early hours, you know, just after Lucy went into the building with Terry."

It was hard to tell these Amish people apart as they all looked so similar, but Jack trusted her instincts. He considered that if it was the same guy, they had another clue as to where Lucy had disappeared off to.

"Do you think that Amish man could have taken Lucy?" Laura said.

"I would say there's a fair chance of that," Jack said. In fact, he was kicking himself for not having thought about it when he'd seen him earlier, if it had been him. He was still a bit misty about the wherefores and whys at that point though.

They watched as the Amish man disappeared down the road, imagining he was headed for a community close by, which gave Jack an idea, "Let's head back into town and see if we can get a cab to the Amish community."

"Do you think they'll let us in?"

"Maybe. They are a private bunch, but if we play the tourist card they might show us about."

"What if they take us prisoner?" Laura looked concerned.

"First sign of anything like that and we just hit our travel-band return buttons and get out of here, no way am I risking anything happening to you."

When they got back into town, as luck would have it, a Cab was parked right out front of the Cafe. As they approached it, the driver came out the café and was about to climb into the cab.

They hurried over to him, arms aloft, "Good morning," Jack shouted, getting his attention, "Are you available for hire?"

"Sure thing! Where're you folks headed?"

"I promised my daughter we could visit the Amish community, we're on holiday from England and Laura is doing a school project on their way of life," he tried to sound convincing.

Laura managed to keep a straight face, giving Jack a dig in the ribs, unseen by the cab driver. "It really would be helpful," Laura added. "I need to get good marks for this," she was performing now, Laura at her best, bringing a smile to Jack's face.

"I'm sure they'd be delighted to show you about little lady," he replied in his American drawl. "They're a private folk, but generally friendly." He opened the back door for Jack and Laura to get inside. "I know the community leader, guy called Joseph Macabre, I'll introduce you."

The cab driver said his name was Joe and gave Laura a big smile before putting the shifter into drive. A little further down the road they saw the horse and carriage they'd seen leaving Terry's earlier. Jack noticed then that the carriage had a thin yellow line outlining the doors and panels which made it quite distinctive.

Laura pointed, "Do all the carriages look like that, Joe?"

"Yeh pretty much. That's Joseph's son, Jacob," he waved as they passed.

"Is he a nice man?" Laura enquired innocently.

"Bit of a renegade if I'm to be honest, been away in the city for a while, at college."

Jack asked, "I hear some of the young one's do opt to enter society for a time, is that normal?"

Joe chuckled, "Yeh I guess they want a taste of what they see as freedom, till they realise they already had it."

Jack got the impression Joe was quite close to the Amish and wanted to know more about Jacob, "You say he's a renegade, how so?" He tried not to sound too inquisitive.

"Can't say, just my impression of the guy," he gave Jack a wary look.

Jack was certain he had plenty to say, he could read it in Joe's expression, so he pushed a little more, "I thought I saw him earlier coming out of that road by the bridge. Is that another part of the community?"

"No. Where we're headed is the only one in these parts He was probably delivering produce, they do have some dealings with the locals," Joe looked back at him in the rear-view mirror, a suspicious look which Jack picked up on right away.

Laura noticed the look too, jumping in, "What about TV and stuff?"

"They don't have no television, nothing like that. As I said, they're just a simple folk," smiling again, happier with the line of questioning. "They have horses to plough the fields and pull the carriages. They grow all their own produce and breed all kinds of animals. They also build their own homes from the wood they cut down themselves on their land."

Up ahead the Amish community came into view. It was nothing like either of them had expected, their beautifully built homes expanding in every direction, covering several acres.

Laura looked mesmerised, "Wow, is that where they live?"

"Yep, all their own work too."

He took the next right turn into a large driveway with a gated entrance. The gate was open but he parked outside.

"They don't allow motor vehicles on their land," he explained, as if reading Jack's next question.

Just over to the right they could see several carriages parked side by side and behind them the stables. Some Amish women were attending to the horses. Climbing out of the Cab, Jack noticed a very attractive young woman in her late twenties, her long blond hair tied back with a bow. She smiled then looked away quickly.

Laura jabbed him in the ribs, "Down boy."

Joe led them to a large colonial looking wood built house, an older man stepped out from the porch and walked over towards them with a welcoming smile on his face. He was quite tall and carried himself as if in authority. Jack guessed this was probably Joseph, who Joe had indicated was the community's leader.

He straightened his jacket and looked across at Laura, she nodded.

Let the games begin.

Chapter 11

Joe introduced Jack and Laura to Joseph Macabre. He was at least six foot five tall and probably weighed about 16 stone. What one would call a gentle giant, you could tell immediately.

"Pleased to meet you, Mr Macabre, I'm Jack Clarke and this is my daughter Laura," Jack said, keeping up the act, noting he had a firm handshake.

"Good to meet you, Jack, please call me Joseph."

For such a big man, he had a gentle and kind voice and his posture suggested he was a proud man. Laura gave him a little curtsy, whilst Jack struggled not to laugh. She was playing her audience.

With the introductions taken care of, they paid Joe his fare and followed Joseph back to his house. Going inside, it was very simply furnished but beautiful at the same time. Following him into the kitchen, they all sat around a large oak table, big enough to seat at least ten people.

Joseph asked, "Would you like some tea?"

Laura gave Joseph one of her dazzling smiles, "Do you have lemonade?"

"Yes, we make it ourselves, my wife, Mary, made a jug earlier," he went into the walk-in larder and came back with a jug of home-made lemonade and some glasses.

Laura's eyes were darting all around the kitchen and dining area, "So where's your fridge and do you have a microwave?"

Joseph smiled, "We do not have any of these things. We have fresh food every day which we grow and produce ourselves. Everything is cooked on a wood burning stove," he said, pointing.

"You must work really hard," Laura said.

"And we are rewarded for our hard work with our good life."

Joseph went on to tell them some history about the Amish way of life. Laura appeared to hang on to his every word, asking the occasional question.

"Come, let me show you around," Joseph offered after they'd finished their drinks. Jack and Laura followed him back outside to where a group of Amish men were busy building a house.

He explained that Sunday would normally be a day of rest, but this project was a little behind due to recent bad weather.

Jack noticed Jacob walking towards them and quickly made sure his travel-band was tucked under his shirt collar. He gestured to Laura to do the same.

Joseph introduced him, "This is my son, Jacob."

Jack shook hands with him, noticing that his grip was loose and sweaty. Jacob eyed them both suspiciously at first, but he seemed to keep his composure.

Joseph asked, "Whereabouts in England do you come from?"

"We're from the Midlands," Jack half lied. In fact, he was a London boy, but he didn't want to complicate matters and throw up any red flags. It was obvious Joseph and Jacob had noticed the different accents, but made no comment.

Joseph nodded as Laura went on to tell him about her school project. He seemed relaxed and attentive whilst Jacob's hard dark unfriendly eyes stared back at them. Jack was good at reading people and decided they needed to take care around Jacob.

After a brief chat, Jacob excused himself. Jack made a mental note of which house he headed for as he felt it quite possible Lucy could be found there.

After the guided tour, Jack and Laura were impressed with the Amish way of life and their general attitude. Everything about the place was well organised and clean. These people obviously had pride and respect, qualities lacking in normal society.

It was hard to imagine bad within this group, although you're always going to get the odd one from time to time. Jack just wondered how dangerous Jacob could be, he still had Laura to consider.

Joseph was explaining to them how they have their own schools and education system. However, some still chose a different route, but most would return and never leave again.

Completing the tour, Joseph insisted they stay and eat with him. It was lunchtime, but for Laura and Jack it was more like teatime. They gratefully accepted his hospitality, heading back to Joseph's home.

Mary, Joseph's wife, was in the kitchen preparing the food along with her two teenage girls. Joseph introduced his wife and the girls, Madeline and Melinda, it occurred to Jack that the men in his family had names beginning with J and the ladies, M. He wondered if there was some relevance to that.

Jacob returned and they all sat down as Mary served the food, which included a massive joint of ham and a large chicken joint along with a large tray full of crispy roast potatoes. Then three pots of vegetables were placed on the table along with a gravy boat.

Jacob didn't seem to show any further interest in Jack and Laura, which suited them. Joseph and Mary were excellent hosts though and Laura was getting on well with Madeline and Melinda.

After a splendid meal, Jack decided it was time for them to leave. Joseph organised for an older gentleman, Franklyn Johnson, to take them back into town in a horse drawn carriage, bringing a huge smile to Laura's face, excited at the prospect.

They all shook hands with each-other. Laura reached out to shake hands with Madeline, the younger of Joseph's daughters when Jack noticed Laura's travel-band slip down a little.

Madeline looked a little shocked and leaned forward to hug her. As she released, her hands ran down Laura's arm and she pulled Laura's blouse over the travel-band. It was all done very smoothly, but pointedly.

Madeline shook hands with Jack and as she did so, he felt her fingers touch his travel-band. She seemed to tap his wrist. All this was done in such a way that nobody else would have noticed, looking around Jack was certain of that, but he was confused.

Was she trying to send him a message?

Was she protecting Laura?

Jack decided he'd speak to Laura a little later and see what she thought.

Climbing into the carriage, Franklyn invited Laura to sit up front with him whilst Jack felt like a lord sitting in the rear. Laura was getting another history lesson on the Amish, which she listened to with genuine interest. Arriving in town, they were quick to thank Franklyn much, shaking his hand warmly.

After he'd left, Laura said, "How cool was that?"

"Better than we could have planned, but what did you make of Jacob?"

Laura scowled, "A bit shifty and horrible."

"And Madeline? You know she saw your travel-band, don't you?"

"Yeh I do. She covered it, I thought I heard her whisper something, sounded like, *'who are you,'* I'm not sure."

Jack had a look of concern, "I didn't hear her say anything, but if you say so, I believe you," giving Laura the benefit of the doubt. He told her how Madeline had tapped his travel-band when shaking hands with him.

Laura looked perplexed, "She may have said something else. I can't be sure."

"I would say she was the cleverest of the bunch, maybe she saw through us?" Jack said. Laura shrugged.

They made their way down the alley, checking around us to make sure they were alone and returned to the blue-room. It was late and the tide was sure to be in and therefore exiting could be a problem, deciding they were stuck in the cave for the night.

They could both use their mobiles though so Laura let her mom know all was well and Jack texted Leila telling her he had a bad throat and would be taking Monday off. She texted back saying she would cover for him.

Jack said, "Just a thought?"

"Oh no, not again, what now?" Pulling a face.

"Where's the bathroom?" He asked.

They both looked around, then Laura pointed to a button on the wall at the far end to the left, just behind the bed. She pressed it and the door slid open giving up a pretty decent wet room.

Jack noticed a fold out screen next to the bed and unfolded it to give Laura some privacy. He'd take the sofa.

"My turn," Laura was looking around, "Where's the TV?"

Searching the apartment, they spent the next ten minutes looking, when Laura found a TV remote in the bottom drawer below the desk. Pressing the standby button, a panel on the wall opened and there hung a massive TV screen, probably about sixty inches.

"Sorted," they said together, falling onto the sofa.

"We'll make a fresh start in the morning, it's a little late to be gallivanting around when we're both tired," Jack said.

She agreed, having got used to the idea that they were just *'pausing the game'* so to speak. Jack got some drinks from the back pack and they relaxed to watch TV, confident they'd find Lucy the next day.

Chapter 12

After a good night's sleep, Jack felt refreshed and ready for their new day. Laura was still asleep, which was no great surprise with all the excitement from the previous day. Making two cups of tea, he flicked on the TV.

"What's all the noise?" Laura moaned, appearing from behind the screen.

"Made you tea," Jack said.

"I'm hungry."

Jack laughed, "Nothing new there," getting back up to see what was in the fridge. "Out of bacon I'm afraid. Eggs okay?"

Laura shook her head, flopping onto the sofa, grabbing the remote for the TV and flicking the channels. "Any biscuits left?" Jack passed her what was left inside the pack.

"So what's the plan today, Pop's?" Dipping her biscuit into her tea.

"Let's go back to the early hours, when we saw Jacob leaving. I'm certain we missed the switch," Jack said, silently kicking himself for such a simple mistake. As far as sleuths were concerned, he was a beginner. But he was learning fast.

Finishing breakfast, they headed for the blue room. Laura adjusted the dials on the control-station and they watched. As they'd suspected, Terry came out of the other side of the apartment building with Lucy walking beside him.

She didn't look alarmed.

Terry opened the carriage door and she stepped inside, he followed her in. Laura adjusted the image closer - just as they saw

Terry produce a cloth from his pocket and quickly put it over Lucy's face. She went limp at once and he laid her out on the floor of the carriage.

Jack said, "Chloroform!"

"What's that?"

"It's a liquid you put on a cloth and when you breathe it in, it sends you to sleep."

Climbing back out of the carriage, Terry said something to Jacob who then closed the door and climbed up front, setting off. Terry walked back into the building and disappeared.

They didn't bother to track him as it was no longer important. So instead they followed Jacob back to the Amish community on screen. Arriving there he went past the main entrance and pulled into a lay-by of sorts, which was right behind his house.

Getting out, he grabbed Lucy and slung her over his shoulder like a sack of potatoes and carried her into his house.

Laura pointed out, "She's not got her travel-band on."

"I bet you Terry took it," Jack said.

"We need to find it," Laura quickly adjusted the image to Terry's place.

His home was a single level building, quite large though. His Chevy Impala was parked on the drive, and adjusting the image to inside, they found Terry in the kitchen preparing a snack. His keys were on the side, but there was no sign of the travel-band.

Finishing his snack, Terry headed for the lounge and grabbed a bottle of whisky from the liquor cabinet, along with a glass. Sitting down on his leather sofa, he poured himself a drink. Clicking on the large screen TV which hung on the wall, a news channel came on, CNN.

Jack and Laura watched as he sat fixated to the TV for a while, then drained his drink, stood up, removed his jacket, then poured another drink. He stood there for a moment longer, staring at the screen, then picked up the remote and clicked off the TV, heading for his bedroom.

His jacket remained on the sofa.

Laura pointed to the sofa, "I bet the travel-band's in his pocket."

"I'm certain of it, so here's what I'm going to do, and I need to you to back me. I'm going to zap myself there. You're going to watch to make sure he stays where he is. If he moves, you come and warn me and we'll both get out fast."

"Okay, be quick," Laura said with a worried look.

"It'll be fine," Jack promised. "Here goes."

In Terry's lounge, Jack picked up Terry's jacket and checked the pockets. The band was right where they expected and he was back beside Laura in less than twenty seconds, looking pleased with himself.

"How was that for quick?"

"Yeh good I guess. But I had another thought," Laura said, frowning.

"What's that?"

"Well, when we return from anywhere, we always come back in our real time, right?"

Jack thought about it for a moment, "I get it, if Lucy uses her travel-band she'll go back to 2003 and not here with us in 2008 as she would only have been gone a short time."

"Right, but listen, we have to go to the blue-room in 2003 and then go and save her, that way we all go back together."

This was getting complicated for Jack, but Laura seemed to have a handle on it, her lightning quick mind making perfect sense of things. Copying the exact coordinates to the Amish village, they adjusted the dials on the control-station and sent themselves to the blue-room, 2003.

Laura entered the coordinates and finely adjusted the view to Jacobs home. Searching, they found him in the kitchen. Laura scrolled the view till they saw Lucy laid out on the sofa in the lounge, ten feet away.

Jack said, "This has got to be quick, in and out."

"I know, watch your back."

"Thanks, Laura," he activated his travel-band.

Standing beside the sofa in Jacob's house, Jack quickly attached the travel-band to Lucy's wrist and pressed her blue button, just as Jacob came into the room. He stopped dead, a look of surprise as well as recognition on his face.

"What are you doing here?"

"Just going," Jack said, pressing his blue button.

Back in the blue-room they could see Jacob frozen to the spot, a look of utter astonishment on his face.

"That was very smooth. James Bond couldn't have done it better," Laura laughed and punched Jack in the arm.

Lucy was still sound asleep and Jack was planning to take her back to her house in 2253. His head was still buzzing though, finding it difficult to work out. Laura, of course, already had.

"We can take Lucy straight back to 2253, to just after she disappeared. That way she will be back in her original time. We can take her to her house so when she wakes up she'll know she's safe."

Jack thought about that for a moment. "That's good, but Lucy is unconscious and we should stay with her and tell her what's happened."

"So, shall we go to 2253 or back to our time?" Laura shrugged.

"Back to 2008," Jack said after a moment of thought.

"You'll have to programme both your travel-bands."

"Good point," he clipped a new travel-band on Lucy's wrist and one on his own.

"See you there," Laura said disappearing.

Hitting his and Lucy's green buttons together, he was beside Laura moments later, sending the travel-bands back to the blue-room in 2003. With that done, Jack carried Lucy to the apartment and placed her gently on the bed, making her comfortable. She was breathing fine and looked okay generally. They just had to wait for her to wake up.

Jack would like to have thought the job was done, but he figured this was most likely just the beginning.

Chapter 13

Checking the time, it was ten thirty am. Lucy was safe and sound asleep and Jack and Laura were hungry, having missed breakfast.

Laura rubbed her stomach, "The fridge is empty, have we got any food left in the bag?"

"All out. We need new supplies. Why don't I get us a MacDonald's?"

"They don't serve burgers till after eleven," poking out her tongue.

"Okay clever clogs, how about a bacon butty then?"

She nodded, "Are you going in your car?"

"Nope, I'll use the blue-room, quicker," Jack checked his pockets to make sure he had some cash. "Will you be okay for a few minutes with Lucy?"

"Go, before my stomach thinks my throats been cut," she joked.

Jack knew where a burger van was well placed for him to get there and leave without being seen, heading for the blue-room. He located it and sent himself there. He was back with Laura five minutes later with bacon butties and 2 Styrofoam cups of tea.

They sat and ate their food, waiting for Lucy to stir. It must have been the waft of the bacon that helped, but five minutes later she began to stir.

Sitting beside her, Laura held her hand. Lucy's eyes opened, a look of confusion expressed on her face, Jack thought she was about to scream. Instead she groggily said, "Who are you?"

"It's a long story but your safe now. I'm Jack and this is Laura."

"We rescued you," Laura said, giving her a big smile, still clinging to her hand.

Lucy sat up rubbing her eyes, she looked confused. "How did you find me?"

Jack explained it all to her - how he and Laura had decided to explore the cave and consequently found the loose rock which had uncovered the manhole cover. Jack went on to tell her how they'd seen the diary and worked out how to use the time-portal and their visit to the Amish.

"Once we were sure who'd taken you, the rest was easy," Jack continued. "We just went back to where Terry knocked you out and followed Jacob to the Amish community."

"Don't forget how we got Lucy's travel-band," Laura added. "Jack went to Terry's house. He waited till he went to bed and then stole it from his jacket pocket. Then we came and got you."

"Did anyone see you?" Lucy asked, still looking groggy.

Jack admitted they had, "Jacob saw me just before I disappeared before his eyes."

"Have you told anyone else about this?"

Laura shook her head, "Nobody, we've been too busy looking for you."

"Well I guess I should be grateful you came along when you did, I don't know what would have happened otherwise. It could have been years before anyone else came looking, if at all."

Laura and Jack looked at each-other then back at Lucy. Laura said, "Its July 2008, our time, you disappeared in 2003."

Lucy gasped, "What are you saying; I've been away for five years?"

"Well yes and no, we have no idea what would have happened to you - we didn't have time to check that out."

"It's okay, I get it," she looked more aware.

Jack asked, "So why did you get in the car with Terry?"

"He told me Emily had sent him and he was going to take me to her, I had to go."

"I don't understand. Couldn't you have found her with the time-portal?"

"The what?" Lucy looked confused again for a moment, before smiling, "Oh I see, you've named it, sorry, still a bit groggy in the head." She told them what had happened to the time-portal and her subsequent repair. "I booted it back up, but I couldn't find Emily because of a malfunction which caused it somehow to have lost a minute in time." Jack remembered Laura mentioning the discrepancy with the minute.

Lucy continued, "I felt sure I would still find Emily, but then this car pulled up beside me, and, well, you know the rest."

"It makes no sense," Jack said, "It sounds like he knew you would come, how could he?"

"I don't know, I've just been thinking the same thing. I need to go to the blue-room."

They followed her in and she tapped coordinates onto the control-station's screen. The image of the location where she'd previously appeared surrounded them. She zoomed out a little for a wider view.

"Look!" Laura said pointing at a car in the Exxon garage forecourt, "Isn't that Terry?"

He was obviously waiting for Lucy - they were sure of that. The question was, how did he know to be there at that exact time and why?

Jack asked, "Has the time-portal ever malfunctioned before?"

"Once, that's how I knew to adjust the time forward a minute."

"And what happened on that occasion?"

"I didn't investigate it as the lost minute wasn't important then."

Laura interjected, "I know computers are all about ones and zeros, just a thought, how do you know how much time you really lost. It could have been one hour, or one day or even a month or a year."

Lucy considered this for a moment. "The commutations are endless, there has to be another way."

Jack said, "I say we start with Terry."

"But he'll know we're coming, Jacob would have told him," Laura said.

"Not if we go back to before then!"

"Oh yeh, keep forgetting," Laura said laughing.

Lucy asked, "What are you suggesting?"

"That we go back to the day before he met you and ask him outright where Emily is and see how he reacts."

"And what about Laura, it could be dangerous?"

Jack considered that for a moment. He had to keep Laura safe at all costs, but he knew she wasn't going to like being left out, especially now, but he felt it would be better for him and Lucy to go without her. Before he had a chance to say anything though, Laura stormed out of the blue-room.

Jack followed her into the apartment where she threw herself onto the sofa, sobbing her heart out, "We're concerned that it could be dangerous and you might get hurt," Jack tried to explain. "And anyway, if something happened to Lucy and me, who would save us?"

"You're just saying that to make me feel better."

"No. I'm saying it because it's true. You are the reason we found Lucy so quickly. None of this could have been done without you. That and It's my job to keep you safe. Oh, and did I mention I love you?"

"Love you too," she said, leaning against him.

"Look, we can't do this till tomorrow, so why don't we take Lucy home with us and spend the rest of the day together. Your Mom will be expecting me to go to work tomorrow. We don't want to attract attention to ourselves, do we?"

"Guess not," forcing a smile.

Lucy was standing at the door listening. "I could do with something to eat."

"Cool, come on then," Laura was excited now, quickly back to her normal self, "Let's go."

Chapter 14

It was just after noon when they left the cave. Lucy was looking around with interest.

"It all looks so different, there's no ledge from the path."

Laura said, "I know, we noticed that when we went to your time."

"When did you do that?"

"When we were figuring out where you were from."

The car was where they'd left it fortunately. Torquay had a terrible crime rate, theft and vandalism rife. A further indication of how society was breaking down and the government had no answers. If it wasn't for Laura, Jack would have moved closer to work and away from there.

Lucy looked up and down the road, "This is totally different, my house is just down there," she pointed.

"We know," Laura said, "We went there too, very nice. Love your swimming pool."

Lucy chuckled then suddenly looked sad, "I don't know what will happen if we don't find Emily, especially now Dad's gone."

"We'll find her," Jack said with confidence, "We're a team now, isn't that right Laura?"

"Team-time," Laura smiled, grabbing Lucy's hand. Jack was happy to see them getting on so well.

They headed back to Jack's place, via MacDonald's for Lucy, where they thrashed out a plan, making sure Laura was fully included in her back-up role. It was a simple plan, but often the most effective are.

Marion arrived home mid-afternoon and surprised them by coming to the door. She'd obviously seen the car and knew Jack wasn't at work. Seeing Lucy, she smiled, looking over at Jack, who had to come up with a cover story.

"Heh, good weekend? I'd like you to meet Lucy, my cousin. She called me yesterday and asked to come down, so I took the day off."

"Oh that's nice, hello," Marion shook Lucy's hand, "So is everything okay?"

Jack assured her it was. They had a cup of tea together then she went home, asking Laura to be back for seven. The cover story seemed to have worked.

Laura was shaking her head at Jack, "Cousin? Is that the best you could come up with?"

"Best I could do on short notice," he said, laughing.

"Well, would my cousin mind showing me about," Lucy said, teasing Jack.

They took Lucy on a tour of the town. She was shocked at what she saw and it was obvious things had changed a lot in her time, apparently for the better.

Jack made sure he took Laura back home at the given time. She asked, with a worried look, "You promise to call me tomorrow and tell me what happened?"

"I promise. We should be back before lunch."

Jack texted Leila to tell her he would be taking another day off but would be back Wednesday for sure. She texted back telling him Mark was on the war-path but she would cover for him again. Jack knew he was giving his boss, Mark, ammunition to attack him, but he had no other choice.

The following morning, Jack and Lucy arrived at the blue-room quite early. It wasn't a very nice day, cloudy and drizzling. The path was slippery and the climb up to the cave was even worse.

Lucy said, "It's so much easier coming in from the path onto the ledge, look, I'm soaked." Jack was soaked too, nodding in agreement.

They'd planned to do some surveillance work first, starting the day before Lucy had disappeared. Drying themselves off, they went to the blue-room where Lucy adjusted the controls and zoomed in on Terry's place. Starting in the morning, they watched and waited till he went out. This was about ten. Following him on screen to make sure he was a suitable distance away before they made their next move.

Terry drove back towards Richmond on the main road past the Exxon garage and past the mini golf course then hooked a left. A little further up he went right onto Hull street and down past the shopping mall. He continued downtown which gave them all the time they needed.

Putting on their travel-bands, they sent themselves to Terry's house, having already checked to make sure nobody else was about. Nobody was though. Splitting up, Jack and Lucy gave the place a thorough search, looking for any clues that might indicate where Emily was. Jack found nothing but Lucy called him into the kitchen.

"I found Emily's travel-band," she held it out, "It was in a pot on top of the cupboard."

"Does it look damaged?"

She placed it on the table and pressed the blue button. Nothing happened.

"What does that mean?"

"I'm not sure to be honest, but I'd guess that it was caused by the burnt-out circuit board." Lucy explained in more detail about how the blue-room had shut down after the malfunction and her subsequent repair.

"Well, now we know that Terry knows where she is. I would hazard a guess it involves Jacob," Jack said. "I think we need to re-visit the Amish."

Returning to the blue-room, Jack showed Lucy where the Amish village was, "That's where we're going."

"Let's go then," she placed a travel-band on her wrist.

"Better idea, start at the town. I know a cab driver who will give us an introduction."

Jack told her about Joe and how he and Laura had convinced him they were father and daughter and she was doing a project on the Amish. Adjusting the screen, they sent themselves to the side alley where they'd been the previous day.

"Let's go and get some breakfast, I know the waitress," Jack said, suddenly laughing, "It feels a little like the film, Groundhog Day."

"What's that?" Lucy asked.

"Oh, it was a film about a guy who kept re-living the same day, well before your time."

Lucy smiled, seeing the excitement in Jack's eyes, or was it fear? "Well, I'd prefer we did this first time."

"Let's hope," Jack said, opening the café door for Lucy.

Chapter 15

Maureen approached Jack and Lucy with a cheerful smile. They ordered two fry ups and two teas then sat down by the window. Joe wasn't there yet, but Jack knew he wasn't far away.

Whilst they were eating their food, Joe walked in. He ordered a coffee and sat down at the counter. Jack finished his breakfast and walked over to where he was seated.

"Good morning. Is your cab for hire?"

"Sure, where you all going?"

"We're only in town for the day and are keen to visit the Amish community. I understand its close by."

"Uh huh. Just finish my coffee," he grunted.

"No worries, whenever you're ready."

Lucy had just finishing eating, so they drained their cups-of-tea as Joe waved to say he was ready. They followed him out and into the cab. It did seem a bit weird to Jack that he'd only seen him the previous day, and here they were again, but total strangers once more.

Lucy was making conversation with him regarding the Amish way of life. They passed a few carriages heading into town and they both made appropriate comments. As the village came into view, Joe said he would introduce them to Joseph.

Pulling up in the drive, Jack saw Joseph walking towards them from his house. Lucy was looking over at the stables and suddenly took in a sharp intake of breath. Jack followed her gaze. She was looking at the young blond lady he'd noticed the previous day. Joe noticed too and looked at them both suspiciously.

Jack said, "Oh Lucy is horse mad, she has a seventeen-hand stallion at home," It was probably true as he knew she had horses.

"Must be a handful?" he eyed Lucy warily.

"He's a thoroughbred racehorse," Lucy said confidently, having re-gained her composure. "My Uncle rode him to seven wins. He's nine years old now," It sounded convincing enough.

"Wow, some horse huh," Joe had heavy sarcasm in his voice.

Joseph reached them and they went through the introductions as before, inviting them back to his home for refreshments. On this occasion, Joe came in and joined them.

"Little lady here has got herself a racehorse," Joe said to Joseph. It sounded like he was trying to be-little Lucy and Jack felt a flash of anger, he didn't like the man.

"His name is Black Jack," Lucy said, "My uncle is inclined to gamble and black jack is his game, thus the name. In fact, I have two stallions and four mares." Lucy looked over at Joe, "Do you ride?"

"No Mam, just drive my cab," he looked a little embarrassed.

Joseph said, "You are very welcome to see our stables. In fact, I would love to give you a guided tour if you're interested?"

"Very much so, thank you," Lucy replied.

They all stood and walked outside and Joe slipped away quietly. Jack noticed him heading for Jacobs place. He checked his travel-band to make sure it was safely hidden, as did Lucy. Jack felt confident there was no way they could possibly know who they were as he'd not met them till the next day, when he and Laura had visited.

Then it occurred to him. Terry obviously had a description of Lucy, so Jacob did too and probably Joe. All the J's, Click. He had to be another relative of Josephs. Too old to be a Son, so he was probably a Brother.

Joseph was telling Lucy about the horses and the work they did. Jack noticed Jacob's brown and white, which the blond lady was attending to. Joseph led them over to where she stood.

"This is my daughter in law, Catherine." Joseph said.

Jack watched as Lucy and Catherine locked eye contact, then he knew for sure, this was Emily, Lucy's older sister. She was very beautiful and probably in her early thirties. He felt his heart skip a beat.

Joe was walking back towards them with Jacob now by his side.

"Father, Franklyn would like to talk with you. I will carry on showing Jack and Lucy about."

Joe was standing beside Emily and Jack felt a knot in his stomach, this was trouble. Joseph excused himself and Jacob led them both away from the stables through the rear. Joe was leading Emily the other way, back to Jacob's house.

Jacob asked, "So what do you think of our way of life?"

Jack went along with the charade for the moment, "I envy your way of life, very enriching."

"Please, come this way," he guided them towards his house. "Catherine will be preparing food, please join us. I'm sure we have much to discuss."

It didn't sound much like an invite, more like an order or a threat. Jack looked at Lucy. She grabbed his hand and squeezed it. Jack squeezed hers back.

This was sure to be trouble.

Chapter 16

Laura was sitting on her bed staring out of the window. She was still a bit annoyed with Jack for leaving her out of Emily's rescue. To make matters worse, her friend Ayesha had gone out with her mom for the day. Her other friends, Sara and Bob, were out somewhere as well and Marion was on the computer player bingo.

She checked her watch, it was only eleven and too early to hear from Jack and Lucy. But when would be the right time?

When should she start to worry?

Were Jack and Lucy going to shut her out completely?

Just then her phone rang. She grabbed it quickly and checked the caller ID. It was her dad, who still lived in the Midlands.

"Hi, Dad."

"Hi, Laura, just called to see how you are, what are you up to?"

"Nothing, I'm bored."

"What's your Mother doing?"

"On the computer playing bingo."

"How is she feeling today?"

Laura sighed, "Same I guess."

"Where are all your friends today?"

"They're all out. What's this – an interrogation?"

"Just asking. Look, I'm coming down this weekend," trying to get Laura to open up a bit.

"Okay, But I still think you should move here."

"We've spoken about this, I can't...."

"You mean won't," she snapped.

"Oh, Laura, don't start."

"See you at the weekend then maybe," Laura hung up.

The phone rang, it was her dad again. Laura rejected the call.

Frustrated and annoyed now, she just wanted to get out of there and find somewhere she could scream out loud.

Putting on her trainers, Laura run down the stairs and grabbed her bike from the cupboard under the stairs.

"Mom, just off out on my bike," she shouted, heading out the front door.

"Okay, don't go too far."

In fact, she'd go wherever she wanted, who cared anyway. Laura peddled hard trying to put as much distance between her and home. She wondered how Jack and Lucy were doing. Then the questions started again in her head. Did he still care about her or did he prefer Lucy? She was older and very pretty after all.

She dismissed that quickly. He did care about her; she was sure of that. She kept peddling hard, working off the anger. Before Laura realised, she was riding past the harbour and towards the cove. It was like she was being drawn there, something inside her head guiding her.

Arriving at the cliff edge, Laura was about to take the path down when she heard the tune of an ice cream van. She checked to make sure it wasn't a pink one. Thankfully it wasn't so Laura pulled out her purse and went over to the van and got a can of coke, some crisps and a chocolate bar.

There were fishermen on the rocks, but they were too busy with their catch to notice Laura, so she headed down the path and found a thick bush to hide her bike in and locked it to a tree trunk. Heading down the path to the cove, she climbed up into the cave. The fishermen were still busy, so she went inside and headed for the rear cavern.

"Please move," Laura pushed her foot against the small rock. The larger one started to move then rolled back. She gave it another hard push and this time it rolled over. The twist handle on the manhole cover was a bigger challenge though, but it eventually came lose. Climbing down, she remembered to shut the cover and push the lever, moving the rock back into place.

Going straight to the apartment, Laura checked the log history and the diary. According to the Log, they'd left just after nine. It was now getting on to one pm. She'd expected a new log entry by then, they'd been there too long.

Going to the blue-room, Laura entered their last coordinates and watched as Jack and Lucy landed in the alleyway and made their way to the cafe. She continued to watch as they ate their breakfast and remembered she was hungry herself, so she let the image play out and ate her crisps and chocolate bar, washing them down with her can of coke.

Seeing Joe arrive at the cafe, Laura watched Jack and Lucy go out with him and drive off towards the village. When they arrived at the Amish community, she noticed Lucy staring over at the stables, looking like she'd seen a ghost. They were talking to Joe, who was looking shifty. She wished she could hear what they were saying.

Joseph walked over to greet them and they spoke a little more then went to his house, as Jack and Laura had done when they'd visited previously. This time Joe went in with them and they had a cup of tea together. After this they left the house and Joe walked off towards Jacob's house. Joseph led Jack and Lucy to the stables.

Watching, Laura saw Joseph introducing them to the blond lady Jack had eyed up the day before. Lucy seemed to make eye contact with her for too long, or so it seemed.

She replayed the image, zooming closer. There it was again and the lady was looking right back at her the same way.

Was this Emily?

She saw Jacob and Joe coming back over and they said something to Joseph, pointing back towards the house. Joseph walked away.

Jacob led Jack and Lucy out through the back of the stables and up the path to where the new house was being built. They walked on past and were heading for Jacobs.

What unfolded next left her in no doubt that Jack, Lucy and who Laura was now certain was Emily, were in terrible danger.

As they reached Jacobs house he said something to them and they went inside. Joe was waiting for them. He had a gun in his hand and was waving it at Jack and Lucy whilst holding on to Emily.

Jacob opened a door in the hallway which had stairs that led down to what looked like a cellar. He took Jack and Lucy down and removed their travel-bands. Joe followed with Emily, then they both came back up and locked the door, taking the key and the travel-bands to the kitchen and putting them on the side.

Laura grabbed a travel-band, hesitated for a moment then grabbed another for Emily as she wasn't sure if she had hers or where it was.

Joe and Jacob then made their way to the lounge, which was just around the corner from the cellar door. Seeing her chance, Laura adjusted the image to the kitchen and sent herself there. As quickly as she could, Laura grabbed the travel-bands and the key and went to the cellar door.

She could hear Jacob and Joe talking, as she slowly and silently put the key in the door and turned the lock. Pushing the door open, she squeezed through. Closing the door gently behind her, Laura crept slowly down the stairs.

Chapter 17

Lucy looked scared and Jack wasn't doing any better. They'd just got to Jacobs place and it was obvious from his body language that something bad was about to happen.

"Please come in," It sounded more like an order than an invite.

They followed him into the hall, Joe was inside waving a gun at them. He had hold of the blond girl, who Jack had figured by now was Emily.

He was still kicking himself for not telling Lucy about seeing her when he and Laura had come the previous day, but at the time he'd seen no relevance. Thinking back to the lunch and the way Madeline had reacted seeing Laura's travel-band and tapping Jack's, he felt he should have worked it out, feeling like an idiot.

Joe said, "We didn't think you were ever going to come."

"Don't hurt my sister you creep. Why are you doing this anyway?" Lucy had tears running down her cheeks.

"We've been waiting a year for you to show and here you are. Keep those hands where I can see them and walk down the stairs," he ordered, gesturing to an open door in the hallway which led down to the cellar.

Jack took the stairs, still holding Lucy's hand. Thinking fast, he considered if they should quickly press the blue buttons on their travel-bands and disappear, but neither wanted to leave Emily with Joe, especially as he had a gun on her.

"I'll have those wrist-bands now," Jacob said. Jack thought - '*there goes that idea,*' as Jacob snatched them off their wrists.

Joe came down the stairs with Emily and shoved her towards Lucy, "Say your goodbyes to your little sister," he growled.

"What are you going to do with her?" Emily held Lucy tight, "Please don't hurt her."

"Oh don't you worry your pretty little head about that, we got plans for her cute butt," Joe said sneering.

Jack was about to take a swing at Joe, clearly annoyed, but Jacob shoved him away, heading back up the stairs, locking the door. Lucy was still crying and Emily looked over at Jack suspiciously.

Wrapping her arms around Lucy, Emily said, "I've been waiting for you to show up for a year."

Lucy hugged her back, the tears rolling down her cheeks, "There was something wrong with the control-station - I couldn't find you."

"The time-portal seemed to have lost a minute," Jack said, stepping forward, "We were trying to figure it out."

"Who are you anyway?" Emily didn't seem happy about him being there.

"I'm Jack, long story, but I was helping Lucy."

"It's okay, Emily, we can trust him," Lucy said, wiping away her tears.

"I don't think Dad would have been happy about bringing someone in from the outside to help," Emily said, giving Jack a dismissive look.

"There is something you need to know, Emily," Lucy said.

Just then, they heard the lock click in the door above. They couldn't see who it was, but they were being very quiet. The door shut gently then light footsteps came down the stairs.

Jack smiled, he just knew it had to be Laura. She appeared around the bend in the stairs, smiling from ear-to-ear. She had three travel-bands in her hands.

"I thought you might need these," looking proud as can be.

They quickly put them on, just as the door opened again and Jacob appeared. He saw Laura and looked shocked, she gave him a cheeky wave then they all hit their blue buttons and were back to the safety of the blue-room.

Watching for a moment, Joe came down and was shouting at Jacob. Jack couldn't hear what they were saying until Lucy tapped a button on the screen and their voices filled the room.

"They just disappeared," Jacob said.

"Where to?" Joe was looking about.

"Into thin air Joe, I swear."

Emily hit another button and the image changed to that of the globe. "Forget them, I need to tell you what happened to Dad."

"I saw his dead body," Lucy sobbed.

"It was Jonathan Prescott!" Emily told her how she'd heard a shot just before the computer had pinged and had gone straight to the blue-room. "When I saw Dad's dead body, I followed Prescott and attacked him. In the struggle the gun went off and the bullet hit the underside of the control panel, which caused the time-portal to go haywire."

Lucy asked, "So what happened when you both transferred?"

Laura was standing by Jack's side and looking a bit deflated. He knew they wanted answers, but Laura had just saved their bacon and some confirmation of that would have been appreciated. Bending down, Jack scooped Laura up, giving her a huge hug.

"Well, I was glad to see you, you're my hero."

He thought maybe he was being a little rude, but a thank you from them would not have gone amiss. Lucy caught on quick and Emily looked embarrassed.

"I am so sorry, it's just that..." Emily went to say.

"It's alright, I understand, this is Laura, Laura, this is Emily and by the way, you are the greatest. I hope you know that."

She buried her head in Jack's neck, apparently going a little coy. That was a first. He didn't want to let her go, being that pleased to see her. Emily and Lucy came over and reached out to her. They had a sort of group hug, a bonding moment if you like.

Jack and Laura had done it; they'd saved Lucy and Emily.

Jack felt the relief, but at the same time he suspected this wasn't over. Call it instinct, but he knew everything was about to change.

Chapter 18

Emily found some spare clothes from one of the cupboards in the apartment and headed off to the wet room to get changed. Lucy and Laura sat down on the sofa while Jack made the tea.

Lucy seemed a lot happier now Emily was safe, "Thanks again for saving us," she said, hugging a smiling Laura.

"I had fun, even if 'Mr. careful' nearly called off the search."

Jack shook his head, "Just to re-evaluate. But heh, we're here, aren't we?" Poking out his tongue.

The wet room door slid open and Emily appeared, feeling more like herself now she was out of the smock dress she'd been forced to wear for the past year.

She continued on with her story, "All I remember is falling heavily and when I looked up, Prescott was pointing his gun at me. Then this man pulled up in his car and asked if we needed any help. Prescott grabbed me and told the driver to get back in the car and we both climbed into the back seat."

"The guy you're talking about, Terry I presume, blue Chevy Impala?" Jack asked.

"I'm not sure about the car, but yes, that was him."

Emily went on to say that they'd driven several miles to a ranch style property which, from her description could only have been Terry's place.

"When we got there, Prescott told him that he was a policeman from the future and I was a wanted criminal who'd illegally used the time-portal, as you call it now. He told Terry it actually belonged to the police."

Jack laughed, "He's been watching too many movies."

Emily gave him a sour look which shut him up. She went on to explain how she'd told them that it was likely someone would turn up looking for her.

"When we were in Terry's house, I noticed a newspaper on the side. It was dated 20th May 2002. That's when I knew I'd gone back a year."

"So that's how Terry knew Lucy would be at that spot?" Jack said.

"Not exactly, I had no way of knowing how the computer log history would interpret it. I suppose Prescott figured that out. Anyway, I always hoped and wished a miracle would happen and Lucy would find a way to locate me. Then I saw you and Lucy arrive at the village!"

"It was my second time," Jack said. "Laura and I had already been there, we just re-ran the day. I saw you but didn't put two and two together at the time."

Laura asked, "So how did you end up in the Amish community?"

"Terry was friends with Jacob and he came to his house almost every day. Jacob seemed okay initially and said it would be safer if I came to stay with him. He told Joseph we'd met at Richmond College and passed me off as his girlfriend. I went along with it as I feared I was stuck there for good."

Jack asked, "Did you tell Madeline the truth?"

"Yes, she promised to keep it a secret, but I had to have someone to trust. She said she would help if Lucy showed up."

Jack told them about their lunch and how Madeline had reacted when she'd seen Laura's travel-band. He kicked himself again for missing an opportunity which could have saved them all a lot of time and trouble.

"You weren't to know, don't beat yourself up," Emily still looked a little off with him though.

Laura asked, "So does Joseph know anything?"

"No, he's a gentleman. He's been really kind to me."

"There is something else we have to tell you," Lucy said, getting Emily's attention "Jack and Laura are from the year 2008!"

Emily looked shocked as Jack explained how he and Laura had found the cave and subsequently rescued Lucy. They could see she was shaken.

Jack checked his watch. It was three pm.

"How about we go back to mine and continue this, I'd like to get Laura home." Turning to Laura, "Where's your phone?" She pointed to the computer station. "Check it to see if Mom has called?"

She did and there was a missed call, but fortunately it had only been minutes before they'd arrived back. "Call her back and tell her you bumped into me and you're on the way home."

Laura agreed and made the call, telling her mom she'd not heard the phone ring as they'd had the music loud in the car. Jack shouted, hello, saying they were on the way home.

Making their way out of the cave they headed for Jack's car, grabbing Laura's bike on the way. Lucy and Laura jumped in the back and Emily climbed in beside Jack.

"I'm sorry if I seemed a bit rude earlier. I'm really grateful," she turned to Laura, "And you are one amazing girl," Laura smiled broadly.

Jack asked, "So where is Prescott now?"

"All I know is what Jacob told me. He said that Terry grew suspicious of him, there was a massive row and he took off and never came back."

"So if we need to learn more I guess we have to speak to Terry?"

"He is the only one who really knows I suppose."

"I'm hungry," Laura pointed out.

Not wanting to deny Laura anything after she'd shown such bravado, Jack took a detour to Macdonald's before heading home.

They checked in with Marion when they arrived and Jack introduced Emily, explaining she was Lucy's big sister and had come down to join them. Emily found the thought of being Jack's cousin quite amusing.

Marion didn't question it and told Laura to be home by eight.

Back at Jack's and after they'd eaten, he asked, "What about your Dad? Now that you're both safe, can't we use the time-portal to do something about that? We could also get rid of Prescott in the process."

"He always told us not to use the time-portal for our own gain," Emily said with a sad look.

"But that's not the case here, is it? We could save him and solve the Prescott problem for good," Jack said.

Emily frowned, "It's not that easy, if Lucy and I go back to before it happened - there will be two of us. Then if we change the future and our other selves don't use the time-portal, well, let's just say it could get quite messy."

"I understand. But there has to be a way?" He insisted.

Laura stepped forward smiling, "We could go back and tell your-other selves what's going to happen."

Lucy laughed, "Knowing Emily she won't believe you."

Emily looked alert, "Hang on, Laura might be on to something, we could write ourselves notes?"

Laura was excited at a new level, "We could video you and Lucy and you can introduce us in the video, and do the notes too."

"That sounds like it could work," Jack said.

Emily smiled, "It just might. Okay let's make a plan."

They spent the rest of the evening planning and doing a video. The girls wrote the notes to their other selves.

The following Day, Jack returned to work, dropping Emily and Lucy off at the cove on the way. They were going to return to their real time, making sure it was after they'd first disappeared. This way the portal would interpret that they had returned safely.

The plan would be implemented that coming Saturday.

When Jack arrived at the office, his boss, Mark Jones, was waiting for him.

"Nice of you to grace us with your presence, Jack, I hope we haven't inconvenienced you."

He replied in the same manner, "Always find the time for you, Mark."

"What's been up with you then?"

"Food poisoning, must have been something I ate."

"Uh huh. That was a fast recovery. Meeting in the conference room at ten about the fashion event you were supposed to be organising. And by the way, Leila is taking the lead on this one."

Jack was furious, "I'm the lead event organiser, that's my job."

"The client came in Monday with some last-minute changes. Leila is up to speed now. Accept it."

"Yes I understand. See you at ten," storming off, heading for the staff kitchen to get a coffee, Leila was there.

"The usual?" she asked.

"With a large bourbon chaser," Jack grunted and slopped into a chair.

"Ah, you've seen Mark then I take it!"

"Yeh boss," he swiped, regretting it immediately.

"Sorry, I don't want there to be friction between us."

"Forget it, I'm sorry. It's down to me. I think this will be a good opportunity for you anyway. It'll be fine, boss."

"Thanks, Jack, I appreciate your support," she smiled and his heart melted.

"You've got it, always," he said.

He was quite pleased in a way. After the last manic few days, he was happy to be taking a back seat for a while. The rest of the week did seem to drag on by for him though.

Jack and Leila had sorted out all the details ready for the fashion event. There was no animosity between them and he was glad about that. Her friendship was far too important to him to risk losing it. In fact, they were working well as a team and that was all that mattered.

Emily and Lucy came over Thursday evening via their blue-room and directly to Jack's house. Laura came around too and they all spent the evening together.

Laura had decided exactly what to do with Prescott, and although Jack thought sending him to the land of the dinosaurs quite fitting, they weren't murderers.

She did seem happy and Emily and Lucy growing very growing very fond of her. Jack felt they'd forged a friendship which even time itself couldn't deny them. But their plan was probably going to change all that.

By the end of the week, Jack and Laura were ready to get it done.

Chapter 19

Saturday 26th July

Jack and Laura set off for the blue-room Saturday morning, fully prepared to execute their plan. They'd both found it a little strange saying goodbye to Emily and Lucy and they felt a little sad when they'd left to go back to their real-time Thursday evening.

By changing the past, the Emily and Lucy they were about to meet would know nothing of what had happened, Jack and Laura would be strangers to them. They had the notes and the video which they hoped would convince them though.

Laura adjusted the date on the control screen to the 19th May, 2253, the evening before everything had happened. They needed time to explain everything to the other Emily. She said she'd been in the apartment from seven pm onwards.

Lucy was home and they needed Emily to get her to come and join them without letting Scott know what was going on. This was something Emily had insisted on.

Jack said, "Here goes."

Laura pulled a face, "Hope it works."

They put on their travel-bands and pressed their green buttons together, arriving in the cavern outside of the blue-room in 2253. They waited, knowing the computer inside the apartment would ping. Within seconds Emily appeared at the door. Seeing Laura must have calmed her a bit as she's only little, but Emily looked shocked all the same.

"Who are you and what are you doing here?"

"I'm Jack and this is Laura, we have a message for you, from, well, you."

She looked at them both suspiciously, "Has something happened, something in the future?"

"Well not the future," Jack said, "But yes, you need to watch a video, it will explain everything. We have notes from you as well. Can you ask Lucy to come down, I know she's at home?"

Jack passed her the note she'd written to herself. Emily walked back into the apartment and they followed. She sat down on the sofa, reading the note. Laura sidled up next to her.

"Well, it's definitely my writing," she said, reading it thoroughly.

Laura opened the screen on the video recorder and pressed play. Emily watched herself and Lucy explain everything that had happened. Jack and Laura were in the video too putting in their two-penny worth.

When the video had played out, Emily grabbed her phone and called Lucy. "Heh you, I need your help, can you come down - it's really important Lucy, please, just come - okay, see you in a few minutes. Don't worry Dad, I'll explain everything when you get here."

She turned to Jack and Laura, "She's on her way."

Emily picked up the note and read it again while they sat in silence and waited for Lucy to arrive.

There was a 'thud' as the hatch closed and the rock rolled back, then footsteps coming down the ladder. Lucy stepped inside the apartment. Jack and Laura were waiting for her to react, but she just looked at them both and smiled.

Laura went over to her. "Hi' I'm...."

"Laura, yes I know and you're Jack," Lucy interrupted.

"But how could you, you haven't met us yet, well you know, till now?" Laura was a little gobsmacked.

Emily interjected, "I'll explain that later. Lucy, look at this," she gave her the Video. Lucy sat in silence and watched it through to the end before reading the note to herself.

Laura snuggled up to Lucy and she smiled and put an arm around her. Laura looked pleased and hugged her back. They'd broken the ice again, thanks to Laura.

Emily said, "We could just call the CEP and have Prescott arrested for carrying a fire arm."

"And you don't think he's got some of them in his pocket," Lucy pointed out. "He'd be out in no time and there's no way of knowing what he'd do next."

Laura asked, "Who are the CEP?"

"Stands for Civil Enforcement Personnel."

Jack said, "Like our Police. What happened to them?"

"After the Civil War, they changed the name because it was the police who'd started it," Lucy said.

Jack laughed, shaking his head, "I knew that would come, when was that?"

"2120," Lucy replied, "So what's the plan? You do have one, don't you?" Smiling as if she already knew the answer.

"We do," Jack said and explained it to her. After he'd finished, Lucy seemed to stare at Emily for a while before she nodded.

Emily nodded too, "Okay, let's do it."

Jack and Laura returned to the blue-room back in 2008, altering the time and date on the control-station to 20th May, just before Scott and Prescott had arrived. This gave them enough time to ensure they were all ready and in place.

Getting the image of the blue-room up in 2253. Emily and Lucy were waiting for them as promised. They had the sound on this time and could communicate with them directly.

Emily and Lucy had two way radios. Jack had his crowbar and a set of handcuffs.

Emily said, "I'll be under the manhole cover waiting for Lucy's signal, Lucy will monitor the back cave and tell me when you're there."

"Laura will stay in contact with Lucy from our end," Jack said.

He put on his travel-band and got himself pumped up ready. He wasn't a fighting man, never had been, but he could hold his own and was quick and agile.

Jack couldn't help feeling nervous though. The plan was good but not perfect. The only thing they had on their side was that they could re-run it should something go wrong. Jack wanted to avoid that and get it done first time. He didn't think his nerves would take a second shot.

Lucy voice came through the intercom, "He's coming,"

Laura adjusted the dials on the control station to the back cave. They saw Prescott come in and stand back from the opening ready to surprise Scott.

"As soon as I go, adjust the image back to Lucy," Jack told Laura.

"I will, but please be careful."

He promised her he would as Laura chose a spot for him to appear, just behind Prescott. They knew he had a gun in his right jacket pocket and Jack was very aware of that. Pressing his green button, he found himself staring at Prescott's back. His heart was pumping at a hundred miles an hour. Prescott was a stocky guy of about fifteen stone and six one tall. He must have felt Jack's presence somehow as he turned quickly. His right hand went for his pocket. Jack had the element of surprise though and swung his crowbar, smashing it into Prescott's hand. He yelped in pain and his gun fell to the ground.

Jack went to kick his legs from under him, but Prescott was quick, grabbing Jack's leg and causing him to lose balance and fall. Jack rolled, going for the gun - Prescott kicked it away. As he did, Jack grabbed his foot and pulled him down with him.

The big rock started to roll and Jack had to be quick. Rolling over he went for the gun again. The manhole cover opened just as he reached it. Prescott was on him again though, just as Emily climbed up. She swiftly kicked him in his side and he doubled over, winded. Jack had the gun in his hand now and quickly got to his feet.

"Save it, Prescott, I won't hesitate to shoot you," he wasn't that convinced he would though.

"Who are you?" Prescott said with a look of surprise.

Emily looked at him with fire in her eyes, "That's not important, get down there," pointing to the ladder.

He hesitated for a moment. Jack took a step closer, gesturing with the gun. Prescott bought it and climbed into the cavern below. Jack kept the gun on him as Emily climbed down to join Prescott and he followed, not taking his eyes off Prescott for a moment.

Once they were in the cavern and with the hatch shut and the rock back in place, Jack handed Emily the gun and got the cuffs out.

"Hands behind your back," Jack ordered. He did and Jack slipped the cuffs on.

"What are you going to do?" he didn't look quite so threatening any more.

"You're going on a journey," Jack told him, smiling.

The blue-room door opened and Laura appeared beside Lucy. They were both looking quite pleased.

Jack led Prescott into the blue-room and put a travel-band on his wrist. He removed the one he had on which would take him back to his real time and put on a new one. Laura went to the control screen and entered some coordinates.

An image appeared of HMP Exeter prison, the year 1950. Knowing the cells didn't have toilets, sinks or TV's back then -

that was how the films and TV shows depicted them anyway, just a slab for a bed and a slop-out bucket, it seemed like a good compromise.

Laura chose an empty cell and Jack pressed his and Prescott's green buttons simultaneously. Arriving, they were instantly greeted with a strong smell of damp and stale urine. Jack very quickly swiped the travel-band off Prescott's wrist.

"Have fun," he said, disappearing from Prescott's view.

They all watched for a minute or two as he started to yell. They were sure he was in for some fun and games.

"Shut it off," Emily said eventually. "We've seen enough."

Lucy said, "I'll clear the log history."

"We'll get back to our time," Jack put his original travel-band back on.

"Okay, me and Lucy will come and see you tomorrow," Emily said.

"You promise?" Laura gave Emily a hug.

"I promise," she hugged her back.

"Me too," Lucy said as she came back in. "All done, we just need to get back to the apartment and act like nothing has happened."

Jack and Laura returned to their blue-room and watched as the girls went into the apartment. After a few minutes, Scott walked in, alive and well.

Seeing Lucy, he said, "I didn't know you were here with Emily."

"Just hanging," Lucy replied, giving her dad a hug.

"What did I do to deserve that?"

"Dunno, just felt like it," Lucy laughed.

Emily got up from her seat and hugged him too, "Shall we go out for breakfast?"

"My two daughters together for breakfast, dare I say no?"

"No," They both said together, grabbing an arm each and leading him out.

Jack looked at Laura, she smiled and a tear ran down her cheek. It was all very emotional.

"Breakfast sounds like a good idea," Jack said.

"Sound good to me too," Laura said wiping her face with her sleeve.

Chapter 20

Jack and Laura went straight home to cook a celebratory breakfast for a job well done, pleased they still had their new friends, looking forward to seeing them the following day. There would be much to talk about.

As Jack pulled up onto his driveway he immediately saw the smashed window beside the front door. The door was ajar and it was obvious he'd just been burgled. His heart sank and he asked Laura to go and get her mom whilst he went inside to see what damage had been done.

It was a mess, things strewn everywhere. Jack decided not to touch anything and picked up his phone to call the local plod. They took the details and the officer said they'd send someone around.

Laura and Marion came in a few moments later, "What a mess, have they taken much?" Marion asked.

"I've not had a good look yet, I've called the Police though, so best not to touch anything for the moment."

"They probably won't come till tomorrow," Laura said with a frown.

"You're probably right, Laura," Jack said and Marion nodded. "Where had you two been?"

Laura was pulling one of her funny faces out of Marion's view and Jack had to stifle a laugh, "We'd been to Newton Abbot, I needed a printer cartridge and the shop in Torquay's shut down. We were only gone an hour and a half tops,"

"Sounds like they've been watching you."

"You could be right," Jack said, "We were about to have breakfast too."

"Come around to mine and bring some bacon, I've got the rest."

They left a note on the door in case the police did turn up by some miracle. Marion started on breakfast and Laura made the tea.

"So apart from this, have you had a good week?" Marion asked.

"Not so bad, it was good to see my cousins, been a while." Jack almost cringed at his continued lie.

Laura said, "I really like Emily and Lucy."

"You do seem a bit happier," Marion said with a smile, scuffing her hair. "Glad to see it."

After they'd had breakfast, Jack and Laura went back to his place to survey the damage and see what was missing. He was sure the police wouldn't be that interested and he needed to clean up anyway.

Checking his bill tin, where he normally kept a hundred pounds or so, of course that was gone. The company laptop was also missing along with his play station, portable DVD, an amplifier and some jewellery. Nothing else sprung out. They'd left the TV and Sky box fortunately.

"What about the digital camera?" Laura asked

Jack went suddenly cold, remembering the pictures they'd taken around the rock in 2253. He grabbed the back pack which they hadn't taken that day and checked inside. As Laura suspected it was gone.

"What if they see the pictures, they'll know?"

Jack shrugged, "They may scan through them, but unless they know what they're looking at they won't see anything of relevance."

"Do you think we should tell Emily and Lucy?"

"Best not to right now," Jack shook his head. "It still may not be an issue."

"I hope you're right," Laura didn't look convinced though.

Just then there was a tap on the door. They knew it was too soon for his friend Trevor, who he'd called to fix the window. Opening the door, Jack was faced with an official looking guy.

He introduced himself as DC John Short, "I understand you've had a break in."

"Yes, found out about an hour or so ago, come in, I was just looking to see what is missing."

"I'll need a list of the missing items. So, this happened this morning?"

"Yes, sometime between nine thirty and eleven, we'd just popped out for a bit," Jack said thinking - just popped out to 2253 to stop someone getting murdered. He saw Laura smiling at him and was sure she knew what he was thinking sometimes.

Jack made a list of the missing items for the detective, including the camera. He was fully insured so he knew there would be no issues with replacing the stuff.

John, the policeman, was glancing about, looking to be making mental notes. In fact, Jack suspected it was more likely he was thinking about what to have for lunch.

Laura sat on the sofa being very quiet, eying John warily. Jack noticed John glance over to her, attempting a smile, but she remained straight faced.

"You might want to invest in an alarm," he said, breaking the silence.

"Yes I agree. I'll get one today."

"The more the deterrent the less likely they are to return."

He took the list and said he would call Jack with a crime number for the insurance. Jack thanked him, not expecting to hear anything further from him after that. All the same he decided to take his advice.

Laura got up, pulling a face, "I didn't like him."

"Guess he's just doing his job," Jack said. "Let's pop into town and get the alarm. Could you ask your Mom if she can house sit for a while?"

Laura went next door and returned with Marion a few minutes later. Jack had already switched on his personal PC for her to play bingo on. The thieves had kindly left that too, probably as it was hard to get at.

They had a cup of tea before heading off to the DIY store to get the things they needed. By the time they got back, Trevor had been and fixed the window, which was good news. Jack and Laura set to work.

"I'm feeling lucky today," Marion announced. "I just won twenty pounds. I fancy going into town for bingo tonight, would you mind..."

"Looking after Laura," Jack finished for her. "Of course I don't mind. Emily and Lucy are coming down again tomorrow."

"Laura might as well stay over at yours tonight then. I can go out for drinks with my mate after bingo."

"Sure you're up to it?" He asked.

"Feeling a little better, I think you were right about the drugs, they seem to be working."

"Well, don't overdo it. You can also have a lay-in tomorrow morning huh?"

"I'll go and get Laura's things," Marion gave him the middle finger and laughed, heading out.

"Want me to install the alarm software?" Laura asked.

"That would be great, if you're sure you know what you're doing. I'll fit the sensors."

By mid-afternoon the alarm was fitted and the house looked a little more like home again. Jack allowed himself to relax a little and realised he was looking forward to the following day when they would see their new friends again. Lucy and Laura had connected so well, Jack just hoped he would with Emily, for more than one reason.

Chapter 21

Laura was excited that Sunday morning as she and Jack had planned to take Emily and Lucy for a drive to Lyme Regis, which was a little further up the coast and one of Jack's favourite spots. There was something about the place which he found quite enchanting. It was a typical coastal village and it relied purely on holiday makers to survive.

Emily and Lucy were going to meet them at the harbour in Torquay so they headed off. Locating a parking place was difficult, but they eventually found one. Walking to the water's edge, they waited, not knowing where Emily and Lucy would appear from.

"I can't see them anywhere, I hope they're still coming," Laura looked a little concerned.

"I'm sure they will turn up, Laura, stop worrying."

Just then, Jack felt a tap on his shoulder, it was Emily. Lucy had done the same to Laura. They both jumped in surprise.

"We were tracking you," Lucy said laughing.

Laura pulled a face and wagged her finger at Lucy, "That was cheating."

They all hugged, Jack asked, "How are things at home? Does Scott suspect anything?"

Emily explained that everything at home was good and Scott didn't suspect a thing about how they'd changed events to save his life.

Jack told them about their plans to drive to Lyme Regis and they both happily agreed, squeezing into Jack's little Honda and setting off up the coast road, taking in the magnificent views along the way, much better than taking the motorway route.

On the way, they spoke about their other selves rescue from the evil Joe and Jacob, deciding there were still several unanswered questions, but they would probably have to stay that way as they couldn't afford to risk changing too many events. It didn't matter as the most important thing was that they had taken care of Prescott and he would never bother them again.

Jack asked, "Why did Prescott want your Dad dead?"

"He was attempting to get approval for a nuclear power plant to be built on Thatchers Rock, right above the time-portal," Emily said. "It was due to go through another planning stage soon."

"So this is all about power then. He just wanted Scott out of the way and control of the time-portal so he could guarantee his future," Jack said. "Could the plant still go ahead then?"

"That's up to whoever takes over from Prescott," Emily shrugged. "Once they've figured out he's missing, it's just a matter of time. All we've done is stalled the build, it's inevitable it will still go ahead."

"We'll stop them," Laura said with a determined look on her face, "We're 'team time' and we're invincible."

The look on both Emily and Lucy's faces said something different though, but Jack decided not to pursue it as this was supposed to be a relaxing day out together.

Lyme Regis is a beautiful place and they all had a great day together. Emily and Lucy had friends who lived in that locality, but in 2253 and they were particularly interested to see how much it had changed. Emily explained that, like Torquay and Paignton, much had changed away from the coast, however, the beach and surrounding area looked very much the same.

Rounding off the morning, they had a fish and chips lunch in a pub which was right by the sea front, then after lunch they took

Emily and Lucy on a tour of the shops which sold the usual seaside gifts such as shells, rocks and other similar paraphernalia.

Laura of course wanted to buy everything she picked up, but Jack refrained from spoiling her too much as he knew Marion wouldn't approve. She settled for a Chrystal stone which was grossly over-priced, but he couldn't deny her.

As they were heading back to the car Laura asked, "Can you show us around your time?"

Lucy looked over at Emily then back at Laura with a smile, "We can do that next time."

"You mean it, can we come next week, can we?"

"Sure can," Emily assured her smiling.

"You'll love it Laura," Lucy said. "We'll take you on a tour of Newtown Village."

"Is that like out Newton Abbot?" Jack asked.

Emily laughed, "A little different, but you'll see. Don't spoil the surprise, Lucy."

"Can't wait," Laura said, "I take it you've got a car?"

"Just wait and see," Emily wagged her finger, laughing.

Laura continued firing the questions as they drove home - she was getting quite excited. Jack was too, but he kept his feelings to himself. Not only because he wanted to see how much had changed in their time but also to see Emily again, as he'd decided he was quite taken with her.

Chapter 22

Torquay - 2008

DC John Short had been a cop for over twenty years and a Military Policeman before then. He'd dedicated his life to law enforcement and had always given his best throughout his career.

Things change though.

What with recent government cut backs, he'd seen his career come to a crushing halt. He felt he still had much to give, but the force had decided to let him go, calling it early retirement. The package was inadequate and John felt disillusioned and angry.

During his final few weeks as a cop, John had grown very bitter, seeing younger men pushing him aside. They were arrogant and seemed to take great pleasure in belittling him at every opportunity.

Determined to prove he still had what it took to be a good cop, John worked all hours investigating a recent string of burglaries. Using his knowledge of his beat and of the repeat offenders he'd had the misfortune of meeting over the years, he'd managed to catch the thief.

He'd turned up at the home of Liam Yates with his partner Dan Lawrence that morning. John had arrested Yates earlier, after catching him selling stolen items to a fence. Yates was taken away for questioning whilst he and Dan tore his home apart looking through what was left of his cache.

They had a long list of items taken from his victims. These included things such as TV's, DVD's, Computers, stereo equipment and so on.

Rummaging through the mess of things, John came across a small Olympus digital camera, a very expensive looking one. He had recently been looking at them and this had been one he'd had on his wish list.

John turned it on and started to scroll through the images on the LED screen. Initially the images appeared to be nothing out of the ordinary, just views of the coast.

Something made him pause; something that didn't look right. He looked a little closer at one of the images which was taken from the cliff edge by Thatchers Rock, looking inland.

The image depicted rolling fields and hills. The sky was clear blue with a slight red tinge to it. John had been in Torquay for many years and he knew the area quite well. There was no sign of the housing estate off Thatcher Avenue and the many sea view homes where Torquay's rich folk lived.

His partner Dan was in another room, so he quickly pocketed the small camera so he could have a closer look at it later. The cop in John was telling him something wasn't right and he wanted to investigate it further.

Later that day, with Yates in custody and charged with a long list of burglaries, John scrolled through the images once again. This time taking a little more time to study the pictures properly.

He'd considered that maybe he was wrong and it was just some place that looked the same, but scrolling on through the images he saw a picture of a young girl, one he recognized, but couldn't place right away.

Before leaving the office, he copied the list of stolen items and their prospective owners. Looking down the list and cross referencing items with names, he found the listing for the camera.

Looking across he could see that the owner was a Jack Clarke. He remembered him from his visit the previous Saturday. The guy was a Londoner and he'd had a young girl with him called Laura, who had a West Midlands accent.

John decided that he'd stumbled onto something strange.

He wanted to know more about this unlikely pair and what secrets they were keeping.

Chapter 23

POWER SOURCE.
Saturday 2ⁿᵈ August

Back at work, Jack's week seemed to drag on longer than usual with everything seeming so ordinary and a little boring. He'd got the bug for time-travelling and couldn't wait to get back to it. Of course, it could have been a lot to do with meeting Emily. She'd been constantly in his thoughts, and although Leila's charms weren't hard to miss, he supressed his feelings for her because she was married after all and therefore out of play.

He also knew Laura was looking forward to seeing Lucy. They'd hit it off immediately, both times, and had already become firm friends. Emily was a different story though and he still couldn't figure her out. Maybe that was the reason he was attracted to her. But then, he'd never been able to figure Leila out either from that point of view.

Finally, the weekend arrived and Jack and Laura set off for the blue-room. They were meeting Emily and Lucy by the cliff, out of site from the house, thus avoiding Scott.

Laura dialled up the coordinates and they saw Emily's futuristic car parked beside the road in 2253. Emily and Lucy stood beside the car facing the rock.

They put on their travel-bands and Laura finely adjusted the view so they would land just behind the car and out of site.

"On three," Jack said to a giggling Laura, getting their own back after Emily and Lucy had crept up on them the previous weekend.

Appearing behind the car, they heard Emily say to Lucy; "You know they're going to creep up on us."

Laura jumped out from behind the car and shouted, "Gotchya."

Emily jumped, but Lucy was smiling and remained cool, "Like that you mean," she laughed.

"We had to get you back," Laura said, giving them both a big hug. This was sure to become an ongoing game, but one Jack would never deny Laura, she was their hero after all.

Laura eyed Emily's sleek looking car. It was something right out of a futuristic movie. But then that shouldn't have been a surprise as they were in 2253. It looked a little like a space ship on wheels with its flip-paint job, changing colour in different light. The interior was plush with leather and chrome with a touch screen control panel in the centre of the dash.

"Wow, it's like getting into a lounge bar," Jack said, climbing in beside Emily.

Laura was grinning from ear-to-ear, her rear bucker seat almost engulfing her, "So where are you taking us?"

"We're taking you on a tour of the coast and then into Newtown Village for lunch," Emily explained.

Laura asked, "So what's in Newtown Village?"

"You'll see," Lucy replied with a smile. Laura looked confused for a moment before smiling too. "You'll will like it, Laura, I promise."

Laura had her hand to her ear, "Why can't I hear the engine?"

Emily smiled, "That's because it's an electric car," pulling away silently.

"What sort of range does it have?" Jack asked, knowing electric cars were quite new to his and Laura's time and the range was normally less than a hundred miles.

"It can store enough power to go five hundred plus miles, but whilst the sun is out it's constantly topping up."

"Solar energy huh, how cool," Jack said. "How many batteries does it have then for a range like that?"

"Just the one," Emily replied. "I bet you'll never guess the size of it?"

"The size of a mobile phone," Laura responded quickly.

Emily looked a little surprised, "Lucky guess and you're right."

Laura just smiled and Lucy was laughing. Jack looked a little confused, thinking he must have missed something, so he just kept quiet.

As they drove along the coast it was clear that a lot had changed. Gone were the towns of Torquay and Paignton, replaced with towering steel and glass structures which lined the coast road. There were more ranch style properties scattered about as they headed inland. They were of immaculate design and seemed to meld into the landscape.

The sky was clear once again, with that strange red haze Jack had noticed before. It was warm and the yellow sun seemed brighter than he'd ever seen it before.

Travelling through Torr Hills towards the village, they drove by other electric cars without a sound, this created a peaceful surrounding. Reaching the crest of the hill, the village started to come into view.

Towering up to one hundred levels high were chrome and glass structures. These were linked with walkways, connecting all the structures. Getting closer, they could see there were electric monorail carriages whizzing around the perimeter.

It was built in a square mile area, Emily explained, and no cars were allowed. There were four out of town car parks, each with its own passenger collection point.

Lucy asked, "What do you think?"

"It's totally cool," Laura looked suitably impressed, "I can't wait to have a look around."

Parking in the south car park, they made their way to the monorail collection point. Within minutes a carriage pulled up silently. The doors slid open and they stepped inside. It pulled away and gathered speed effortlessly. It had no sooner done so when it glided to a stop inside one of the towers, twenty levels high above the ground.

Stepping out of the carriage and onto the platform, they were presented with a large active map of the village. The platform led to rolling walkways, shooting off in different directions connecting all the structures.

"Which way are we going?" Laura asked.

Emily pointed to the tallest building which was in the centre of the village, "There's a food complex on the ninety ninth level. There is also a viewing area above it on level one-hundred. We'll take you there later."

Laura jumped onto the moving walkway, having quickly calculated the route to the main tower. Lucy was hot on her heels. Emily and Jack took a more leisurely pace.

"I hope you know how grateful I am for everything you and Laura have done for us," Emily said, taking his arm.

"I'm glad we were able to help, and anyway, I think Laura has gained more confidence though it all. She adores both of you."

"I can't even imagine what would have become of us should you not have found us. I'm just sorry I've no memory of the rescue."

They transferred onto another walkway at the next tower, and one more before arriving at the central tower. The last walkway had a span the length of a football pitch. Lucy and Laura were waiting for them at the other end by the elevator.

Pilling into the elevator, Lucy pressed the button for the ninety-ninth level. It gathered speed smoothly and ascended the seventy-nine levels in a matter of seconds, or so it seemed. Laura felt a little light headed when the door opened.

"Phew, that's quicker than the drop at Chessington," Laura said, holding her stomach.

Emily was laughing, "You'll get used to it."

The food complex consisted of about twenty-five separate establishments, mostly take away. There were four waiter service outlets a bit further up. Tables and chairs were lined up and down the centre of the complex. It was large enough to seat about five hundred people.

Laura grabbed Jack and Emily's hands, pointing to the first establishment with a burger sign. Lucy was already heading that way. They caught up with her and ordered their food. It was served in less than a minute and was piping hot.

Finding a quiet spot, they sat down with their food and tucked in. Jack asked, "So has Prescott been replaced yet?"

"Yes, with a guy called Chris King," Emily replied.

"Is that good or bad news?"

"Not good," shaking her head. "He is every bit as bad if not worse than Prescott."

"So I take it they're still pushing forward with their plans?"

"Not only that, but with our natural resources running so low, it's inevitable it will go ahead as planned," Emily said, a sad look.

Laura asked, "How can we stop them?"

"I'm not sure we can," Lucy cut in, "Unless we can find an alternative power source."

"Why can't you use solar energy like your car does?" Laura enquired.

Emily frowned, "I wish it were that simple, but the village consumes an enormous amount of power and solar energy just isn't enough."

Laura looked worried, "How much time do we have?"

"Not much," Emily said. "There's a planning-meeting Monday!"

Chapter 24

The news was discouraging, leaving them with little or no time to do anything useful. The biggest concern being that Emily and Lucy would lose access to the time-portal.

Jack asked, "If they vote in favour, how long before work on the plant commences?"

"Usually four weeks," Emily replied.

"That's quick. Back in our time they'd talk about it for several years then take that amount of time again before they built it, if you're lucky," Jack said, surprised.

Emily explained that many things had changed since the Civil War of 2120. It had been a bloody war and millions of people had been killed, with mass destruction country wide.

Queen Sophia ruled as head of state in their time and the government was now a civil affair. There were still councils, but not as Jack and Laura knew them. They were truly representative of the people and not faceless bureaucrats and corrupt officials. The regime they once knew so well was no more. Or at least that's how it seemed.

"The CEP had replaced the Police after an attempted rebellion by a group within the force. They were misguided enough to believe they could take over the country, which didn't work out for them," Emily said, pulling a face. "My Dad become a leading figure in the civil movement throughout the south-west. The Civil planning group is just one of his responsibilities."

She explained more about Chris King and his reputation for getting the job done at any cost, willing to take whatever course of action necessary to get his way, very much like Prescott. This had come to light as three of the planning group committee members had resigned the previous week. All three had been supporters of Scott. There were three new members due to be sworn in that coming Monday.

Rumours were already suggesting they were planted by King. Jack was surprised at the speed in which things happened, and if they *were* supporters of the nuclear plant, the vote was sure to go King's way.

Laura said, "There must be something we can do to stop them?"

Lucy shrugged, "The only way that I can see, as I've already said is, to find an alternative power source!"

They considered that wasn't likely, so, they were looking at damage limitation, and even that didn't give them any options Jack could see.

"The situation sounds dire," he said. Emily and Lucy agreed.

Laura was getting angry, "We have to do something - we're a team, aren't we?" The tears welling up in her eyes, Lucy saw this too and reached out, taking her hand.

"What's the likelihood of them finding the cave or destroying it by accident?" Jack asked.

"From the plans we've seen that's unlikely," Emily replied. "But access to the cave would be blocked as they would take control of the entire area surrounding the rock and a mile inland."

He'd already figured that and didn't have an answer. The tears were rolling down Laura's cheeks now. Her caring nature just wanted to see the good in everyone, but sometimes there isn't good in certain people and Jack was sure King was one of them.

They finished their lunch and Emily and Lucy took them to the viewing area as promised. It didn't help lift Laura's mood, in fact they were all a little subdued.

Emily insisted they shouldn't let it spoil their day out, but even with trips to various shopping outlets, nothing seemed to lift Laura from her gloom. The tour complete, they made their way back to Emily's car.

Laura asked, "Can we go to your house?"

"Dad will be there, another time, I promise," Emily replied.

"Does he still have no idea what happened?" Jack asked.

"None whatsoever, thankfully," Emily said, "I'd like to keep it that way for now."

From the expression on Lucy's face, Jack could see that she didn't agree, "I think we should tell him now. I want him to meet Jack and Laura."

"And I would too. Soon, I promise," Emily tried to assure her, but it was clear they had different views.

"Next time we come, I really want to come to your house, you've got to promise," Laura was staring at Emily - a dark look in her eyes. Jack noticed Emily touch her forehead as if in pain, which worried him. She looked across at Lucy before answering.

"I promise we'll sort it out, Laura. I'm just concerned about how Dad will take it. He has always said we shouldn't mess with time, as there would be consequences."

Jack asked, "What sort of consequences?"

"I don't know, honestly. It was enough to stop our ancestors wanting to use the technology. It's only in recent years we have."

Arriving back at the rock. Emily and Lucy gave Laura a big hug and they agreed to meet at Jack's place Monday evening, after the power plant planning meeting.

Back in the blue-room, 2008, Laura and Jack watched as Lucy hugged her big sister, they were both crying. This set Laura off again and Jack consoled her as best he could. They drove home in silence. Jack knew she was worried about losing their new friends, for the second time.

Marion was there to greet them as they pulled onto my driveway, "You had a visitor earlier."

"Oh, who was that?" Jack asked.

"A Policeman!" She handed Jack a card. "His name was Dan Lawrence. He wanted to speak with you about the robbery."

"Did he say what it was about exactly? I was under the impression John Short was handling the matter?"

"He's taken early retirement. He did say they had recovered some of your things though. He's coming back to see you Monday after work." Marion followed them inside, "So what have you two been up to today?"

"We just went into town and had lunch," Laura said, a smile appearing on her face.

"Oh good, did you go somewhere nice to eat?"

"We found a place which does burgers which are out of this world," She answered with a silly grin on her face.

Jack had to look away so Marion didn't notice his astonished expression. Laura did sail close to the wind at times. Marion didn't seem to notice though.

Later, Jack met up with some friends for a game of pool. He had agreed to meet up with Marion and Laura the following morning as they'd planned to go to a boot sale together.

As he wasn't driving, he had a few too many beers, seeing his game grow steadily worse till finally, he rolled home in the early hours, much worse for wear.

He awoke Sunday morning with a very sore head, quite thankful they weren't saving the world that day. The original reason for going to the boot sale was to see if they could spot any of Jack's stolen items for sale. This was often the way in which such things were disposed of.

Marion and Laura arrived at ten and Jack's head was still throbbing. He got no sympathy from Laura though. He didn't have the stomach for breakfast, deciding there would probably be a burger van at the boot sale.

It was quite busy when they arrived with people making their way up and down the many lines of stalls. Most of these were full of inconsequential items which were of no interest, but Laura spotted a second-hand Saxophone, an instrument they both wanted to learn.

By lunchtime Jack's stomach was growling but there wasn't a burger van in site, only a pink ice cream van, which they gave a wide berth. Heading back to Jack's, they cooked up a traditional Sunday roast, the first in weeks with all that had been going on.

Marion and Laura seemed to be getting along better than usual, which came as a relief to Jack. He knew there was no doubt Marion adored Laura, but showing it sometimes seemed to be an effort, although he blamed that on the prescription drugs she was taking. He guessed that was why Laura had turned up on his doorstep months before looking for friendship.

He'd pushed her away initially, largely because how society viewed such friendships, but she wasn't about to give up that easily. He'd soon realised what a talented and clever girl she was. Marion and Jack had become friends and it had gone on from there. There was no romantic connection with them as Marion had told Jack he wasn't her type, and to be fair, Jack felt the same way. But they got along well and genuinely liked each-other.

Jack's marriage had broken down many years earlier. He'd had a wonderful Son though. Laura had met him on a few occasions, but Richard had little time for Laura, that age. Still, she was very fond of him anyway, looking on him as a big Brother.

Jack's job had brought him to Torquay as he covered all the events in the west of England. At the time, the move had made perfect sense as it was a central location for work. But he'd tired of Torbay and had been seriously considering a move.

This was out of the question now, since he felt responsible for Laura, more than that, he'd grown to love her unconditionally.

After their Sunday roast, Marion returned home to her internet bingo whilst Laura and Jack practiced the Sax until Jack felt the neighbours had been punished enough. Giving the neighbours a break, they went to the cinema.

By the end of the day it occurred to them both that it was the most normal Sunday they'd spent together for some time. They hadn't talked much about Emily and Lucy as Jack knew Laura was quite worried still.

Monday's meeting couldn't come soon enough.

Chapter 25

Monday 4th August 2253

It was nine in the morning when Emily left home and headed for the cave in 2253. She felt tense and apprehensive about the Civil planning meeting later that day. If the vote went in favour of the development, which was quite likely, access to the time-portal would be lost forever.

Emily was the eldest daughter of Scott, and at thirty-two, she felt responsible for protecting her seventeen-year-old little sister, Lucy. They'd lost their mom, Carol, two years earlier in a plane crash, which had killed all five hundred and thirty-five on board. She'd been returning from visiting family in Australia.

Accidents of this kind were unheard of and had been for quite some time with advances in technology, but society still had its rebels. It was believed this had been a hijacking gone wrong, however, no flight disc was ever found and even today, it was a mystery what had happened to flight TL305.

As she approached the cove, Emily was immediately aware that something wasn't right. There were several flat-bed transporters pulled up beside the green and men were unloading link fences.

Emily was furious and hurried over to an officious looking man, "What do you think you're doing? Planning hasn't been approved yet. You can't put up these fences."

"I'm just following orders Mam. However, it's inevitable the planning group will approve the plants go ahead, so please stay clear and let us do our work," the officious man turned to walk away.

Emily was beside herself with rage, "I'll have you stopped - you do not have the authority."

The officious man spun around, a look of arrogance, "I have been informed that approval is imminent, so please keep clear."

An angry and frustrated Emily pulled out her video phone and dialled her father Scott, but it went straight through to messaging. "Dad, they're fencing off the area around the cove, what should I do? Please call," Emily pleaded, walking slowly back towards the house.

Lost and upset and with tears rolling down her cheek, Emily felt frustrated. There was no way of telling Jack and Laura what had happened, although she was quite sure they would work it out. This was her only comfort though.

The planning group meeting was due to commence at eleven that morning. There were only two matters to attend to, swearing in the three new members and the vote on the plant go ahead.

The sudden departure of the three former members had come as quite a shock and all three within the same week. This had caused speculation and suspicion and it was suspected that Christopher King had something to do with it. All three had left the village complex within twenty-four hours of their resignation and none had left forwarding addresses.

Corruption within the civil government was extremely rare, but with the Earth's natural resources drying up, the power-hungry breed of nuclear power plant bosses took full advantage of the situation with no consideration for the long-term damage they would cause.

Emily hoped her father would find a way to swing the vote, but even if he did, were they only stalling the inevitable decision for the plant to go ahead?

Lucy was sitting at the kitchen table when Emily returned. She could see her big sister had been crying.

"What's happened?"

Emily told her about the link fences going up and the officious man.

"Have you called Dad?"

"Left a message."

Lucy jumped up from the table, "They can't do this Emily - we have to stop them."

"I know, but how? The man was quite confident approval was imminent and I have a feeling he may be right."

Emily put her arms around Lucy and hugged her tight. They were both sobbing now, neither having any answers.

In Newtown Village, Scott was already seated at the conference table. He'd been sitting there for an hour deliberating. There were eight group members including Scott. At the last meeting, the vote had gone five to three against the plant, but King had insisted the group had the opportunity to hear the revised plans. King had managed to get the second hearing by using his connections in London, namely Scott's boss.

A close colleague and group member, Bill Brady, had indicated to Scott he was about to withdraw his support for the plant. This was encouraging, but the problem was the three new members. The former members had all voted against. If rumours were to be believed, and Scott had every reason to think so, the new members were all in favour, which would be enough for the nuclear plant to be approved.

The group members started to arrive. Bill came in first and gave Scott a nod and a smile. Steve Russell followed, he was behind Scott too. All three new members arrived together, Mandy Glover, Martin Stiller and Lewis Mackenzie. There seemed to be an air of familiarity between them. Next to arrive were Stewart Robin and Sylvia Knight, both were known supporters.

The meeting was brought to order and Scott introduced the new members. They were each sworn in before going on to the main part of the meeting.

"We have just one further item to attend to, the Thatchers Rock Nuclear Plant. Before we go to vote, I have a statement from Christopher King, the CEO of Prescott Nuclear Fusions."

He read out the statement, which basically covered the positioning of the plant. It also went on to explain the effect on the immediate surroundings and the revised section which covered the Rock itself. Thatchers Rock had been a landmark for thousands of years, this would be preserved, but the cove access would remain secured and inaccessible.

This of course meant access to the time-portal would not be possible. This was quite intolerable, but Scott could see no solution. He looked around the room, they all seemed eager to continue.

"Shall we vote?"

Each member had a small sheet of paper in front of them. For or against is all they had to write. Each sheet of paper was folded and handed to Scott.

He opened Bills first, against. Next was Steve, also against. Both Stewart and Sylvia remained in favour. He had three remaining in his hand, he opened Mandy's first, for, then Martin, for, and then Lewis, for. His was the final vote - but it didn't matter.

Scott's heart sank, the decision to approve the plant had been made. Work would commence in fourteen days. There was no appeal process in normal circumstances, although he was now quite certain that the three new members were plants by King's people. Proving that was going to be difficult though. But this would be the only way to get them back to the table.

Scott felt powerless. He knew Emily and Lucy would be devastated at the news.

He wasn't looking forward to going home and having to face them.

Chapter 26

Monday 4th August 2008

Jack arrived home from work Monday evening and found Dan Lawrence on his doorstep waiting, recognising him from Marion's description.

"Jack Clarke?" he enquired.

"You must be Dan Lawrence," Jack shook his hand, "I understand you've recovered my stolen items."

"That's right. You can pick them up from the station next week. We have the thief in custody, he's already pleaded guilty."

"Good work, come in. So, what happened to John?"

Dan gave Jack his card and explained that with recent cut backs, some police officers had been offered early retirement packages. Whilst John had been ten years away from his official retirement date, he had taken up the option, be it stubbornly.

He went on to explain that it had been John who'd caught the thief trying to fence stolen items at a local second hand shop. On searching his home, stolen items from several burglaries had been recovered.

Dan handed Jack a short list of the items recovered which belonged to him, there were just three items listed, his company laptop, play-station and portable DVD player.

"There's no mention of my amp, jewellery or my digital camera?"

"I'm afraid this is all we recovered of yours, he'd probably already fenced them."

This was his worst fear, as if things couldn't get any worse. "So when did you get the guy?" Jack was desperately trying to figure out a way to locate the camera.

"Last Tuesday morning in town."

He pushed on, "Is he a local man?"

"Yes, he's well known to us."

Jack needed more, "How local?"

"Warren Road, that's all I can say."

That was probably enough for him to work with so he thanked Dan, who gave Jack a receipt to take into the station the following Tuesday.

Considering whether he should mention something to Emily and Lucy about the camera, he decided they had enough on their plates with their own situation. He put the kettle on and a few moments later Laura appeared.

"Who was that?"

Jack repeated the conversation he'd had with Dan and the bad news about the camera.

"We have to find it?" Laura said.

"I agree, so where do we start?"

"At the thief's house, we can use the time-portal to see when the police did the search and go from there."

It sounded perfectly reasonable, "I guess I'm going to have to take another day off?"

"Will your boss let you?"

"He should as the next event doesn't start till Thursday and I've already done the prep work." Jack thought for a moment. "I'll call Mark first thing tomorrow and ask for two days' holiday, I'll tell him we're going to London to see Richard, he'll be okay with that."

"Where is your next event?"

"It's in Edinburgh. I fly up first thing Thursday and should be home by Friday evening at some point."

"I wish I could go with you," Laura pouted.

Jack would have preferred not to go with everything that was going on, but with Mark on his back he had little choice. "Next time we have an event closer to home I promise."

"I'll hold you to that," she said, smiling now. "I still have four weeks' holiday left before I start year seven."

"We'll see, I'll find out on Thursday what's coming up, I promise," Jack said.

"Cool. Mom's cooking dinner, you're invited."

That came as a relief to Jack as he didn't feel much like cooking. Laura left him to shower and change before joining them for dinner. He was certain that by the time he returned home, Emily and Lucy would be there waiting for him. But when he arrived back there was no sign of them. By eleven he was quite worried, although there was little he could do till morning. He imagined the worst and had little sleep.

The following morning Jack called his boss, Mark. For a change, he seemed to be in a good mood, agreeing to give Jack the time off, providing he and Leila had the next event covered. Jack assured him they had, hanging up before he changed his mind.

Putting the kettle on for a cup of tea, Laura appeared moments later with a worried look on her face.

"They didn't come did they?"

"No sign, but we'll know soon enough when we get to the cave," he said getting another mug out for Laura.

"Something bad must have happened, what if they can never use the time-portal again?"

"Let's hope there's a simple explanation," Jack wasn't convinced there would be though.

Laura scowled at him, "We better get going then."

Gulping down their teas, they got their things together and headed off for the rock and to the time-portal. Once inside, they dialled up the green above the rock in 2253. The image appeared and it was clear what the problem was right away. The whole area was fenced off and there was a high level of security.

Laura re-adjusted the image to Emily and Lucy's home. Nobody was there, so they decided to check out the burglars' house in Warren Road.

They didn't know the time the police searched the premises, however, they did know it had been the previous Tuesday. Starting at nine and flicking forward, they noticed a black Seat Ibiza parked outside one of the houses about half way along. Dan and John both had one, which meant this had to be one of them.

Having mastered the controls, Laura had the image adjusted to inside of the house and quickly found John and Dan in a top floor flat. They watched for several minutes before noticing John pick up a small object. Laura zoomed in to see what he was holding. It was Jack's Olympus digital camera.

He turned it on and started to scan the images. Frowning, he looked to see where Dan was. Unsighted, John slipped the camera into his pocket.

Jack's worst fear was realised. He was certain John had seen something to make him curious enough to steal police evidence. He had little doubt about recovering the camera, it was John he was more concerned about.

Jack was just thinking about their next move when Laura decided she had it sorted. "We can follow him home after work and see where he puts the camera, then take it when he goes out again."

Simple but effective the plan, Jack agreed.

"In the meantime, shall we......."

"...check on Emily and Lucy," Laura continued.

Jack had noticed she'd done that a lot lately, that and second guessing. Laura adjusted the image to Emily and Lucy's home, but they still weren't there. Laura wanted to go and wait for them but Jack knew they should be more concerned with John and what knowledge he thought he had.

For the next couple of hours, they followed John's progress. They had no idea when he might go home and didn't want to miss an opportunity. Their eyes were aching from watching the image on fast forward, deciding to stop for some lunch.

Laura sat at the desk and pressed the button on the remote which slid open the panel revealing the large TV monitor. She leaned back in the chair and flicked through the channels whilst Jack made sandwiches and tea.

Checking his watch, Jack said, "I think we should give it another hour or so and head off before the tide comes in too far."

"We have to check on Emily and Lucy before we go, maybe if they're not in we can leave a note or something."

"Sounds like a good idea. Try and think where we can leave it so Scott doesn't see it though."

Suitably fuelled from their food break, Jack and Laura got back to John's progress, watching as he left the station again, but only to make several more house calls before returning once more. After a while they decided he must have been on a late one and called it a day.

Laura dialled up Emily and Lucy's home one last time. Still nobody was home so she wrote a note to Lucy, "Where shall we leave it?"

"I was thinking maybe the stables?" Jack suggested.

"In Black Jack's stable?"

They both knew that Lucy, being horse mad, would be sure to regularly visit the stables, so Jack agreed. Laura slipped on a travel-band and delivered the note. She stayed a short while and stroked the horses. Jack wanted to join her but she seemed happy on her own.

Eventually they left, and only just in time as the tide was coming in fast and the cove was already a foot deep.

Jack dropped Laura off around her friends, where she spent the rest of the afternoon, He was glad she had something to keep her mind off what was happening in 2253, and their own problem in 2008 with John.

When Jack got home, he had a look on the internet to see if there was any information regarding John. There was nothing he could find though, but that wasn't an issue. They'd get back to John the following morning and still have more than enough time to do that and hopefully visit Emily and Lucy too.

One thing was certain, Jack had to get the camera back before he saw Emily again as he knew she would throw-a-wobbly. Having already experienced her dark side, he didn't want to annoy her again so soon and blow any chance with her.

Chapter 27

Tuesday 5ᵗʰ August 2008

After another sleepless night, Jack dragged himself out of bed, thinking about the note they had left Emily and Lucy, hoping they'd seen it. Laura would be waiting for him so Jack showered and dressed then headed next door for a cup of tea. Tapping on the door and walking inside, he come face-to-face with a strapping sixteen stone chisel faced man he hadn't seen before.

"Morning," is all Jack could manage as he slipped past him, wary of his evil looking expression. He continued upstairs, fortunately.

Laura popped her head around from the kitchen, "Morning, Pop's, Tea?"

"Love one," joining them in the kitchen. Marion was at the kitchen table with her lap top computer switched on to her beloved bingo.

Jack asked, "How are you?"

"I'm okay. Did you meet Damon?"

"We passed in the hall," pulling a face at Laura.

She pulled one back, "That's Mom's new boyfriend."

"Cool," he lied, having taken an instant dislike to the man, "How did you meet?"

"We first met a few years ago, back home," Marion replied, "We bumped into each-other in town yesterday, I had no idea he'd moved down here."

Laura passed Jack his tea and whispered, "Drink it quick so we can get out of here."

He did and they were gone before Damon came back down.

"Have you eaten?" Jack asked.

"I had a bowl of cereal, but I'm still hungry."

"No surprises there then," he laughed. "Shall we grab some bacon sandwiches on the way?"

"Yes please," Laura rubbed her stomach.

Finding a burger van beside the road, they collected their greasy breakfast and headed off to the rock, devouring the bacon butties on the way.

It was a typical English August summers day, dull, windy and raining. Jack got an umbrella from the boot of the car and they carefully walked to the cliff's edge. The pathway down looked very slippery and Jack feared it might be unsafe for Laura. There was nobody about, not even a fisherman.

"This is going to be fun," he said.

"Don't be a-woos," Laura shouted, racing on ahead.

She took the path too quickly and slipped up almost immediately. Jack rushed down and scooped her up, she was trying so hard not to cry by putting a hard face on. He hugged her anyway.

"We can always come back tomorrow."

"No, please, I'm okay," she pulled away and dusted herself down.

"Okay, but let's take it slow and hold on to me."

"Yeh, Yeh," Laura wiped her face and put on a smile. Jack admired her for being such a tough kid, as well as being damn stubborn.

They continued down without further incidents and carefully climbed up to the cave and into the dry. They were both soaked from head to foot and Laura was covered in mud from her fall. Fortunately, they had clean clothes and towels in the apartment. This was England after all and quite normal for summer.

Jack took his things into the blue-room and left Laura to shower and change. Having dried off and changed himself, he went to the control-station and dialled up Emily and Lucy's home. Zooming in to the kitchen he could see Emily sitting at the table.

Clipping on a travel-band, he sent himself to the back door and knocked. Emily looked pleasantly surprised when she saw who it was.

"I'm glad you came, where's Laura?"

"In the shower. She had a slight accident which involved a lot of mud." Jack told her what happened. "Is Scott here?"

"No, he went with Lucy into Newtown Village."

"Okay, back in five with Laura," pressing his blue button, hoping Laura hadn't sprung him. A few minutes later she appeared, all cleaned up and looking like herself again.

Seeing Emily, Laura quickly put on a travel-band, "Come on then," she disappeared into the image and Jack followed.

Emily was just bringing three cups of tea to the table and smiled, "Just in time!"

"How did you know?" Laura asked then nodded, turning to Jack, "You came here while I was in the shower!" He admitted to her he had and she gave him a wary look.

Laura hugged Emily, "Did you find my note?"

"Lucy did when we got home last night. She's looking forward to seeing you. You only just missed her."

They sat down and Emily explained what had happened in the planning meeting, which explained the fences.

"So I take it the three new members are corrupt?"

"I would say so, but without any proof we have nothing."

Jack thought for a moment. "What would it take to get a new vote?"

"We need to prove an association with Prescott Nuclear Fusions or Chris King."

Laura asked, "What can we do?"

Emily pondered for a moment. "If I were to get the personnel files for the new members..."

"We could check them out using the time-portal?" Laura continued for her, her mind lightning fast, or was it something else?

"Okay, I'll have them by morning. If Dad's here, we'll meet you up the road a bit."

"We'll find you," Jack said.

Scott was due back any time, so Jack and Laura headed back to the blue-room to continue following John about. The image was just starting to get dark as John left the station for the evening. Following his progress down the coast road, they watched him take a left turn then pull onto a driveway, which they assumed was his home.

Having parked, John entered the house and Laura adjusted the dials so they could follow him inside. He took off his jacket and hung it up, and was about to walk away when he stopped and returned to his jacket. He reached into the pocket and removed the camera, placing it in an old battered leather brief case by the front door, before continuing through to the kitchen where his wife was preparing dinner.

"We know where he lives now," Jack said.

"So let's go forward to when they're both out," Laura suggested.

"So long as he doesn't take the camera with him when he leaves," Jack said.

Fast forwarding from six am the following morning, John finally left the house at eight, without the camera. His wife left an hour later. They followed her to make sure she wasn't coming straight back, which they concurred she wasn't. Satisfied, they put on their travel-bands and arrived at John's house. Jack went to retrieve the camera from the leather case, but it wasn't there.

Laura called out, "The case is in here under the computer table."

Relieved, he joined her. Laura had the camera in her hand, a smile on her face, "I expect he's downloaded the pictures." She booted up the computer and scanned the files, "Here they are," opening the file.

"Hope he didn't make a copy, can you check."

Laura was clicking away and finally announced that it was the only one, "Shall I delete the file?"

"Yes and don't forget to empty...."

"The recycle bin, yeh, yeh. Everything's done," Laura turned off the computer. "Let's go."

The day had turned out to be a successful one and it was only lunchtime. Grabbing their dirty clothes, they headed back out. The rain had stopped and the sun was fighting its way through, so the exit was much cleaner than their entry. Jack dropped Laura off at her friends once again, letting Marion know before going home to think.

Finding something on the new committee members might be easier than proving it, so he had to come up with a flawless plan. He felt sure they would. His optimism was kicking in again as he saw a glimmer of hope to hold on to.

Chapter 28

Wednesday morning was dry and sunny from the start. This made the route down to the cove much easier for Jack and Laura. However, with the better condition came tourists and fishermen, so they took their time as they passed them before climbing quickly into the cave and disappearing.

Emily and Lucy were home, as was Scott. Jack waited till he walked out of the room for a moment and went to signal Emily they were coming. She saw him and held up her hands indicating she'd be ten minutes. Waiting up the road a bit, Emily and Lucy appeared a short while later. Laura and Lucy hugged - Lucy swinging her round to her delight as Jack steered Emily away.

Emily handed Jack a file, "This is everything we have on the new members. The information is logical and a bit too tidy. You'll see what I mean when you read it."

"And is this uniform for all three?"

"As if the same person wrote their CV," shaking her head, "You'd think they would have tried harder to conceal who they were."

"Arrogance. That might be to our advantage though."

Laura came over and asked, "Are you coming back with us? I've got a spare travel-band."

"And so have I," Jack said holding up his arm.

Emily whispered, "We hoped you'd ask," clipping on her travel-band. Laura ran back over to Lucy. Emily continued, "I think it will do Lucy good, she so adores Laura."

"And Laura adores her too. Why don't we go back to my house so they can spend some time together and come back to the blue-room after lunch?" Emily agreed.

Back at Jack's home, Laura and Lucy went next door to see Marion whilst Jack and Emily prepared lunch.

"They seem to have made quite a connection," Jack said.

"She's good for Lucy. I've always been the older sister looking after her. Now she can look after Laura, not that she needs it, quite an independent person."

"It hasn't helped with her Mom being ill," he said with a sigh. "Although I know Marion does the best she can."

"You're there for her."

Jack shrugged, "As much as I can be. I know Laura tires of my cautiousness at times, but that's the way it has to be."

"She'll understand one day. Anyway, back to our new committee members. I suggest this afternoon we gather as much Intel as we can, even if it's flimsy. It still might piece together."

"I agree, there has to be something to incriminate them. By the way, you were going to explain something about Lucy?" Remembering the comment Emily made when they'd met the second time in the apartment.

"I would, but!" she said pointing out of the window at Lucy and Laura returning.

They had lunch then headed back to the cave to start investigating the committee members. Inside the blue-room, Emily entered the coordinates for Mandy Glover's home first. The lady obviously had money, looking at the massive spread she had, not to mention the house itself. The whole structure was constructed of glass and granite and appeared to grow out of the ground.

There didn't seem to be anyone home so they all clipped on a travel-bands each and pressed their green buttons simultaneously. Splitting up, Laura covered the reception rooms while Emily and Lucy went to explore upstairs.

Jack checked out what looked like a study. There was a large desk with draws both sides. He went through each one but found nothing of consequence. It was the same in the dining room and games room, nothing.

Meeting back in the massive kitchen, Jack said, "I found nothing."

"We didn't either," Laura said with a shrug.

"What's that," Emily pointed to a picture on the wall beside the refrigerator, "I recognize the background. Lucy, isn't that one of Prescott's plants?"

The picture was of Mandy Glover along with two men in suits. They were standing in front of an office building.

"It looks like the Portsmouth plant," Lucy studied the picture. "We went there with the school last year. That's the main office block, I'm certain of it."

This rather confirmed their suspicions, but it still wasn't enough to tackle Mandy Glover with.

Next, they headed for Martin Stiller's home, which was a small but nicely furnished apartment in Newtown Village. Repeating the process, this time it was Laura's turn to find a clue.

"Got a letter with a different address on the letterhead."

They all gathered around to look. It was a central London address, which meant money. After returning to the blue-room and dialling in the new coordinates, they were surprised to learn that Martin wasn't single, as his information suggested, but married with three children.

He had a large four story home, very close to the city square mile. They even had staff, who were busily cleaning and cooking in various parts of the house. They decided to get back to Martin at the weekend as the search was bound to be more complicated with the house unlikely to be empty at any given time.

Lewis Mackenzie's place was next. He also had an apartment in Newtown Village. Not only that, it was in the same tower as Martin and of similar design and size.

They'd only been there a minute when Lucy produced a piece of paper from his desk draw. It was a company memo from Prescott Nuclear Fusions, addressed to Lewis. Dated the month before, it included details of his transfer from Portsmouth to the south-west, to join the *new location team*.

Emily took a photo of the document, "Seems we found the weak link."

Laura shouted, "Got another photo."

It was of Lewis and Mandy, again standing outside the Portsmouth HQ building. Emily copied the image, "This should be enough to persuade Dad to call for an investigation."

"But we have to consider that we obtained the evidence illegally?" Jack pointed out.

"Good point, but I'm sure we can use the information to good purpose, flush them out into the open," Emily said, sounding a lot more optimistic.

It all made sense to them, so they finished up and went back to the blue-room. It was getting late and the tide would be coming in at any time, so they decided to call it a day and meet Saturday to continue their search. Emily and Lucy put on travel-bands and sent themselves back home. They returned the bands moments later.

"Let's get out of here before we have to swim out," Jack suggested to Laura.

The tide was already coming in fast and flooding the cove. They had to paddle their way back to the path. Laura managed to stay upright though and they headed home.

"So when are you back," Laura asked, knowing Jack was off to an event the following morning.

"Hopefully Friday evening at some point, I'll text you, I promise."

"Please text me tomorrow."

"I will, so long as you promise me you'll spend some time with your friends." Laura assured him she would as they arrived home.

Saying good-bye, Jack headed inside to grab a bag and started to pack ready for Thursday morning. Leila was meeting him at the airport. He usually looked forward to being away for a few days, especially with Leila, but with all that was going on, work was most definitely taking second place in his mind.

Saturday couldn't come soon enough for Jack.

Chapter 29

Laura went home to let her mom know she was back. As she opened the door, Damon was waiting in the hallway. She did remember him from home and had never liked him. Not that she'd ever been asked.

"Are you in for the evening now, Little Madam?" He growled.

"I was going to knock for Ayesha to see what she was doing tomorrow."

"Do that in the morning, your Mom's getting tea ready, go and help her," he said, blocking the door.

"I'll call on her after tea," Laura slipped past him.

He grabbed her firmly by the shoulders, "I said tomorrow, don't argue," he spat.

Laura pulled away and ran into the kitchen. She remembered all too well what a temper he had on him. Her mom was sitting at the kitchen table playing bingo on the laptop.

"Just sit down and do as he asks."

Laura went to argue then noticed her mom's eye was swollen and blackened. She reluctantly sat down, feeling frustrated. "What's for tea?"

"Your favourite, Casserole," Marion got up to check the oven, "Get the plates out will you, boo."

Laura did as she was asked and laid the table. Marion served the casserole and they sat down. Laura had lost her appetite by then though and just wanted be go to her room and be alone.

Damon came into the kitchen and stood over Laura, who was picking at her food, "I suppose you've been eating rubbish around his place," he said referring to Jack. "I've spoken to your Mom about this. I think you should stop going around there."

"Why, I haven't done anything wrong, have I, Mom?"

Marion just put her head down, ignoring her plea. Laura was fighting back the tears, feeling confused and hurt.

Damon was still wound up, "It stops now, are you listening," he shouted, "And that's the end of it."

With that, Laura got up from the table and ran upstairs to her room, slamming the door shut behind her. Damon went to follow.

"Don't, Damon, please. Leave her be, I'll talk to her tomorrow."

"You're too soft on her. She shouldn't be hanging around with that guy anyway. You don't know what they're up to," Damon sat down to eat his dinner.

"I trust Jack. He's good with her. Laura and I have been getting on better lately too. You shouldn't judge him so quickly."

Damon gave her a stern look, "I'm here now so we don't need him anymore, alright?"

Marion just looked down at her food, deciding it wasn't worth winding him up again and getting another thump in the face.

Laura was listening with the door ajar, tears flowing down her cheeks. She wanted to call Jack, but she'd left her phone on the kitchen table. Shutting the door gently, Laura flung herself onto the bed and pulled the duvet over herself, shutting the world away.

Laura's heart felt like it'd been ripped out, thrown on the floor and trampled on. Feeling totally lost, she hugged her pillow and cried herself to sleep.

The following morning, Laura was up early and crept downstairs to the kitchen to retrieve her phone. It wasn't there. Her stomach tightened and she felt sick, the phone was her lifeline. She searched through the kitchen draws, but there was still no sign of it.

A door opened then slammed shut upstairs and heavy footsteps descended. Laura put the kettle on and grabbed three mugs as Damon walked in.

He still looked grouchy, "I'll have tea if you're making one."

"Where's my phone?" Laura took three tea bags out of the jar.

"You'll get it back when you show some respect, you've had it your own way for far too long."

"That's not fair, it's *my* phone," Laura raised her voice in anger and frustration.

"Don't argue or you won't get it back at all," he shouted back.

Pouring the tea, Laura placed one in front of Damon, "I'll take Mom her tea," she grabbed the other two mugs of steaming tea from the side.

"Don't think you're going to soft soap her, the decision has been made."

Laura didn't answer, walking past him with the two steaming mugs of tea. He grabbed her roughly and both cups went flying, crashing to the ground in the hall. Laura screamed out loud as the hot tea scolded her hands.

Marion heard this and came rushing down the stairs. Looking quite worried, she asked, "What's going on?"

"She's giving me attitude; I won't put up with that."

Laura ran upstairs to her room and closed the door. She could still hear Damon shouting. Her mom was trying to calm him down but his voice was just getting louder. Making a quick decision, Laura packed her school bag with clothes and essentials, got dressed and went to the door to listen.

The voices were still loud, but muffled. Laura crept down the stairs. The kitchen door was closed now, so silently, she wheeled her bike to the front door and opened it gently. Pausing to make sure she'd not been heard, Laura pushed her bike onto the road and very quietly shut the door.

Jumping on her bike with her bag over her shoulders, she peddled as fast as she could to get away from there. She didn't know where she was going yet, but her internal antenna was already guiding her. All Laura knew was that she didn't want to go home whilst Damon was there.

It was a good half an hour later when Marion came out of the kitchen to go and change. Right away she noticed Laura's bike was missing. Panic struck her hard as she knew all too well how she would react. All Marion could hope for was that Laura would calm down and be home later, so she decided to cover for her with Damon.

Marion opened the front door and shouted, just loud enough for Damon to hear, "See you later, have a nice time." She shut the door quickly, just as he burst out of the kitchen like a raging bull.

"Where does she think she's going?"

"To see her friend Ayesha, leave her be, please Damon, you hurt her this morning you know."

"I'll be having words with her when she gets back, I'm not putting up with her cheek."

Marion grabbed his arm and steered him back into the kitchen. "Okay, we both will later, but Damon - she's my daughter, let her calm down."

Marion felt her stomach tighten and knot up. She'd always known Damon had a temper, but he'd got worse since she'd last seen him. He also had a side to him that she adored, but at the end of the day, Laura was her daughter and she loved her unconditionally. She knew Jack felt the same way about her. Marion just wished that Damon could see that and then everyone would get along.

Damon could see he'd upset her and pulled Marion towards him to give her a hug.

She pulled away immediately, "I'm going to get dressed."

"I'm sorry babe. I just want us to be a family, is that too much to ask?"

Marion didn't answer, heading upstairs and making her way to Laura's room. She looked around and noticed her school bag was missing and clothes were strewn everywhere. Walking over to the window, she stared out into the street. Tears rolled down her face, her head was spinning, hers eyes blurred. She felt herself sinking as she collapsed onto the bed and sobbed uncontrollably.

Laura had been riding blind for quite a while and her legs were just starting to ache. She slowed down a bit and looked around her, realising immediately where her autopilot was taking her. She was almost at the rock.

Arriving there, Laura hid her bike in the same place as before then made her way down the path via the bushes to avoid passers-by. Safely inside of the cave, she climbed down into the cavern below and shut the hatch. She immediately felt protected and went to the apartment. Checking the fridge, she could see that Jack had topped it up. Quite hungry now, Laura grabbed a packet of pepperoni sausages and a can of coke then sat down and flicked on the TV.

Relaxing in the comfy chair, she ate her food, washing it down with the coke, feeling much better. She wanted to call Jack and tell him what had happened, but without her phone she couldn't.

Deciding, Laura put a note in the diary and went to the blue-room. She dialled in her coordinates and clipped on her travel-band. Taking a deep breath, she pressed the green button.

Chapter 30

Thursday 7th August 2008

Jack met Leila at the airport and they checked in then grabbed some breakfast. Their flight was called a short while later and they were soon on board and in the air, heading for Edinburgh.

The event was due to start at noon and the plane touched down at nine. Hailing a cab and heading for the conference centre, they arrived there thirty minutes later.

Meeting with the event staff, who'd arrived earlier to set things up, Leila went through the order of the day. This was a catalogue company fashion event to publicise their autumn/winter range. After a brief meeting to ensure there were no issues, they met with the company representative.

Everyone seemed to know the order of things, so after checking on the stage and lighting, Jack and Leila went for a coffee before people started to arrive.

Leila asked, "How was your last few days' holiday?"

"Oh just a quiet one pottering about at home," he lied.

"So when are you going to bring Laura along to meet us?"

"She asked the same question, I said I'd take her to an event closer to home."

"What about the games event at the end of the month, that's local. She'd love that, don't you think?"

"I'd quite forgotten about that," Jack said, remembering Leila had done most of the leg work, but agreed it was ideal, looking forward to telling Laura about it later.

People were starting to take their seats. Jack and Leila did their final checks before taking to the stage. Jack made the introductions and then passed the microphone to Leila for her commentary. Finding a good spot in the audience, he sat down.

Models came and went and they were all beautiful women. Cameras flashed and people applauded, Jack's mind was elsewhere though. He had to find a way to stop Chris King from building the power plant and with what they'd found so far, he felt sure they could prove Kings Involvement.

This would still only delay things though. There were sound reasons for this location, technical issues which were beyond his comprehension. His mind continued to wonder whilst he automatically joined in the applause at the appropriate time, until finally, they stopped for a break.

Joining Leila for some lunch, Jack checked his phone for messages. There were two from the office but not one from Laura. He imagined she was out with her friends and having fun.

The afternoon session went by slowly and with no hitches. Jack was glad to get back to the hotel and relax. They had agreed to meet the catalogue company's rep for dinner, not that Jack liked these stuffy suck-up dinners but it was necessary to play the game, one they were very good at as a team.

Jack was having breakfast with Leila in the morning when she asked. "Did you tell Laura about the event?"

"No, I'll tell her when I see her, but I'll text her now and say hello."

He tapped in a quick message telling her all was well and that he missed her. His phone rang almost immediately.

Jack smiled and answered. "Heh you, you okay?"

"It's Marion, Laura's gone missing."

Jack's heart skipped a beat, "When, what happened?"

"She went out yesterday morning on her bike and hasn't come back."

"Have you called the police?" Jack asked as Leila's head jerked up.

"Yes, they've been looking for her."

Jack thought for a moment. He was sure she wouldn't have taken off without good reason. He asked, "Did you have a fall out or something?"

Marion hesitated, long enough for him to realise something was up, "Damon has told Laura she can't see you again."

Jack was upset now and feeling responsible, "Why, what's his problem?" He felt his anger flare and checked himself immediately.

Marion explained briefly what had been said which had caused Laura to run. He still thought she was holding things back, but agreed to head home right away.

Leila saw the worried expression on his face, "Is everything alright?"

"No, that was Marion. Laura's gone missing. Been a major fallout from what I can gather."

"You should go, I can handle things here."

"Thanks, I hate to ask with all the covering you've done for me lately."

Leila gave him a hug, "Call me when you've found her, from what you've told me about her she's a pretty smart kid. Try not to panic."

Jack rushed off to pack his bag. Leila called a cab and he was on the way to the airport in no time. Calling the flight desk on the way, he managed to get a flight back in an hour. Checking in at the airport, he waited patiently in the departure lounge.

It seemed like an age, sitting there twiddling his thumbs, frustration building up inside him. Jack was worried, but something kept telling him she was safe. He'd convinced himself she was cooling off somewhere, probably in the apartment at the rock. The only thing that concerned him with that was if someone had found her bike. The police would then concentrate their search around the rock and this would effectively cause a major headache getting to the cave unseen.

This would also leave the time-portal blocked from both ends.

Soon everyone boarded and once in the air, Jack began to think again. He was worried about their relationship and started to question himself again about how other people viewed such friendships. Maybe Damon was right and she should stop seeing him.

He was responsible for her disappearance, or so it seemed. On the face of it, he'd encouraged her to keep secrets, namely the time-portal. But they'd become embroiled in a situation together. Then there was Emily and Lucy, they were like family to him now.

Before he had a chance to beat himself up some more, the fasten seat belt lights came on and the plane landed. Jack was off and through customs with his carry-on bag at speed. It wasn't long before he was behind the wheel of his little red Honda CRX and belting down the motorway.

Driving straight to the rock, Jack was certain he would find the answers there. Parking, he walked down to where Laura had put her bike the last time, making sure nobody could see him as he checked, and as expected, it was there and fortunately well out of site.

Looking around, there wasn't too many people about, so he undid the combination lock, took the wheels off, as they both had quick release, as did the saddle, then quickly and carefully took the bike back to the car without attracting any attention and put it in the trunk out of site.

This done, he headed back down the path and up into the cave. Entering the apartment, it was hard to miss the empty coke can and pepperoni pack on the desk by the diary. The TV was left on too. Jack read the diary and saw at once where she'd gone.

Making his way to the blue-room, he saw Laura's travel band on the floor, which she must have returned. He pulled up the last coordinates, which, as he expected, was Emily and Lucy's home. Scanning inside their home, nobody was about, but once he scanned the surrounding area he was quick to find Laura and Lucy in the stables.

Putting on a travel-band, Jack sent himself outside as he didn't want to spook the horses. Calling out to Laura, she came running out.

"What kept you?" She jumped into Jack's arms and hugged him.

Jack just hugged her back, lost for words. Whilst he knew she'd be okay, seeing it was a relief. Lucy came out, smiling.

Jack said, "Your Mom called me this morning. She's reported you missing to the police. What happened with Damon, I understand he's been on your back?"

"I hate him, he's horrible," Laura started to cry.

"We couldn't tell you Jack, especially as Laura sent her travel band back as soon as she got here," Lucy said defensively.

"I know, fully understand. I just have to figure what we're going to tell Marion."

"I'm not going back, don't make me," Laura pleaded.

Jack was worried now, this was a difficult situation and he didn't know how to handle it. He felt lost and Laura was looking at him like he was the enemy.

"Where's Emily?" Jack asked.

"She's in town with Dad," Lucy replied.

"Does he know about Laura?"

"I told him she was my friends little sister, who's about the same age fortunately. I said it was just for a few days."

"And he bought it?"

"I know he's suspicious to be honest, he's very perceptive."

Laura suddenly piped up, "Damon's been beating my Mom up."

"When did this happen?" Jack asked, a look of shock.

"I didn't see him do it, but Mom's got a black eye and she looks scared. He hurt me too," she was sobbing. Lucy put an arm around her to comfort her. Jack just felt useless.

"I don't know what to do," he shrugged.

Just as he said that, Emily and Scott came down the path. Scott had already seen Jack so there was no point in doing a disappearing act. That and he'd spotted the travel-band.

Emily spoke up quickly, "Dad, this is Jack. It's alright, I've told Dad everything," She looked over at Lucy and she smiled. Jack stepped forward and shook hands with Scott.

"Good to meet you, Jack, I understand I owe you my thanks."

"Not necessary and good to meet you too, Sir, I'm glad Emily has told you, relieved in fact."

"We have much to discuss, let's go back to the house," Scott said.

"I'm glad we can finally talk," Jack said, knowing that having Scott on-side would be a tremendous help.

Heading back to the house, Jack explained to Scott about the current situation with Laura and what had happened at home for her to run. Scott could see he was worried and assured him he had his full support, which meant a lot to Jack.

Laura said, "Can't you tell Mom I'm with Emily and she can tell the police I'm okay?"

"It's not that easy, Laura, they would want to check to make sure." Jack knew handling the police was going to be difficult enough. That and they'd quite likely call in the social services, where lots of questions would be asked.

Jack could see trouble ahead.

Emily said, "I have an idea. If I come back with you and Laura, I'll explain that Laura called me and asked me to come."

"But what if the police want to check you out?" Jack asked.

Scott seemed to have other thoughts, "Do you know anyone in the force who could help?"

Laura and Jack looked at each-other and she gave him a suspicious look. Jack continued anyway. "Well, there is someone, but I'm not sure if I trust him."

"Is it someone we can use short term?" Scott said.

He considered that for a moment, seeing where he was going with it as an idea started to form in his head, "Maybe, I'll have to think of a way I could approach him though."

Laura said, "I don't like him," Jack assumed she'd realised he was thinking of John.

"Neither do I, but I agree with Scott, we do need help."

Emily asked, "How do you know him?"

Jack thought for a moment, glancing over at Lucy. She didn't look very happy with him so he decided to tell them about the burglary.

"My house was broken into recently and he was the officer handling the case. In fact, it was John who caught the guy."

Scott asked, "Did they take much?"

"Just a few bits," he noticed Lucy still frowning at him. He'd decided he would tell them about the camera, but not then as he was more concerned with getting Laura back to their time.

Jack looked over at Laura, "Let's go back with Emily. I'll book you both into a B&B then I'll go home and speak to Marion. Maybe she can get the Police to back off."

"You won't make me go home, will you?" Laura said, looking worried.

Jack promised her that he would try and defuse the situation with both the Police and Damon. Checking his watch, it was already two pm and Marion would be waiting.

Emily stood up, "I'll get my things."

"I'll go back to the blue-room and get you a travel-band." Jack said, handing Laura hers.

With Emily packed and the three of them with their travel-bands on, they said goodbye to Scott and Lucy, setting off back to 2008.

Jack's heart was pounding. He knew things could turn bad in a heartbeat, and that worried him.

Chapter 31

Taking the car, Jack dropped Emily and Laura off at a small B&B just down from the rock. The other option would have been to take them to a hotel the other side of town which was owned by a friend of Jack's. However, there were too many CCTV cameras on the way and that could get dangerous.

The little B&B was tucked away, which presented less of a risk. He didn't know the people there and that made it easier, the less people involved the better.

Laura was still wary of Jack and he felt a bit hurt. It frustrated him that she didn't fully understood the ramifications of him being caught with her at that time. Questions would be asked and it would be hard to explain.

Emily saw Jack's concern and whispered, "I'll talk to her. You better go and see Marion."

He agreed and said goodbye till later and headed home. Marion was waiting for him.

"Hi, sorry I'm later than expected, any news?" He innocently enquired, more lies.

"No nothing. I was hoping you would have some ideas," she eyed Jack warily.

"Other than driving about and talking to her friends, I have none," he lied again, which made him feel nauseous.

"We've already spoken to them, so have the police."

"Where's Damon?"

"He's at work, why?"

Jack thought for a moment, "This disagreement Laura had with him concerning me, how serious was it? Was he violent towards Laura in any way?"

Marion gave him a guarded look but said nothing. Jack opened his front door, "Come in a have a cup of tea, I think you have something to tell me."

Marion hesitated for a moment then followed him inside, sitting down while Jack made a cup of tea. He pulled out his cigarettes and offered her one, which she took.

"He'll get mad if he knows I've spoken to you," Marion looked genuinely frightened.

"Then we'll keep it between the two of us. Come on, Marion, this is your daughter we're talking about here, so what really happened?"

Tears started to roll down her face as she told Jack more of what had occurred the previous day. He acted surprised and hurt, keeping up the front.

"Has he been violent in any way?" Jack asked.

Marion looked up sharply. "No! Why would you think that?" She answered too defensively and a little too quick, making him suspect she was keeping something from him.

Jack pushed a bit more, "So Laura hasn't seen you two go off at each-other? Remember, I know what you're like with that temper of yours!"

Marion went silent, sipping her tea and pulling on her cigarette. He was about to prompt her when she opened-up.

"We had an argument Thursday night and Laura heard it."

"Did he hit you?" Jack asked, a little more firmly this time.

"More of a slap, but I hit him back."

He knew she was lying and was about to tackle her again when Marion's phone rang, it was Damon. He stayed quiet till she ended the call.

"He's on the way home," Marion had panic in her voice, "I better go, sorry."

"Okay, I understand. But, Marion, if he's violent, you must get rid. I'm thinking of both of you when I say that. I thought you knew this guy anyway, what's changed?"

"He has. Look, I'll speak to you later," she went to leave.

"I'll have a drive around in a bit," Jack was looking for an excuse to go out again. She nodded and disappeared back to her house.

Unpacking his bag, Jack got changed. He'd promised Emily he'd find a spare phone so she could contact him. With that sorted he was about to leave when there was a knock on the door.

Opening it, he was a little surprised at who he found standing in the doorway, although he'd half expected the visit, "Hello John."

This was probably his best chance to find out what John thought he knew and to see if there was a chance they could ask for his help, both with the Laura situation and with what was happening in 2253.

Jack decided to appear friendly and open to see how he would react. "So how's retirement suiting you and what do I owe the pleasure?" He invited him inside, "Would you like a cup of tea?"

John looked a little taken aback at his reaction. "Err, um, yes fine. Look, can we talk?" He looked uncomfortable.

"Sure, John, oh and thanks for nabbing that thief. Dan told me you were responsible for catching him. I can pick my things up next week. No sign of the camera though," Jack remarked, watching John's expression, "I don't suppose you know anything about that, do you?"

He saw a flash of anger from John, but he didn't snap, "I know you're up to something, you and that young girl. I saw the pictures."

John was looking at him with a stern expression, something he probably did as a policeman all the time. Jack found it laughable but didn't let on. After all, he needed John's help.

Making a quick decision how to deal with him, Jack decided to blow his socks off and tell him everything. It was risky, but he felt John wouldn't have come around unless he was up for something, he just didn't know how mind blowing it was going to get.

Jack put their teas on the table and they sat down.

"The pictures you saw were taken around Thatchers Rock a couple of weeks ago."

"I worked that much out, but they're, well, different."

"I know, let me explain. The pictures you saw were of the rock, but in the year 2253."

He looked at Jack suspiciously, "But how?"

"I know you're going to struggle with this, John, but it's the truth. Laura and I found a, for want of a better word, a time-machine."

He laughed, expecting Jack to do the same, but he had a serious look on his face.

"We can go anywhere in the world, past, present and future, and in a blink of an eye. About that, we have the camera," Jack said, producing it.

Anger flashed across John's face again, "How did you get that?"

Jack told him how he and Laura had followed him home using the portal and then how they'd found the camera. John thought he had something on him, but not now.

Jack needed to keep him on side though, so came back at him from another angle, "I need your help John."

He sat silently at first, just staring at Jack, then finally he spoke.

"Would this be about Laura?"

"Yes John, as you obviously already know, she's gone missing."

"So, where is she?" His eyes bored into Jack's.

"That I can't answer at this moment in time, but I do need you to do something for me."

He repeated to John what Marion had told him about Damon and what had led to Laura's disappearance. He listened patiently.

"So you want me to check him out and find some dirt? What's in it for me?"

"A trip to the future and an opportunity to earn some money for a little consultancy work."

"Yes alright, I'll look-into this Damon guy. I'm still not sure if you're on the level, but I'll be back tomorrow when I want to see this time-machine of yours," Jack could hear the sarcasm in his voice.

"Sure thing, John, but make it Sunday for the time-machine. By the way, we call it a time-portal. I'd like the info on Damon sooner please."

"You know where Laura is don't you?"

"I have a good idea, what can you do to help out there?" Holding eye contact.

"If you know she's safe, I will try and get the heat off, unofficially."

"You'd do that," Jack was surprised and started to like him a little.

"Yes I can. So, one more time, where is she?"

Jack smiled and nodded, "Okay, but you'll struggle with this. She's safe in 2253 for now, staying with a lady friend of mine. I saw her earlier," not mentioning for the moment they were at the B&B.

Jack told him everything Laura had said. He listened intently and genuinely showed empathy. John sat quietly for a few minutes, thinking. Jack remained silent till he seemed to have decided.

"Alright. I'll let them know back at the station that I've located her and I'll do a confirmation visit later. I'll need to see her, Jack – that's the only way they will back off."

"I appreciate that, I do," a feeling of relief. "I'll have to think of something to tell Marion."

"Doesn't she know anything?" he looked surprised.

"Nothing about the time-portal, she does know my lady friend though. Marion thinks she's my cousin."

"You lead a complicated life," he frowned, shaking his head. "I'll speak to you tomorrow," he held out his hand and Jack shook it firmly.

Giving John a few minutes to disappear, Jack left to meet Emily and Laura. Checking around to make sure he wasn't being following, he saw nothing, going around the houses a bit anyway, just to be certain.

He parked a street away from the B&B, still being careful, then went directly to their room. Once there, he bought Emily up to speed regarding the camera and John's visit.

Emily was a little angry with him, "Do you think it was such a good idea to tell him so much."

Jack was defensive in his response, "I didn't think I had a choice. We need him to take the heat off Laura, that and I actually think John can help us with the situation in 2253."

He explained his thoughts to her and she reluctantly agreed, "I don't think Dad's going to be too pleased."

"I appreciate that, leave him to me."

Jack promised her he would accept responsibility for John and keep a close eye on him. He spent a little time with Laura and assured her that everything was going to work out alright, telling her what he'd asked John to do regarding Damon.

"I really hate him. I'd rather go into care than go home if he's still there," being her normal stubborn self.

"I know, I understand. It won't come to that, I promise," he tried to assure her.

Jack agreed to pick them up in the morning so they could continue with the investigation into the three new committee members, especially Martin Stilling and his posh family home in London.

He didn't expect to hear from John till the afternoon, and he knew Marion would still be freaking out, although he couldn't tell her anything for the moment. Not something he was happy about, but he couldn't risk Laura going home while Damon was still there through fear of what he might do to her.

Chapter 32

Saturday 9th August 2008

Jack was just making a cup of tea in the morning when the phone rang. It was John, "Morning. Don't tell me you already have the information on Damon?"

"No, not yet, but I have managed to call the search off for Laura. I still have to do a physical meet."

"Yes of course, I appreciate that. I'll arrange that for later today, you have my word," feeling much relief.

"I should have some information on this Damon Humphries character by then."

"Thanks again, John, I'll speak to Marion, she's freaking out and I should tell her something."

Checking outside he could see that Damon's car had gone, he knocked on Marion's door.

The door swung open, "Have you found her?"

She looked so pale and scared. Jack knew he had to put her out of her misery, "Yes I have, she's was with my cousin, Emily."

She eyed him suspiciously, "When did you find out?"

"Just now. Emily didn't have my mobile number so had no way of calling," he lied. "Remember I've been away."

"I should tell the police," she pulled the phone from her pocket.

"No need, I've sorted it, they're seeing Emily later. I explained everything."

"I hope she's not in trouble?"

Jack assured her Emily would be fine, feeling the discomfort of the continued lying. He just wanted to blab the lot there and then, but controlled the urge.

Marion said, "I have to speak to Laura."

"Yes of course," he dialled the number of the mobile phone he'd given to Emily the previous evening.

Laura answered. Jack said, "Hi, it's me. The Police search has been called off and your Mom's with me, she wants to speak to you."

Marion grabbed the phone from him, "I've been so worried, why didn't you call me and let me know you were safe?"

Jack couldn't hear what Laura was saying, but he could tell that Marion was about to explode, so he interjected, "Marion, calm down, let me talk to Laura."

"She's refusing to come home," Marion said, crying in frustration, handing Jack the phone.

"Laura, I'll be up in a bit, just need to speak to your Mom."

"I'm not coming home," is all she said before ending the call. He was starting to feel that maybe their relationship had been damaged too much and this was the end of it. He hoped he was wrong.

"When is Damon back?" Jack asked.

She noticed his mood change and answered directly, "He said he'd be home about lunchtime. What shall I tell him?"

"Nothing for now, buy me a few hours please Marion, I'd appreciate it. I'll get this sorted."

She wasn't happy about it, but agreed, so Jack set off to meet Emily and Laura. Arriving there fifteen minutes later, Jack repeated everything to them.

"John will need to see you, Laura, I've agreed to that," he added.

Laura looked angry and was about to launch one at Jack when Emily calmed her, explaining that he had to allow it. She wasn't happy though and made that quite clear.

They sat in silence on the way to the cove, arriving there a few minutes later. Making their way across the green towards the cliff edge, they were surprised at how many people were there that day. Venturing down the path to the cove, they noticed a group of teenagers playing ball right beneath the entrance to the cave, making it impossible to get to the blue-room whilst they were there. As they drew closer, from their shouting and laughing, it became obvious they weren't English.

"They're French," Laura announced as a beach ball came their way. Laura caught it and said something to them Jack and Emily didn't understood. They shouted back and she ran over with the ball to join them, laughing and smiling.

Emily said, "I didn't know she spoke French."

"I learn something new about her each day," Jack said, shaking his head.

"She is very talented, Dad commented on that."

"Yes, and very highly strung you might have noticed," Jack sat down on a nearby rock. Emily joined him.

"I did notice she can be quite stubborn."

"She doesn't understand what I have to deal with. I love her dearly, but I feel I'm under constant scrutiny from her and whatever I do is wrong."

Emily put her arm around Jack, "I'm sorry I added to it by getting angry with you before, I know this hasn't been easy for you."

"It's turned my world upside down, but in a good way too. It's just that I don't always get it right," Jack was struggling to hold back the tears.

Emily gave him a reassuring hug then leaned forward and kissed him lightly on the cheek, hugging him again. Jack felt himself blush, enjoying the attention, it was hard not to notice how beautiful she was.

They watched Laura playing ball with the French girls and boys. After a while they stopped and talked to Laura, she was gesturing with her hands and talking fluently in French, somehow. The next minute they headed up the path, waving goodbye.

"How did you manage that?" Emily asked Laura as she came over.

"I told them there was a beach ball competition further up."

Jack noticed this was aimed at Emily and she was ignoring him now.

They waited till it was all clear before making their way to the blue-room where Emily entered the coordinates for Martin's house in London. He was there along with his wife and children as well as the staff.

"I suggest we look at yesterday as it's likely they were out being a week day," Emily busily adjusted the dials.

Starting in the morning, she skipped forward to eleven am, when there were just two members of staff left in the house. This wasn't ideal, but probably their best chance. It was quite a large house and on four levels. There was a lot of area to cover, so they scanned the property and chose the likely places to search.

Emily and Laura decided they would do the searching whilst Jack kept a look out. They put on their travel-bands and went to the first location when it was clear. They were on the second floor and the two members of staff were downstairs doing their choirs.

A thorough search confirmed this was Mrs Stilling's office, which held no surprises. The next target was the bedrooms. These were two doors down from the office. Jack stayed in the hall while Emily and Laura had a good look around.

Still with nothing, they decided to return to the blue-room as their next target was on the ground floor, another study. This was going to be tricky as a member of staff was on the same floor, but at the other end of the house.

Taking their chance, they continued. Again, Jack stood lookout while they searched the room. Almost immediately Emily found a folder on the desk. The Prescott logo was embossed on the cover. She quickly took photos of the documents inside. Laura pointed at some pictures on the wall. One was of Jonathan Prescott, Mr and Mrs Stilling and another lady, who Emily said was Prescott's wife. Emily copied these too.

Suddenly Jack saw the cleaning lady coming out of the dining room and heading their way. He quickly got Emily and Laura's attention, but in the process of waving his arms about, he knocked over a vas on the cabinet beside him. It crashed to the ground. They all instinctively hit their blue buttons together, just as the cleaning lady came through the door, looking around suspiciously.

Emily said, "That was close."

"Were you trying to get us caught," Laura shouted at Jack. He decided not to respond, considering things couldn't get much worse between them.

Emily showed Jack and Laura the images she'd taken from the study. These included letters from Prescott to Stilling about the new plant.

They now had a firm link, probably not enough to take back to the planning management group in London, but a starting point for further investigation.

This was where John's expertise would come in and Jack was sure he was up for the challenge.

Chapter 33

The small B&B was quiet that lunchtime as most of the guests were out for the day. Jack was starving, having missed breakfast with all that was going on. They headed for the dining room and sat down.

While they were studying the menu, Jack's phone rang, it was John, "I've got major dirt on your man."

"Excellent, where are you?"

"I'm about to leave the station. I could come straight to yours?"

"Have you eaten? We're near the rock, come and join us for lunch."

He agreed and Jack told him where they were. Laura gave him another of her wary looks.

"Why did you tell him to come here?"

Jack explained that he had some information regarding Damon and would tell them all about it when he got there. Laura just scowled at him.

Emily could see Laura's behaviour was really starting to upset Jack and turned to Laura with a firm expression, "Laura, Jack is trying to help. Why are you so angry with him?"

"I don't like John, he's going to make me go home and *he's* going to let him," glaring at Jack.

"How do you make that out," Jack said, confused. "I'm trying to get rid of Damon for you, but you disappearing the way you did has caused problems that needed solving."

She snapped and yelled, "You just want to get rid of me."

"Laura, you are so wrong. If I could adopt you I would, I couldn't love you any more than I do and I promise you I don't want get rid of you. But you must understand, I had to do something and John was our only hope. Without him I don't think they would have let me see you again, especially if the social got involved." He was close to tears, "Please Laura, we'll sort it, I promise," holding out his hand, which she took, stepping forward.

"Sorry, I didn't mean to upset you."

Jack gave her a big hug. Looking over at Emily, who was smiling. He noticed her long blond hair flowing over her shoulders, her blue eyes hypnotizing him for a moment. Laura started to smile too, watching Jack.

Emily dug him in the ribs gently, "Shall we order?"

Jack was still mesmerised and Laura started to laugh, "Do you two like each-other, don't you?"

Emily blushed whilst Jack attempted to prepare a suitable response. Emily beat him to it, "Of course we like each-other, and we both love you."

"You know what I mean."

"Just friends," Emily winked at Jack, causing him to blush a little. He was glad to see John walking through the door, waving him over.

Emily stood up and introduced herself. Laura went quiet again, eying John with a sour look on her face.

"So you're Laura?" John asked, holding out his hand to her.

She didn't take it, instead blurting out, "You stole Jack's camera - we saw you do it."

John looked a little stunned, lost for words for the moment. Jack decided to get him off the hook, "We're just about to order; what would you like?"

They ordered their food and John told them what he'd found out about Damon. He was separated from his wife in Birmingham, which they already knew, but were unaware of the circumstances. She'd had a restraining order taken out against him because of his continued violence. Adding to this, there was a warrant out for his arrest for breaking the order and for an attack on another lady.

"I've arranged for officers to go and arrest him. He will not get bail, that's guaranteed."

"How can you be so sure of that," Emily said.

He just tapped his nose, "We do things differently down here."

Laura looked a little more relaxed now, like a weight had been lifted off her little shoulders. Much to Jack and Emily's surprise she smiled at John and thanked him, shaking hands with him this time.

After they'd finished lunch, Jack decided to call Marion. She answered immediately, "Is Laura with you?"

"Yes and Emily is here too. Are you okay? You sound distressed."

"The police have arrested Damon."

Jack didn't react, remaining silent for a moment, not quite sure what to say.

"You already know I take it?" she sounded annoyed.

"Yes I do, Marion. So, tell me who's more important, Damon or Laura?" cringing at his remark, wondering if she was about to explode. It got the right response though.

"Well, Laura of course."

"Exactly. Look, we'll be back shortly and we can talk then. Please don't be angry with me."

"Don't be long then," Marion said, hanging up.

"Would you like me to come back with you for support?" John asked.

Jack declined, thinking it best he and Emily handled Marion - such was their complex web of lies.

"Thanks for all your help John. Pack a bag and meet us at mine tomorrow, you're going on a trip."

He looked quite excited as they went their separate ways.

Marion was waiting in Jack's driveway as they pulled up. Jack noticed immediately she had a bruised and swollen cheek.

Laura said, "Did he do that?"

"It was an accident."

Jack was furious and snapped, "Do you want to be a victim all of your life?"

Marion looked at him with shock. He lowered his tone a bit, "He could have done that to Laura, would you have called that an accident too?"

She flushed, annoyed with Jack again. Emily quickly stepped between them, "Marion, I'm sorry I didn't contact you, I wanted to speak to Jack but I didn't have his mobile number, sorry."

"It's alright Emily, thanks for taking care of her," she reached for Laura to hug her.

"Yeh alright, whatever," Laura wriggled away.

Jack and Emily sat Marion down and told her the whole story about Damon. She looked horrified, agreeing that getting rid of him was the right thing to do.

A little later, Marion and Laura left to talk things through. Emily and Jack sat and discussed how they were going to use John to gather evidence. Jack felt certain they would prove that Mandy, Martin and Lewis were corrupt.

"If Dad agrees, we could get John to impersonate a member of the London planning group security manager's office. He should be able to provide John with a new identity, with papers to support. He could then use his detective skills to shake things up."

"Sounds like a good plan," Jack said.

Satisfied, they had a night cap before retiring. Emily was staying over in the spare room where Laura normally slept.

"I'm really grateful for everything you know," Emily leaned forward and kissed him on the cheek.

"You're welcome," he stuttered, blushing, "Just happy everyone is safe."

She scuffed his hair, kissing him on the lips, "I'll see you in the morning," slipping away silently.

Jack was left sitting there with a silly grin on his face for at least ten minutes, before remembering that he had to call Leila. He'd promised to let her know Laura was safe.

"Thank God she's okay, what a horrible man that Damon sounds. So, are you okay?"

"I'm good, all good." Jack was about to tell her about Emily but something stopped him.

"Okay, I'll see you Monday," she hung up.

Jack sat there for a while longer thinking, but he was so tired as well as love struck, his thoughts just kept going around in circles. He succumbed with a massive yawn and hit the sack.

The following day was sure to be interesting.

Chapter 34

Sunday 10th August 2008

Waking up Sunday morning, Jack could hear Emily going down the stairs and quickly hopped out of bed and into the shower before joining her.

There was a cup of tea waiting for him, "I could get used to this."

"Just luring you into a false sense of security, then I'll turn you into my slave," Emily said with a wicked smile.

She looked so beautiful, Jack imagined any man would fall for her charms and be putty in her hands.

There was a knock on the door. It was only eight thirty, turning out to be John, bag in hand. Jack silently cursed him for being so early.

Emily made him a cup of tea then headed upstairs to get ready. Jack wasn't sure whether to text or call Laura, he thought maybe she should spend some quality time with her Mom and sort things out.

However, ten minutes later she arrived, "Morning all."

"Heh you. What're your plans today?"

"I'm coming with you, Mom's still in bed."

Jack imagined the stress from the last few days had probably made her unwell again, worried for Marion. Preparing breakfast for four, they sat and ate. John was watching Jack closely and he wondered if John thought he was only delaying the inevitable let down, was he in for a shock.

An hour later they arrived at the cove, which was clear of people this time. Jack pointed to the cave, "That's where it is, John."

"How do you get up there?"

"We climb," Laura laughed at him before rapidly ascending the rock face to the cave, showing off.

John followed somewhat slower, with Jack and Emily behind him. He was looking about, "So, where is it?"

Jack knew he still had his doubts, which he considered was typical of the type of people in his line of work, they seemed to have closed minds and no imagination.

"Follow me," Laura led the way.

By the time they'd caught up with her in the rear cavern, she'd already moved the bolder and the hatch was open. Jack figured Laura had done it that way so John didn't see how. She was most definitely back on form.

They climbed down and went directly to the blue-room. Laura placed a travel-band on John's wrist and handed Jack and Emily one too. Putting her own on, she adjusted the dials and the image zoomed down to Emily's home in 2253.

"So what happens now?" Johns asked, the look of doubt replaced with apprehension.

Laura hinged open John's travel-band and hit the green button, they watched for a moment as he stood outside the kitchen door of Emily and Lucy's home looking nervously around. They couldn't help but laugh when Lucy come to the door and gave John a very strange look before smiling.

Besides him moments later, Laura and Lucy hugged as Scott appeared at the door, eying John, looking for an explanation.

Jack introduced him, "This is John. He's an ex policeman and has agreed to help us investigate the three new board members."

With the introductions sorted, they headed into the house. Emily brought Scott up to speed with what they'd found and explained the plans regarding John. Laura was telling Lucy about her own situation, while Jack stood back feeling a bit left out.

Emily noticed and reached out and took his hand. Scott looked up with an amused expression and Jack felt himself blushing again. Of course, Lucy and Laura were whispering and giggling to make him even more embarrassed, if that was possible. Jack just poked his tongue out at them both.

Finishing their tea, they left John and Scott to talk details. Lucy had promised Laura they would go for a ride on the horses. The four of them made their way to the stables and saddled up their respective mounts.

Laura's ride was a sixteen-hand grey called Tiger. Emily had a beautiful seventeen-hand black stallion called Gemstone. Lucy of course had her seventeen-hand black stallion called Black Jack, but she chose to ride a slightly smaller sixteen and a half hand golden brown beauty called Monkey-Magic, which she handled expertly and confidently.

Jack's ride was a seventeen-hand grey called Precious. "Watch out for her," Emily trotted up beside him. "She's got attitude."

With that, Emily patted Precious on the backside and she took off at great speed, trying at the same time to buck Jack off.

He held on tight though as he'd a little more experience with horses than Emily knew, having ridden many times before, but they weren't to know that. He soon got the measure of Precious and they all rode on for miles taking in the scenery.

Laura was back to her normal self and getting to grips with her ride, Tiger. She seemed to have it well under control which didn't surprise any of them.

Arriving back, Scott had already given John his new identity papers and they'd sorted out the finer details.

John was looking quite excited. Jack asked, "Glad you came?"

"I should never have doubted you."

"So how do you feel about the general plans?"

"It all sounds quite straight forward. It's what I do best."

"Good, because tomorrow is going to be a big day," Scott interrupted. "We have till Thursday latest if we are effectively going to delay things."

"I understand, I won't let you down," John said.

Jack pointed at John's travel-band which was still on his wrist. He slipped it off and handed it to Jack, who passed it to Emily.

"Best keep that safe," he suggested. She slipped it in a drawer whilst John had his back turned then removed her own and returned it to the blue-room 2008.

"We should go," Jack suggested to Laura.

She nodded, giving Lucy another hug, "I'll miss you."

"I'll miss you too," Lucy said, clinging to her.

"Thanks again for what you did for us, John," Jack said.

"Glad I could help," John said, shaking hands with him.

Jack and Laura headed outside, Emily and Lucy followed.

"Will you miss me?" Emily said, circling her arms around Jack.

"I will," is all Jack could manage. Emily leaned forward and kissed him, whilst Lucy and Laura giggled.

Jack didn't want to go after that but he knew he had to get Laura back. "Come on you, let's get going."

"When are you coming back?" Emily was clinging to him still.

"I'll try and get a half day during the week."

"Do your best to," she kissed him again.

"I definitely will," Jack said, a silly grin plastered over his face.

Getting back to the blue-room, Laura said, "Do you think we can stop the plant build?"

"I think we can definitely stall the build, re-locate it maybe. That would be our best bet," Jack said.

"I hope so," a tear welling up in her eye.

"It will all work out, Scott and John will see to that, you'll see," Jack said, roughing her hair.

Chapter 35

Sunday 10th August 2253

Scott made sure John was fully briefed before driving him to Newtown Village, dressed smartly in his one piece tailored suit with shiny silver buttons up to his neck. He looked a little uncomfortable but it was necessary for the plan to work.

His cover ID as a security manager from the London HQ was safely inside of a slim metal case the size of a laptop. Inside the case was also a questionnaire tablet which Scott had prepared.

Using his cover, John would interview all the committee members. This way it would not arouse the three new member's suspicions that this was aimed specifically at them.

The reason for the '*vote audit*', as they called it, was decided because of the sudden swing vote as well as the recent changes to the committee. Scott knew they didn't have much time before someone would check John out, and dependent on what contacts King's people had at London HQ, it was possible they could expose John as a fraud.

Scott had tried to cover his bases as best he could with the many contacts he'd established over the years. His only hope was the surprise factor would be on their side and that, hopefully, someone would get the jitters.

They arrived at the south terminal and parked then transferred onto the monorail system. Scott gave John a small video phone which had the London HQ insignia on it. He'd acquired this from a former member who'd retired a few months before.

Arriving at The Tamworth Park Hotel, Scott introduced John to the lady on reception.

"Rachael. This is my colleague John Short who is down from London HQ. I would like a single executive suite please.

Rachael busily typed in Johns details onto the computer terminal. "Here we go Mr VanDaley, suite 27, level 53," she handed him an entry card.

Scott paid for the room and they made their way to the elevator. John was taken aback at its speed and smoothness, arriving on level 53 feeling slightly light headed.

Suite 27 was a very spacious affair with a magnificent view across the village through the large panoramic window. The living area had a large bed and a leather sofa, of the finest quality. The bathroom was awash with glass and marble with everything one could hope for.

There was a massive TV screen sunk into the wall with a space age looking remote control hanging beside it. Beside the door stood a drinks dispenser and a mini bar which Scott made sure John knew how to use.

"I'll memo the planning group members as soon as I get back home. We don't want to give them too much time to figure out what's going on."

"What time would you like me to be ready in the morning?"

"Eight sharp please, John. I'll start you off with Steve Russell, he's on our side. This will hopefully demonstrate this isn't aimed at any specific individual. Oh, and by the way, breakfast is six to eight on level 4. You can have it in your room but I want you seen publicly."

After a superb night's sleep, John showered and changed into his new suit. He made his way down to level 4 and sat down to enjoy the full works breakfast special. Satisfied he'd been noticed, John made his way back to reception where Scott was waiting.

The planning office was situated at the north end of the village in one of the smaller towers, which had fifty levels. They used the active walkway to get there so they could talk on the way. The journey was almost a mile but took only minutes to achieve.

When Scott and John walked into the planning office reception, Steve Russell was already there. Scott knew Steve would be a bit defensive but he couldn't afford to risk letting him in on the plan. Instead, he passed the interviews off as HQ ticking boxes and demonstrating their superiority.

"John will go through the procedure with you," Scott explained. "I'll be in my office if you need to speak with me afterwards."

John walked over to the large conference table and beckoned Steve to sit. He was still feeling a bit out of place, so this was a good warm up for him. He decided to start off with some non-threatening questions to lighten him up. All the questions had relevance though.

"What are your feelings about the nuclear plant Mr Russell?"

Steve frowned, "I know it's necessary with our natural resources drying up, but I object to the location because of the historical relevance of the rock."

"Are you in any way connected to the anti-nuclear convention?" They were a group of individuals who would object to any new plant, tree huggers with no real answers or solutions.

Steve was taken aback, "Certainly not, I'm a realist."

John continued with a few more relevant questions before ending with, "Do you or any of your family members have any connection to Prescott Nuclear Fusions?"

He knew Steve was on the level but it was important to be well practiced for when it mattered, with the three new members.

Steve confirmed that he didn't have any such connections, looking a little irritated by the questioning. As a group member, all the questions being asked that day were included in their confidentiality agreements in some way shape or form. John passed Steve the tablet and asked him to sign.

"Is this routine or do you have an agenda?" He asked.

"Just routine, thank you again for your cooperation," John shook his hand.

As Steve left, he let out a long sigh, one down and six to go.

The next person to be interviewed was one of the new members, Mandy Glover. She glided in dressed sharply, looking professional and sleek. John immediately felt his nerves tingle.

"Good morning, Mr Short, I hope we can do this quickly, I have more important things to attend to."

"I'm grateful you could come at such short notice," John tried to calm his jangling nerves. He quickly explained the procedure and went through the first few questions, which got minimal response.

He studied her facial expressions and body language with each question asked before going on.

"Do you or your family have any connections to Prescott Nuclear Fusions?"

Mandy angrily said, "That would be against group rules," not giving a direct answer.

Her eyes dilated a little as John pressed on, "Do you or any member of your family have any connection with the plant?"

"Most certainly not," she snapped.

Finally, thought John, an answer. Her body movements indicated that she was showing signs of discomfort, but Mandy kept her composure.

John continued, "If there were an alternative power source, would you reconsider your vote?"

Mandy was on the defensive again, "But there isn't, is there?"

"It's just a simple question Mrs Glover," he studied her facial expression - starting to feel more confident. He kept eye contact, waiting for her answer.

"In the absence of an alternative, I am in full support of the plant."

"Just one more question, would you profit in any way from the decision to go ahead with the plant?"

Mandy went red with rage. She stood up, obviously rattled, "Again no. Will that be all?"

"Thank you, I appreciate your time," he slid the questionnaire tablet towards her. "If you could just sign here please."

Mandy was rattled, no longer the professional who'd glided in minutes earlier. She knew all too well that by signing the tablet, she was committing a crime.

The punishment for such a crime was at least five years' imprisonment. Mandy had no choice though and scribbled her name in the box, hoping it was just routine. A confirmation tick appeared next to her signature confirming its authenticity.

"Thank you, Mrs Glover," John stood and offered his hand. She hesitated before shaking it rather feebly then hurried off, almost tripping up on her way out the door.

John stifled a laugh but remained poker faced. He felt certain she would attempt to call the other new members to warn them.

What Mandy didn't know was that Emily was in an empty office one level below and had a powerful scanner which was also capable of jamming signals. It had a range of a hundred metres. She'd been listening to the meeting through her ear piece.

As Emily expected, the scanner lit up moments later. The device recorded the call from Mandy's phone. Emily listened in as Lewis Mackenzie answered. Mandy quickly told him about the meeting with John and the use of the questionnaire tablet.

Lewis was obviously shaken, he sounded panic stricken, "What shall I do?"

"Just keep to the script and don't lose your nerve or we will all be in trouble. This guy is a pro."

"Should we contact Chris and let him know?"

"Not right now, let's see what develops. That and do we want that animal on our backs. You know what he's capable of. Do you honestly think he had nothing to do with Jonathan's disappearance?"

Emily was smiling to herself. She knew Chris King had nothing to do with sending that dinosaur of a man to where he belonged, but she was pleased they suspected him.

Lewis sounded exasperated, "Okay, I'm not due in till this afternoon, I'll handle it."

Mandy hung up and called Martin. The phone went to messaging. "Call me as soon as you get this, it's about the audit meet." She left it at that, hoping he would call her back before he had his meeting with John.

Unfortunately for him, he was already in reception. Emily had jammed the signal to make certain he couldn't receive the call.

John's next meeting was with Bill Brady while all this was going on. He went through the questionnaire much as he had with Steve and Mandy and met with no issues whatsoever.

Sylvia Knight came in next. Scott had warned John that she was a long serving member and he should tread carefully as Sylvia had many friends in civil government who had a lot of power. She was also in favour of the plant.

John went through the questions in a casual manor. Sylvia's answers were well thought out and slick. Scott had felt sure she was not involved in the vote rigging but John was getting a different feel about her.

He changed tact a little, "Are you aware of any reason for the sudden departure of the three former members in just one week?"

Sylvia looked flustered, be it just for a moment, but enough for John to suspect she wasn't being entirely honest.

"I have no idea; I didn't socialise with them."

"So in the two years you've worked with them you didn't think to question their decision to leave so suddenly?"

"That's up to Scott, ask him, as I have already said, I didn't socialise with them. I suggest if you want to continue with this line of questioning, we do so with my lawyer present."

"That won't be necessary, Mrs Knight, thank you for your time."

John passed her the tablet to sign. She scribbled her name and left without another word. He was certain she had more to tell. He decided he would speak to Scott about it at lunch.

Martin Stilling came in next. John could tell from his manor immediately that he was a very well educated man with an unshakable air of confidence. He gave nothing away and even thanked John for his due diligence.

If John hadn't already known Martin was connected to Chris King, and even with his years of experience in investigating people, he could easily have found him more that believable.

John met Scott for lunch and told him everything he'd learnt. Scott listened intently but made no comment. They had lunch and then returned to the office for the final two meeting.

Next up was Lewis. He was due to meet John at two, but by quarter past it was becoming obvious he wasn't going to show.

At half past, Stewart Robin arrived. Whilst he'd been a supporter of the plant, John felt certain he would change his vote in an instant should a viable alternative power source become available.

Meeting again with Scott they discussed the absence of Lewis. Scott tried to reach him on his phone but it went directly to messaging. Deciding to visit his apartment, they checked in with the apartment complex manager, where they learnt that Lewis had cleared out before lunch.

Scott had a wry smile on his face. He knew he had enough evidence to call an emergency meeting with his superiors at

London HQ. His tactics would no doubt come into question, but Scott was confident they'd do the right thing.

John headed back to the hotel to collect his things. Scott had agreed to meet him at five and take him back to the house. His part of the job was complete and John felt he'd done well.

Taking the elevator to level 53, he made his way to suite 27. Just as he got to the door, and as he was about to put the entry card into the slot, he felt cold metal pressing against the back of his head.

"Just open the door and step inside, now," Lewis ordered, pressing his gun harder to John's head. John did as he was asked, not wanting to agitate him.

Once they were Inside, Lewis pushed John onto the leather sofa, "I want all the information you've been gathering or I'll kill you," he pointed to the metal case.

"I don't have it. I've already sent it to HQ," John showed him the inside of the metal case.

"Don't lie, where is it?"

"I've already told you, you're too late. Give it up Lewis, we know everything."

Lewis raised his gun to shoot, but John could see the hesitation in his body language. He was about to lunge at him when the door flew open suddenly. Lewis spun around and come face to face with a fully garbed civil enforcement officer, gun in hand. Lewis went to raise his gun but he was too slow, a shock bullet, much like a Taser, but with no wire, stunned him into paralysis. Lewis collapsed to the floor.

John looked at the officer with much relief and thanked him. The officer holstered his gun, John asked, "What sort of gun is that?"

"It's a Livingston 98 Stun pistol, he'll be okay in about an hour," the enforcement officer said, grabbing Lewis's unconscious body.

Scott appeared at the door moments later, "Good job you still had the case," he gestured to the metal case open on the floor. "Emily planted an active listening device in there as a precaution. After packing up, she'd forgotten to take out her ear piece, which was quite fortunate."

"Spying on the spy," John said and laughed.

Scott laughed too, "Let's get you out of her, Emily will drive us home. I have a call to make."

Chapter 36

Monday 11th August 2008

Jack arrived home quite late Monday evening. He'd tried for an early one as he wanted to see Emily again and to find out how their day had gone, but Mark Jones, his boss, had decided to call a meeting which went on some.

Checking the time, it was just after nine pm, a little too late to be texting Laura, so he decided to relax A few moments later though, and whilst he was deep in thought, the phone rang.

It was Marion. She invited him over for a chat. When Jack arrived, she looked more relaxed and her black eye and swollen cheek were healing steadily.

"I have something to ask you?" Marion looked very seriously at him. Jack prompted her to continue, "It's about something Laura said concerning you and Emily."

He felt uncomfortable suddenly. Marion offered him a smoke and passed him his tea, "She's not your cousin, is she?"

Jack shouldn't have been surprised he'd been sprung, He played for time anyway, hoping he could come up with a good cover story, "What exactly did Laura tell you?"

"She let slip she saw the two of you kissing. So, who is Emily to you and why lie?"

Considering the question. Jack knew if he lied, it would reflect badly on both him and Laura. He didn't want to do that.

At the same time, if he told the truth or even a half truth, Marion would completely freak out.

She continued to look at him with an amused expression on her face. Jack smiled, "No, she isn't."

"And Lucy?"

"No!"

"So why tell me they're your cousins?"

Failing miserably to come up with a convincing cover story, he arrived at another weak offering, "Lucy is the daughter of a friend of mine and Emily is her older sister. My friend, Glen, is in prison, long story. Lucy was in some trouble and I offered to help."

"What sort of trouble?" Marion looked concerned.

Jack was still trying to think of that. He took the easy line, "The normal, boyfriends and drugs, that sort of thing. Emily came down to make sure she was okay and, well, we kind of hit it off."

"So why not just tell me that?" she gave him a stern look.

"Because I thought you might not want Laura near them because of the circumstances," trying hard to sound convincing.

"I'd like to have known, but I wouldn't stop Laura from seeing you because of that. I won't have you lying to me though."

"No, you're quite right, I'm sorry."

"So what's your friend in for?"

"Arson, he burnt his house down."

Sharon looked shocked "Was anyone hurt?"

"No. It wasn't occupied at the time. It's all to do with a disagreement concerning a divorce settlement."

"Oh," is all she said, looking a bit stunned.

Jack wondered if he was digging far too deep a hole and went on with the lie, "His ex-wife got greedy, he was backed into a corner and nobody would listen to him. It was a call for help," cringing at the new lie.

They sat in silence while Marion considered what he'd told her. Jack tried to change to subject, "Any biscuits, I'm starving?"

She smiled at last, "I take it you've not had dinner?"

He shook his head. With that, Marion made him a sandwich, "So are you going to visit your friend in prison?"

Jack quickly thought of a suitable response, "I would, but he's in London somewhere. Emily is getting me the address. I will write to him though."

"You should, he'd appreciate it I'm sure. Next time, tell me the truth."

He nodded, thinking all he'd done was to make the lie a hundred times worse. He was trying to think of a way to fill Laura in with the details as soon as possible.

After finishing his sandwich, Jack headed home. Just as he got in the door, his phone buzzed with a message. It was from Laura, it read - *'Nice story, good job I heard everything.'* Jack smiled, shaking his head.

How did she do that?

The following morning Jack was up early, having decided to see Emily before he went to work. Slipping out of the door at seven, he climbed into his car and was about to put the keys in the ignition when his phone rang.

It was Laura, "You're going to work early."

"Actually I was going to see Emily on the way."

"Hang on, I'll be there in five," she said and hung up before Jack could respond. He sent Marion a text to let her know.

The roads were empty at that time as was the cove when they arrived. Inside the blue-room, they checked to see if Emily was up. To their surprise, they were all up and seated around the table in the kitchen.

They slipped on their travel-bands and went to the back door and knocked. Lucy sprang up immediately, opening the door, "I knew it was you," she said, giving Laura a big hug.

Emily was right behind Lucy and circled her arms around Jack while Scott looked warily his way before smiling. John was looking happy with himself and was quick to tell them about the previous day's events, not forgetting Emily's very important role.

Scott took over, "We already had them banged to rights, but Lewis hasn't stopped talking since his arrest. He's given us everything in exchange for a deal."

Laura asked, "What about the time-portal?"

"The fences will be coming down. We have another meeting arranged for next Monday."

He explained that the planning group HQ would chair the next meeting and bring with them four temporary members to replace the four fraudsters.

"Why four?" Jack asked.

John smiled, looking quite smug. "Sylvia was also involved, had been from the start."

They hadn't checked into her as everyone had assumed she'd no connection to the other three. Scott had to admit he was very surprised too.

"Turns out she was Prescott's step sister. I have no idea how that was missed. It was her job to steer the group, but not all of them would play ball. So, the sudden departure of the three old members was because they were being blackmailed."

"What now?" Jack asked. "Can you get them to stop the plant altogether or even re-site it?"

"Certainly we have delayed things. As for an alternate site, until we get a response from Chris King, I can't be certain, but it is possible."

"Won't King be in trouble for his part in all this?"

"He's denying knowledge. He claims it must have been organised by Prescott before he disappeared." This made Jack laugh. By disposing of Prescott, they had effectively given King an alibi.

Jack and Laura spent a little more time there as he didn't have to be in work till ten. Lucy took Laura to the stables and Emily grabbed Jack's arm and steered him outside, whilst Scott gave him another wry smile.

"Sounds like you should be working for M15," Jack said.

Emily looked strangely at him, "Who are they?"

"Like secret police in my time, undercover work, spies. My girl the spy, I'm in awe."

She looked a little embarrassed, "Oh well, it was necessary."

"I wasn't judging you, in fact I'm really proud to know you," Jack gave her a hug. They stood there for some time holding each-other. Jack felt good to have her so close and he knew he was falling in love.

They walked to the stables to see the girls, who both giggled as they approached, hand in hand.

"We better get going as I have to go to work," Jack said.

"Wish I could stay," Laura said.

"I'd say yes if I could, but your Mom wouldn't be able to contact you."

"I know. Come on then, can we get a big-mac breakfast on the way home."

"I guess so, okay," he laughed. "Come on then."

John had decided to stay on for a few more days. He and Scott were getting on well and the girls had a genuine respect for him now. Even Laura was starting to like him.

After they returned to the blue-room, Jack rang Marion. She answered groggily, "Morning Jack, what time is it?"

"It's nine thirty, did you get my text?"

"Yes, is Laura going into work with you?"

"Can do, we were just about to go for breakfast, hope you didn't mind."

"That's fine, I'll go back to sleep then," she said and hung up.

Marion sounded so down and with everything that had happened of late, Jack knew the stress was getting to her. The new prescription the doctor had given to her seemed to be working initially, but now he wasn't so sure.

After grabbing breakfast, they joined the morning traffic and headed to the office. Leila was just getting out of her car as they pulled up in the office car park, Jack waved.

"Who's that?" Laura enquired, eying him closely. He quickly explained as Leila walked over towards them.

"Finally, I get to meet the famous Laura."

"Why, does he talk about me a lot?" She said with a silly grin.

"All the time! Has he told you about the games event yet?"

Jack admitted he hadn't, with all that had been going on, it had slipped his mind.

Laura looked at him daggers, "Were you going to tell me?"

"Of course, when I remembered."

"It's okay, he's like that all the time," Leila pointed out smiling. "So would you like to see what we have planned?"

Laura agreed she'd like nothing more so Jack left them to it and went to his office. Mark was just coming out of his as Jack passed.

"Morning, Jack, have you sorted things out at home?" He was referring to Laura and Jack's sudden departure from the event in Edinburgh.

"Yes thanks. I've brought Laura in with me today. I hope that's alright with you."

"So long as it doesn't interfere with your work anymore than it already has."

He assured him it wouldn't and that Leila was getting some valuable feedback from her. Mark just shrugged and walked off.

The event was due to start on the last Monday of August and would go on till the weekend. Jack had already decided he would take Laura in on the first day, which was press day. He would then take all the girls at the weekend.

Managing to clear his desk by lunchtime, Jack headed off for a bite to eat with Laura and Leila, who'd become inseparable by then. Throughout lunch Jack noticed Leila was giving him searching looks and he wondered if Laura had accidently let something slip. He knew she wouldn't have said anything deliberately, but Leila was as sharp as a razor and missed very little.

After lunch, Jack showed Laura around the offices and warehouse whilst Leila went into a meeting. She wanted to know all about the different parts of the business, especially the coming games event.

"The first day is Press-day," Jack explained. "I'll take you in again at the weekend," which met with her full approval.

With their plans made, all they could hope for now was that the planning group back in 2253 would vote to re-site the plant and that would make it a slam-dunk week. What more could happen?

Chapter 37

Wednesday 13th August 2253

Emily was up early and decided to take a walk down to the rock. To her surprise the flat-bed trucks were back loading up the link fences. There was no sign of the officious man she'd met the last time so she sat on the green and watched them till they'd finished loading and left.

With Thatchers Rock and the cove back to normality, Emily headed home. Her dad, Scott, was in the kitchen making some breakfast and she quickly told him the good news.

"I expected as much, King is on the back foot and trying to cover up."

"Do you think we can prove he organised the new committee member's infiltration?"

"I doubt it," Scott sighed. "Not while he can continue to hide behind the absent Prescott."

"Pity, I wish we could bring him and his corrupt organisation down."

Lucy walked in and Emily quickly told her about the fences. This brought a smile to her face, "Can we go and see Jack and Laura later?"

"If that alright with Dad?"

Scott chuckled, "I'm sure you'd like some time with Jack?"

Emily blushed, not being able to find a quick retort, which amused Lucy no end.

"I'll take John a cup of tea," Scott said as he walked away smiling to himself. Moments later he returned with a concerned look on his face.

"What's up Dad?" Emily asked.

"It's John, he's not here," a worried look.

"Maybe he went for a walk."

"I'll have a look out back," Lucy headed out the kitchen door. She checked the stables and the pool but there was no sign of him.

Scott and Emily checked the house thoroughly but still nothing. When Lucy returned, they decided to head down to the cove. They made their way down the path and onto the ledge, which gave them a good view of the cove below, but still there was no sign of him.

"Let's go to the blue-room and run through from the last time we saw him," Lucy suggested.

Emily and Scott agreed and they headed inside to the cave. Once in the blue-room, Emily adjusted the dials and zoomed in on the house and into John's bedroom, just after he'd retired for the evening. He was sound asleep.

They put the image into fast forward and watched as he moved around in his sleep. At five thirty am the image changed though. John literally disappeared before their eyes.

Emily was confused, "How can that happen?"

"He didn't take his travel-band from the drawer, did he?" Lucy asked, remembering Jack had asked Emily to put it there.

They all headed back to the house and Scott checked the drawer. The travel-band was still there though.

"What now?" Emily looked over at her Dad. But Scott wasn't there any longer. "Dad, where are you?" she cried out just as Lucy disappeared before her eyes.

Emily screamed, and then she vanished too.

John awoke from a strange dream. He opened his eyes, trying to make out the time. He noticed at once that the clock on the bedside table wasn't visible. In fact, the bed was different too. As his eyes become accustomed to the half-light, he knew he was somewhere else entirely. He had no idea where though.

He noticed a light above the bed. Searching, he found an on and off button just beneath it. Pressing it to on, the room lit up. It was simply furnished but in a weird way, futuristic movie type weird way.

There was a small round window, much like a ships porthole, opposite the bed. Walking over, he found another button beside the window which was probably for the blind. Pressing it, the blind slid open. He gasped at the view.

It was of planet Earth from space.

Reeling from the shock, John wondered if he was still asleep and dreaming when the door slid open behind him. A woman stood in the doorway smiling. She looked human in every way to John, even if the clothes were a bit out there.

"How are you feeling?"

"Where am I?" is all John could manage, a little panic stricken.

"You're on board a Stoffian space ship," The woman replied calmly. Her accent and use of words didn't suggest she was an alien. "My name is Marnia."

"How did I get here?"

"We transferred you here through our active portal, don't worry, no harm will come to you."

John checked himself over quickly just to be sure, two hands and feet, arms and legs, all there. "But why me?"

"All will be explained to you soon. I have bought you some clothes," she put them on the bed for him. Marnia then pointed to another door in the small room, "You may use the cleansing facilities. I will return for you in an hour."

"Do you have anything to drink?" John realised he was quite thirsty.

Marnia pointed to a weird looking contraption by the door, "We have entered your Earth preferences. Just speak what you require and the device will dispense it for you," Marnia smiled and gave John a curtsy, then left him to get ready.

Walking over to the contraption, John asked for a coffee with milk and sugar. A mug of steaming coffee appeared moments later. He took the drink and tasted it. To his surprise it was exactly what he expected.

Finishing his coffee, he checked out the cleansing facilities. Pressing a button, the door slid open to reveal a good size and very futuristic looking wet room. Feeling brave, John decided to give it a whirl.

Ten minutes later he walked back into the main room feeling refreshed and invigorated. He was awake and alert now. Changing into his new clothes, he checked himself out in the mirror, "Different," he mumbled to himself.

John asked for another coffee and added, "Toast would be nice." Moments later, both the coffee and two slices of toast appeared. "Butter and marmalade," he added, not expecting a further response. Two small containers appeared.

He chuckled to himself, looking around for a TV, he just knew there had to be one. Finding another button, a panel slid open revealing a large screen, "News channel," he asked. The picture lit up and a newscaster appeared.

Sitting on the bed, he ate his toast and waited for Marnia to return.

Still screaming, Emily suddenly became aware of here new surroundings. She was in a small room which was simply furnished. There were no windows in this room but there was sufficient light to see around her.

Emily shouted out loud, "Dad, Lucy, where are you?"

Moments later a door slid open and a woman appeared, dressed from head to toe in silver.

"You are Emily VanDaley," the woman stated rather than asked. She found that odd.

"Who are you and where are my Dad and Sister?"

"I am Marnia, please come with me, I will take you to them."

Emily followed Marnia into the hallway. They walked past several doors and stopped at a large double door. Marnia pressed a button and the door slid open and they walked into a spacious conference room, be it of futuristic design. There was a massive full width panoramic window looking out into space and onto the planet Earth below. Emily stood there for a moment, quite stunned.

Scott and Lucy were seated at a large floating glass table beneath the window. Two men were seated beside them. Both men were dressed in one piece blue suits with orange embroidered on the shoulders and cuffs.

"Where are we?" Emily took the seat beside Lucy.

The two men stood up to introduce themselves, "I am Stirk and this is Yamme. We are from the planet Stoffia. We have travelled from another universe on a peaceful mission."

Scott asked, "Why are we here? More importantly, what can we do for you?"

Yamme smiled, "It is what we can do for you."

Chapter 38

Scott looked confused for a moment, "I don't understand, please explain."

Stirk said, "Our ancestors and your ancestors have met before, a long time ago. You are the keepers of the crystal-vortex."

Scott looked stunned, "You mean the time-portal?" Having accepted Laura's new name for it.

"I understand you call it that, yes."

Lucy enquired, "Why do you call it the crystal-vortex?"

Yamme said, "The power source which runs the vortex is called crystallite. It controls the vortex which allows you to shift seamlessly in both time and location."

Lucy was none the wiser as Marnia bought over a tray with five glasses filled with light blue liquid, placing the tray on the table.

"Thank you, Marnia, please let us take refreshment." Stirk lifted a glass, as did Yamme. Scott nodded to the girls and they took theirs, "To our new friends."

Emily took a sip and was surprised, "This is really nice. What is it?"

"We call it nepelite juice, it is from one of many natural springs on our planet. I understand you have something similar, you call it water."

"Oh, spring water," Lucy smiled.

Scott asked, "Tell me more about this crystallite?"

Stirk nodded, "Crystallite is a sustainable source of power. We have an abundant supply of these crystals on Stoffia."

Emily asked, "You mean you have enough to last indefinitely?"

"Not exactly, each crystal has a reproductive energy which enables it to last forever!"

Scott and the girls were genuinely blown away. Scott asked, "So basically you're saying the crystals need nothing to maintain their power?"

"Much like your solar energy, it is reliant on the sun alone. However, the regeneration process is faster and the collective energy more efficient. This brings us to the reason we are here. Your own power sources are running out and you are only left with one alternative, which I understand is both dangerous and highly polluting."

Scott explained, "This is true, we have been trying to stop a nuclear power plant from being built near our home."

"Yes we are aware of this, directly above the crystal-vortex," Yamme said, "This is the reason why we decided to come and offer you a solution."

Scott looked shocked. He knew this would certainly solve the problems facing them. Not only that, it would make Kings nuclear power plants totally redundant.

Now that was good news.

Scott wanted to know more, "How much crystallite would be provided and how exactly would it work?"

Yamme explained the finer details, "Imagine the size of a football field. I understand this is still a popular sport here on Earth. The crystallite will fill one of these much like a lake. The depth would be the equivalent of a two-story building. This will be enough to power the entire south-west. Four of these will power the entire country and it is non-polluting energy."

Emily asked, "How will you transport it here?"

"We have many transporter ships which can carry up to a thousand people. In addition, each ship is capable of transporting a quarter of what is required for the south-west!" Yamme replied.

Emily was silently taking this all in. This was going to be good for the south-west, but more importantly, it would solve England's energy problems forever.

She was a little worried though, "This is a very generous offer, but I can't imagine for a moment you are providing it as a gift. So, what will you want in return?"

"Something you have an abundance of," Stirk said, "Human life!"

The room fell into silence as the announcement sunk in.

Yamme took over and went on to explain, "The crystal-vortex was created over two hundred and sixty years ago. Initially it was used by the chosen few. However, the technology fell into the wrong hands in recent years. This resulted in our planet being held to ransom. There ensued a long battle. Finally, all the crystal-vortexes were destroyed and we managed to overcome our enemies. But our losses have been substantial and the result is that ninety percent of the planets population has been wiped out."

Lucy enquired, "How did so many die, did it involve nuclear weapons or something similar?"

"No, it was largely due to the excessive use of the crystal-vortex which created a great number of time shift variations. This resulted in worm-holes being left in the atmosphere, which reacted much the same way as the tornado's your world has in some parts. The loss of life from these alone was on a massive scale."

"Could we cause the same to happen on Earth?" Emily looked concerned.

"Not as things are, however, it is a risk you face as the more people who know of the vortex, the greater the risk."

"We have been careful," Lucy said defensively.

"You lost control of the vortex," Stirk pointed out, "The three of you owe yours lives to the two known as Jack and Laura."

Stirk went on to explain that they'd been watching for the past month and had seen everything. They'd decided to choose this time to summon them after careful consideration and with the knowledge of what planet Earth could offer in return for their technology.

The Stoffian's needed to re-populate their planet with people of a certain calibre. They would have to have skills such as Scientists, chemists, doctors, engineers and trades people.

"We have one more condition," Yamme said, "Your crystal-vortex would have to be destroyed and all those who are aware of its existence will return to Stoffia with us. This will happen after the crystallite power source has been successfully arranged and you have assisted us in providing fifty thousand human."

"You mean you would want us to return to Stoffia with you?" Scott said, a look of astonishment.

"Yes, that is correct. You should inform Jack and Laura they must come too. This is the agreement."

Chapter 39

Wednesday 13th August 2008

Preparation for the games event was proving to be challenging and Jack didn't arrive home till just before ten Wednesday evening. He much preferred this kind of event to the fashion events they'd had a run of lately, looking forward to taking the girls.

Pulling onto the driveway and parking, he thought he heard talking coming from the house. His immediate thought was that he was being burgled again, but with no sign of forced entry and a silent alarm, that was unlikely, considering it was possible he'd left the TV on. Putting the keys in the lock and opening the door, to his delight, Emily was standing there with a big smile on her face.

"Hello, you're late! I've been waiting ages."

Jack gave her a huge hug, "If I'd known you were coming I'd have been here long ago." They stood there for a few minutes just holding each-other.

"I have some news," Emily announced, tearing herself away.

"Is this about the nuclear plant?"

"It's about the power source."

Jack was a little confused. "Is it going ahead now?"

"Not with Prescott's company."

Now he was totally confused, "I don't follow, there's another company involved now?"

Emily grabbed a bottle of Merlot and some glasses and they sat down. She explained what had happened that day in 2253, from being '*beamed*' aboard a space ship and the crystallite technology.

"That's incredible, fantastic news, totally weird and off the planet," he said, "So what do they want in return?"

"My first question too. They want something we have an abundance of, can you guess what that is?"

Jack scratched his head and thought for a moment, "Water?"

"No, they have that covered," she laughed. "They want human life!"

Emily repeated what they'd told her about their war and the massive loss of lives, "They want to re-populate Stoffia, but having lost ninety percent of the population, they're in need of fifty thousand humans."

"Are you going to be able to do that without involving your civil Government?" Jack asked.

"No, they should be involved, but we are going to need yours and Laura's help though."

"What can we do?"

"Think of ways in which we can find forty thousand people," she said with a shrug. "The government will be responsible for finding the first ten thousand. Do you have any suggestions?"

"I'll have to put some thought into that. Do you think the government will go for it?"

"Dad is meeting with them tomorrow to discuss the proposal," Emily said, pouring them both a glass of Merlot. "But with pollution at the highest level in the planets history - caused by the waste product from nuclear energy, I don't think they can say no."

"What other conditions are attached to this?" Jack knew there was always something.

Emily gave him a wary look, one he didn't recognize, "What do you mean?"

"I mean the kind of people?"

"Oh I see, sorry. They want scientists, chemists, doctors, engineers and trades people. The government will take care of the first four and the rest is down to us."

Jack was a little suspicious of her reaction, having learnt a lot about body language and how to read people. Whenever someone tried to hide something, or lie, he nearly always knew.

"So what did you think I meant?" He asked.

Emily gave him that wary look again, then smiled, "Nothing, that's it," she lied again. He could see it in her eyes but decided not to pursue it at that time, deciding he'd speak to Laura about it the following day and see what she could figure out.

They prepared some supper and sat down to talk about the mechanics of the operation, from how the Stoffian's were going to transport people back to Stoffia, to when the power source was likely to be up and running.

Yawning, Jack asked, "Are you staying?"

"I'd like to if that's okay, I'd also like to spend some time with Laura tomorrow if that's alright too?"

"That's fine, I'm sure she'd like that, what about Lucy?"

"She's coming in the morning, so you and I can be alone tonight."

It took Jack a few seconds to realise what she meant. He didn't need to answer though as Emily saw the delight in his expression.

Waking up in the morning, Jack wondered if he was still dreaming.

Emily opened her eyes and smiled. "Morning."

He pinched himself, but she remained there, "Morning to you too," he kissed her gently.

Just then they heard sounds coming from downstairs, Jack checked the time, it was only seven thirty.

"And that will be my little sister, she's an early riser."

They both got dressed and went to join her.

Lucy had a knowing smile on her face when they come down, "Morning lovebirds, did you have a nice sleepover," she laughed.

Emily shook her fist at her playfully, "I'll get you back for this."

"In your dreams," Lucy taunted. "So did Emily tell you about the Stoffian's?"

"Yes, I'm still trying to take it all in."

"Did she tell you about John?"

Jack looked over at Emily, "What about John?"

Emily shrugged and smiled, "I meant to tell you, but...."

Lucy went on "Stirk and Yamme are holding him till we agree terms. They want to take him back to Stoffia."

"Oh," he felt suddenly bad for John, "Is he alright?"

"He's fine, they're taking good care of him, that's all they would say."

Jack felt an unspoken conversation going on between Emily and Lucy. He decided not to question it right then though, but he'd be more aware going forward. It wasn't the first time he'd felt that.

Preparing breakfast together, they discussed ideas on how they were going to find forty thousand people, until it was time for Jack to go to work. As he went to leave, Laura appeared.

Jack said, "Emily and Lucy are inside."

"Excellent. Are you going to work?"

"Yes, I'll be back around six," He lowered his voice. "I think they're keeping something from us, see what you think."

She whispered back, "I'm sure they wouldn't do that, but I'll find out."

"Thanks. They have another surprise too, I'll let them tell you all about it. See you later, love you."

"Love you too, Pop's," she slapped him on the back.

Jack headed off to work. When he arrived and as he pulled into the car park, he noticed Leila was sitting in her car. Getting out and walking over to her, as he grew closer, he could see she was crying.

"Heh, what's happened?" Climbing into the passenger seat beside her and taking her in his arms.

"It's Roger, he's left me," she said sobbing.

Roger was her husband of only two years. It had been a whirlwind romance. Jack had only met him twice and got the impression he was a womaniser. He'd decided not to share his thoughts and mind his own business at the time.

"So why did he leave?" Jack asked.

"He's gone off with my so-called friend Carrie."

"How long has that been going on?"

Jack had met Carrie on a few occasions. She was a petite and very attractive blond in her mid-thirties. Carrie and Leila had gone to school together.

"They've been seeing each-other for six months."

Jack pulled her closer and comforted her as the tears exploded once again. He was surprised that Carrie would do such a thing to Leila, bearing in mind the length of time they had known each-other. They'd always seemed so close.

After a few minutes, Leila pulled away and wiped the tears from her eyes with a tissue, "I wish I could just pack my bags and disappear, any suggestions?"

Jack smiled, thinking he had the answer to that, but he decided not to mention it though. She'd think he was crazy, "Let's go and get a coffee," he suggested instead.

They made their way inside and headed for the kitchen. Leila went on to tell Jack over a coffee that she'd gone home early the previous evening to surprise her husband, Roger. Instead it was

Leila who'd got the surprise when she found them in bed together. They admitted their affair immediately and both had left ten minutes later.

Jack had known Leila for five years through work. She'd been there a year longer than him and had worked in the marketing department. He'd hand-picked her as his number two. The main reasons for this was her professionalism and character. However, at five foot six tall, slim with long black hair and stunning looks, Jack had to admit that he'd always had a soft spot for her. Then Roger had come along, so he'd put his attraction aside.

Holding her so close had bought back some of those old feelings though. "Let's go and sort out the gaming event stand positioning," Jack suggested. He didn't know why, but he was having guilty thoughts and imagined Emily watching them.

Leila grabbed his hand and squeezed it, "I'm glad I have your friendship."

He smiled. "You always will. Let's take your mind off thing, for a while at least!"

They made their way to the board room and went through the floor plans for the games event. With the distraction, Leila seemed a little happier. But Jack felt a little confused at his own feelings, keeping that to himself.

By mid-afternoon they'd made good progress and the stand order was established. Jack suggested they should have an early one.

"Trying to get rid of me," Leila said, pulling a face, mimicking Laura as this was something she would say to wind Jack up, playfully.

He explained that he'd promised to look after Laura and was therefore heading home early himself. He knew he should have told her about Emily at that point, but with her breakup, he thought it best to hold back on his happy news.

When Jack arrived home, the girls were all in the kitchen cooking dinner. "Good day at work?" Emily hugged him tight.

"Very productive, but I couldn't wait to get home," he kissed her and all memories of the day disappeared from his mind as he stared into her gorgeous blue eyes.

Laura and Lucy sat on the sofa giggling at them as usual. Jack couldn't imagine life being any better. After dinner, Emily and Lucy slipped on their travel-bands ready to go back to 2253.

"We'll see you Saturday," Jack said.

"We should know more about how the government reacted to the proposal by then," Emily replied.

"They're likely to agree, aren't they?"

"I would have thought so," Emily said. "I'm sure a great number of people would be happy to volunteer."

Jack couldn't imagine leaving Earth, but as a scientist, he would have thought it to be a life changing opportunity, one they would never experience again. He looked over at Lucy and noticed her eying him oddly.

They said their goodbyes before Emily and Lucy pressed their blue buttons and were gone. Laura and Jack kept waving though, knowing they would be doing the same in 2253.

Jack said, "What are you up to now?"

"Mom's in bed, she's not feeling well. Can I stay? Mom said it would be alright."

"Sure, where's your things?"

"In the spare room," she laughed.

He texted Marion to let her know it was fine for Laura to stay.

"So did you get any vibes from them?"

"Kind of, nothing I could really understand, but I think it's to do with Stoffia."

"In what context?"

"I'm not exactly sure, although I'm certain Lucy knows, but she kept changing the subject."

Jack wondered what it was they were hiding from them, finding his mind wondering to Leila again and the badly timed feelings he'd had, be it for a moment.

Laura gave Jack a strange look, "So, what aren't *you* telling me?"

Chapter 40

It was fast becoming obvious to Jack that he couldn't lie to Laura. He was also aware that it was more than a coincidence she could consistently be able to read people and situations.

Laura seemed to know when things were wrong or out of place. Jack had started to take it for granted a little because of his own skills, but Laura's seemed to go several steps further.

Jack had foolishly assured her he was keeping nothing from her the previous evening. On the way to work the following morning, he was regretting his decision.

Laura sat beside him with an amused expression on her face. He felt a pang of guilt run through him, hesitantly saying, "Laura, you know I'd never lie to you."

"So you say," she smiled, watching him.

"Well, sometimes it's not that simple, especially when it's something I'm struggling with. I'm not sure I can share feelings I don't fully understand myself."

Laura smiled back, "Is this to do with Leila?"

Jack felt the knot in his stomach tighten, how did she do that? He decided to come clean and tell her everything, as he felt he had no choice if he was to continue earning her trust. Jack assured her that he hadn't been lying but maybe he'd been economical with the truth. With everything they'd been through in recent weeks, she'd earned his respect, so he knew it was the right thing to do.

"So do you love Leila?" Laura asked, still smiling.

"I've always been very fond of her, but we've never hooked up. I really do love Emily though and I wouldn't two-time her."

"But you're angry with Emily because she's keeping something from you," Laura pointed out, continuing to watch him closely.

"Well, she is keeping something from both of us, I just can't figure out what it is."

"Leila is very pretty and I think she's really nice too, but I don't want you and Emily to break up." Jack remained silent and she continued. "We should ask Emily outright at the weekend and see what she says." He had no argument with her logic. In fact, it made perfect sense.

Arriving at Jack's office, they noticed Leila's car in the car park. Laura took off at speed in search of Leila so they could organise equipment hire for the games event. Jack got himself a coffee and went to his office.

Mark appeared at his door a short while later, he walked inside and sat opposite Jack, "I see you're busy babysitting again."

"I'd hardly call her a baby," Jack said defensively, "And anyway, she is making herself useful."

"So are we on target with this event? It's of paramount importance that we get this one absolutely right."

"We are ahead of target and below on budget to date. I have complete confidence it will go smoothly," Jack gave him a concerned look, "Why the panic?"

"You've been taking a lot of time off recently, what with your problems at home, and Leila is clearly an emotional wreck."

"Okay, I hear what you're saying, but I do have the situation under control," Jack said a little too aggressively, standing.

Mark stood and took a step back, "Keep it that way, and if you have any issues I want to know immediately."

Jack agreed and headed off to join Laura and Leila, who were just finishing off the order confirmation, which fortunately agreed with their original estimates.

"You don't need me then?" Jack said.

"I wouldn't say that," Leila replied smiling. Laura had that amused look on her face again and he could only manage a stifled chuckle.

By the end of the day Jack was exhausted from the emotional sparing. He managed to tear Laura away from Leila, who was becoming quite attached to her.

When Jack said, "See you Monday," as they were leaving, he noticed at once how disappointed and hurt she looked.

So, he added, "Call me if you want to talk." He wasn't sure if she took it in the way that it was meant though. Laura continued to find all this quite funny, but was saying very little.

Jack had arranged to go out with friends for a game of pool that evening so when they arrived back at Jack's, Laura went straight home.

Leila called during the evening and they chatted for a bit. Jack was sure she was angling for an invite down and whilst he wasn't against it, he knew he couldn't bring her into their complicated situation.

Jack was having breakfast with Laura and Marion Saturday morning and was pleased to see Marion was looking a little better, although she was still happy that Jack was taking Laura off her hands for the day. He knew she gave the impression she didn't care about Laura, to some people at least, but it wasn't true. He blamed the drugs.

Jack and Laura set off shortly afterwards and made their way to the blue-room and forward in time to 2253, where they joined Scott, Emily and Lucy, who quickly brought them up to speed with the Stoffian's proposition.

Scott explained, "The civil leader, Peter Crane, has agreed to the Stoffian's proposal and will provide ten thousand people for re-settlement covering the agreed professions. This will be done in a low-key manor though, as it will not be public knowledge. The first crystallite power station will be operational within two months. They have given us a further four months to complete the re-settlement programme."

"That doesn't give us much time," Jack said, wondering where to start. "Can we find forty thousand people in that time without attracting too much attention ourselves?"

"I thought we might ask Joseph for his help," Emily was referring to the Amish community leader in Richmond, VA, where Jack and Laura had rescued her other self from.

Jack quickly considered it and realised she was on to something. They were all skilled trades people and generally honourable. In addition, there were other Amish communities scattered across the States.

"But he won't know us because of the time shift," Laura pointed out, "And what about Jacob?"

None of them were about to forget Jacob after what he'd done to Emily and Lucy, along with Joseph's brother, Joe.

"Laura's right, we should be careful," Emily said. "However, if Joseph is open to a new settlement for his people, Stoffia would be ideal. The planet runs on its own natural resources and the Amish would retain their independent living standards. I'm certain they would become a genuine and accepted part of the population."

It made perfect sense, and if Joseph were to agree, they could approach other like-minded communities in both the past and present time. This could easily result in at least half of the people required.

This would still leave a lot of people to find and with only five of them, it was going to be a tough call. Jack's own work commitments were also a consideration, not to mention Laura, who was due to start at her new school in two weeks.

Lucy asked, "So who is going to speak to Joseph? I'm not sure I want to go."

"I will," Scott offered, "With your help, Jack. Emily, I want you and Lucy to locate other communities around the globe. The

Stoffian Transporters can carry a thousand people on each ship and there are ten of these on the way to us. They will arrange all transfers."

Laura had a sulky expression and asked, "What about me? I want to help too."

Scott smiled, "I assumed you would be coming with me and Jack!"

"You mean it," Laura's face lit up in excitement.

"So long as it doesn't interfere with your school work and attendance," Jack pointed out. That gave them two weekends before the games event, including the current one.

Laura asked, "So when are we going to see Joseph?"

"Tomorrow. Remember, with the time-portal, or as the Stoffian's call it, the crystal-vortex, we have total control of time," Scott said.

Jack asked what had happened to the three former new committee members and Sylvia. Scott informed him that due process had already been completed and they were all serving lengthy jail sentences far away.

After they'd finished their update, Lucy took Laura to the stables. Laura was looking forward to riding Tiger again. Scott had a meeting with Stirk and Yamme so Emily and Jack decided to take a drive to Newtown Village.

They discussed their plans in more detail and Jack suggested other groups of people she could consider. He still felt Emily was holding back about something. Not knowing what, he didn't know how to approach it. After spending several hours together, Jack was still none the wiser, hoping Laura would have better luck with Lucy, who he felt was more likely to open-up.

Lucy and Laura had returned from their ride by the time Jack and Emily got back from the village. It was just gone two, so Jack suggested they head home. To his surprise, Laura agreed immediately.

They returned to the blue-room and were making their way out when Laura stopped and pointed down into the cove. The French students were back and there were even more of them this time, which meant they couldn't climb down without being noticed.

"What shall we do, wait?" Laura said.

"We could, but the tide will be coming in soon, so they should leave. Alternatively, we could go back to the blue-room and transport ourselves to a quiet spot up above and send the travel-bands back."

Laura laughed and thumped Jack in the arm, "Why haven't we done that before?"

He shrugged. He didn't have an answer to that. Laughing, they made their way back to the blue-room. Minutes later they were in the car and heading home.

They'd arranged to meet Scott the following morning to visit the Amish. Jack was looking forward to seeing Joseph again, although he hoped Joe or Jacob wouldn't be there.

Chapter 41

Sunday 17th August 2008

Laura awoke Sunday morning and was about to jump into the shower when she heard her Mom downstairs, coughing badly. The voices in her head were telling her something was badly wrong and she rushed down to find her Mom laid out of the sofa, a blanket draped over her.

"Are you okay?" Laura asked, going to her Mom's side.

"Rough if I'm honest, I think I've caught a cold. Could you make me a cup of tea, boo?" Marion said.

Laura was hearing something else in her head which contradicted that. She went to the kitchen and made her Mom a cup of tea, taking it back to her, but Marion was so weak, she hardly had the strength to lift the cup.

Worried at a new level now, Laura decided to get Jack, heading next door and banging on his door. He came straight to the door, noticing how worried she looked.

"It's Mom, she's in a lot of pain. I don't know what to do," tears were rolling down her cheeks.

Jack wasn't sure whether to call an ambulance at that stage but decided to check in with Marion first to see how serious it was for himself.

"Is she dressed and out of bed?"

"Yeh, what shall I tell her?"

He grabbed his car keys, "We can take her to accident and emergency if necessary."

"What about Scott," Laura said, remembering they'd arranged to meet him to see Joseph. "He'll be waiting?"

"This is a little more important, let's go and see your Mom."

Marion was laid out on the sofa still, clutching her stomach and in a lot of pain. She was white as a sheet so Jack decided at once they should take her directly to Torbay Hospital.

"I'll be okay," Marion said defensively.

"Let's see what the hospital has to say about that, come on, you can't mess with your health. You could be having an adverse reaction to the new drugs."

Marion agreed reluctantly, so they headed off to the hospital. It was only five minutes away and fortunately when they arrived, there was only a few people waiting. Because of the distress Marion was in, they immediately wheeled her into casualty.

Laura and Jack waited whilst they assessed her. Laura was clearly upset still. All he could do was to be there for her as she clung to his hand tight.

Jack was aware Scott would be waiting for them in the blue-room and he wondered if he might have decided to look for them. No sooner had the thought crossed his mind, Scott walked into the waiting area.

He hurried over to Jack and Laura, "I thought something was wrong so I came straight here. How is Marion?"

"We don't know yet; they're assessing her now!"

A few moments later a 'white coat' appeared. "Hello, I'm Dr Janna, I've examined Marion and I've arranged for some tests. We would like to keep her here whilst we investigate further and to monitor her condition. Would you like to see her for a few minutes?"

Laura jumped up, still holding Jack's hand tight, "Please come with me."

"I'll wait for you both here," Scott suggested as they went through to casualty.

Marion was still as white as a sheet but they'd obviously given her something for the pain, as she looked a little more comfortable.

"Sorry to worry you, Laura," she whispered as Laura gave her a big hug. Marion looked over at Jack, "Please take care of her for me."

"Of course, you just do as the doctors tell you and you'll be home soon," Jack said.

Five minutes later they joined Scott in reception. They were coming back to visit Marion that evening, once she'd been settled into a ward.

"I don't mind if you two want to stick close to home today, I can do the trip to Virginia," Scott offered.

Laura quickly said, "I want to go, please."

"There isn't much we can do here," Jack said, shrugging.

They agreed to meet Scott back at the blue-room. He found a suitable place and disappeared. Jack and Laura were there half an hour later, dressed in their Sunday best to impress Joseph.

Scott was waiting for them and the blue-room image was already zoomed in on the Amish community in Virginia. Joseph was there looking a little older than the last time they'd seen him.

"This is your real time," Scott explained. "I didn't think we should confuse matter and go back to 2003."

It made perfect sense to them, so they chose a suitable spot beside Joseph's house to appear. Jack knocked on the door and Joseph answered. He saw a flicker of recognition on his face and Laura was smiling broadly.

"Hello, my name is...."

"Jack, yes I know who you are," he said, smiling warmly, "And you must be Laura."

Jack was taken aback as he'd assumed the time shift would have wiped his memory. He quickly introduced Scott.

"So you remember us?" Jack asked.

Joseph explained, "Yes, I do remember something. My son, Jacob, told me about a man and a young girl. He remembered your names. He was very confused at the time. I put it down to stress as he'd had his mind polluted by the city folk. But I remember you, Jack, and an older girl."

Jack remembered Lucy telling him it was more than possible they would remember the last time they'd seen them, and whilst the time shift would have altered their minds of all forthcoming events, Jacob would sure remember them disappear before his eyes. This would have left him with confused memories.

Laura walked towards the food larder and pointed, "Could I have a glass of your delicious lemonade please?"

Joseph laughed, "Have you been in my house before?"

Laura nodded and Jack explained, "It was five years ago, but you wouldn't be able to remember, how is Jacob?"

"He went away soon after the last time I remember seeing you and the older girl. He told me about you and Laura. His wife, Catherine, and my brother, Joe, left with him and I have heard nothing since. I don't even know if they are still alive," he had a sad expression.

In one way Jack was relieved, but it must have been heartbreaking to have lost three members of his family. He looked over at Scott and he nodded, knowing they were about to shock Joseph some more.

Jack told him everything from how Jacob had kept Emily prisoner and had attempted to do the same to Lucy. He explained how they had both got there initially, not forgetting Laura's rescue. When Jack had finished, they sat in silence and sipped their lemonades until Joseph finally spoke.

"I really don't know what to say. How can you ever forgive me? Are Emily and Lucy alright now?" he looked genuinely concerned.

Scott said, "They're fine. It was Emily who suggested we talked. She has a great deal of respect for you Joseph."

In reality of course, Emily hadn't met him. Jack decided it best not to confuse him though and said, "I know you looked after her and you couldn't have known. The time-portal caused a time shift which is why your memory of us is patchy."

Emily had in fact been with them for five years and Lucy four. But explaining that would be difficult as they'd changed all that.

"This isn't why we are here today," Scott continued. "I would like to add that we have the utmost of respect for you and your people,"

"That is kind of you to say. What can I do for you?"

"Well, it's more what we can do for each-other." A pause, then Scott continued, "We have a proposition for you and your community. I think it will be of great interest."

Chapter 42

The trip to Virginia turned out to be a successful one and Scott was impressed with the sales pitch Jack made to Joseph. They felt sure that once he'd spoken to his community they would accept their proposal, agreeing to visit the Amish again the following weekend.

Scott returned to 2253 to let the girls know how the meeting had gone, whilst Jack and Laura headed home for some dinner before visiting Marion. Laura went back to hers to grab some things whilst Jack prepared a meal.

Grabbing her bag, Laura filled it with everything she needed for the next few days. The voices in her head had quietened down a little, but she'd heard her Mom say she thought she had cancer, but how? Jack hadn't heard it, as he would have referred to it, so she had to consider she was mistaken. Wiping away a tear, Laura headed back down-stairs, remembering to grab her school shoes.

Looking around, she felt a shiver run down her spine. If anything happened to her Mom, who would take care of her? She was sure Jack would put up with her for a few days, but what if it was longer? What then, social care? She didn't want to go there, pulling herself together, she headed back to Jack's.

"Got everything you need, school clothes and all that?" Jack asked.

Laura held her bag up, "Yeh, all done."

"Dinner's ready, hope you're hungry," he said, noticing she looked upset.

"I'm not that hungry," Laura said, slopping onto the sofa.

"Well, try to eat a little if you can," Jack said, pulling his oven-proof gloves on and pulling a cottage pie from the oven.

She picked at her food though, clearly worried. Jack cleared up and they headed off to the hospital. Arriving there, they located Marion's ward and found her sitting up in bed reading a magazine. She looked a little more like herself, explaining that the Doctors had done several more tests and the results from these were due in about a week.

It was clear she would rather have gone home and Jack shared her thoughts, but until they knew what they were dealing with and what medication she needed, they insisted she stayed.

Driving home in silence. Laura looked deep in thought and her eyes were puffed up and red. She was clearly upset, "I'm sure your Mom's going to be fine," Jack tried to assure her.

"I don't think so, I heard something."

"What exactly did you hear?"

"Mom thinks she's got cancer," Laura promptly burst into tears.

"I didn't hear her say anything," Jack tried to comfort her, but she just pulled away.

"I know, but I heard it. Same as I heard you say you liked Leila and that Lucy Emily and Scott are going to Stoffia."

Jack was stunned, was it possible Laura was reading people's minds. Was she telepathic?

"I don't understand what's happening," she was still sobbing.

Jack was curious as to what else she might have heard, if she was indeed telepathic. He decided not to push it for the moment though with her being so upset.

"We'll sort it out like we always do," he said.

Laura remained quiet and a little withdrawn. Jack tried to cheer her up with a game of monopoly that evening, but it was clear her mind was in turmoil.

Jack was making tea in the morning when he noticed something move out of the corner of his eye. He knew Laura was still in bed and sound asleep. Smiling, he grabbed another cup from the cupboard, hearing Emily laugh.

"Morning, darling, did you miss me?" She came up behind Jack and wrapped her arms around him.

"Always miss you," he said, turning his head and kissing her.

"So how is Marion, Dad told us what happened."

Jack brought her up to speed and assured her Marion was comfortable and in no immediate danger that he was aware. He decided not to mention what Laura had said for the moment, realising by doing so, he was no better than Emily for withholding things, but this one was Laura's call.

A short while later, Laura padded down the stairs to join them. On seeing Emily, she rushed in and gave her a big hug, genuinely pleased to see her.

"Would you like to come and spend the day with me and Lucy?"

"Can I?" Laura looked across at Jack.

"So Long as Jack's okay with that," Emily said and Jack nodded, certain she'd have more fun than coming to work with him. It meant he'd have to contend with Leila alone though.

Laura went to shower and change, leaving Emily and Jack alone for a moment, "She seems very subdued this morning."

"Just a bit concerned about her Mom, it's a confusing time for her with everything that's going on," Jack said.

"We'll cheer her up," Emily promised, holding Jack tight. He didn't want to let go, but he had to go to work sometime.

Eventually he did manage to pull himself away and headed off to work. Leila was waiting for him outside of the office. She looked very down and her puffy eyes suggested she'd been crying a lot.

Jack asked, "Is everything alright?"

"Roger came home for the rest of his stuff last night," she exploding into tears.

She wrapped her arms around Jack and he felt those uninvited feelings returning once again. They stood there for a few minutes before Jack pulled away gently.

"Come on, let's get a coffee."

"Okay, if you say so," she smiled, then leaned forward and kissed him on the cheek.

He imagined Emily watching them again, which made him feel guilty enough. Not to mention Laura reading minds.

This roller-coaster ride was reaching new levels and Jack wondered what could possibly happen next.

Chapter 43

Tuesday 19th August 2253

Far above the Earth, Stirk and Yamme were meeting with Scott, Emily and Lucy. They sat around the same conference table as before. This time however, the VanDaley family were expecting to be there.

Scott explained that he'd chaired the regional meeting that past Monday to rubber stamp the replacement power-source. Central government had already accepted the Stoffian's proposal. Today's meeting was to confirm the arrangements.

Stirk nodded in approval, "I have ordered the transporters to collect the first wave of settlers. They will be here in two weeks. They will bring with them enough crystallite to power your region."

Lucy was curious, "Where exactly is Stoffia?"

"Stoffia is in the Kirsemmtya universe which is beyond your neighbouring Carhelyan universe," he explained in a matter of fact manner.

Scott asked, "How can you travel that sort of distance so quickly? It takes us several months, if not longer, just to enter the Carhelyan universe."

"We harness our power from what you call black-holes," Stirk replied.

Emily looked concerned, "But aren't they unpredictable, how's that possible?"

Yamme explained, "Our ships project a crystallite pathway into the black-hole which enables us to control its direction. This allows our ships to travel great distances in a matter of days rather than years."

"How accurate can you make them?" Emily asked.

"To within half-a-day at sixty percent power," Yamme stated proudly.

Lucy had questions too, "How do you intend to collect people?" She imagined ten massive space ships landing in the south-west of England somewhere.

"Exactly as we did with you, in fact we can transfer up to five hundred people together if necessary."

Scott considered the next question, thinking of the Amish, "So what if we wanted to bring people from the past?" He told them about their meeting with the Amish in Virginia.

Stirk and Yamme looked at each-other, puzzled at first. Then they both smiled, "We have lost the ability to time travel, as you know, but we do have many of, what you call, travel-bands. With our coordinates programmed into your time-portal, we can use it as a transfer station."

He explained one hundred travel-bands had been saved and that they could design a container which would have a master green and blue button to activate all the bands together. These would be sent into the past where one hundred people would simply press their blue button, which would send them via the blue-room in 2253 directly onto the ship. The process would simply be repeated till all the settlers had been transferred.

Stirk asked, "These Amish people you speak of, what more can you tell us about them."

"They are an independent community who live separately from normal society. They are experienced trade people with many skills including farming, construction, carpentry and teaching," Scott explained. "They are hard-working and peaceful folk."

"What sort of numbers are we talking about?"

"From the Amish alone, it's possible it could be as much as half the required amount."

Yamme asked, "And these are all from a single community?"

"They have similar communities scattered across America, but they share the same philosophy. I'm sure they would suit the model you're trying to achieve."

Stirk seemed satisfied with that, "Very well! When can they be ready to travel?"

"We have a meeting with them on Saturday. Joseph, the leader, will have spoken to his own community by then and others will be contacted once he has accepted our proposal."

Scott went on to tell them that five thousand of the required ten thousand being provided by the government had already been selected and the other fifty percent would be selected in plenty of time.

It was all agreed and they shook hands. Stirk announced, "Please, join us for some food. We would like to show you more of Stoffia and what we have to offer."

Lucy asked, "Can we see John?"

"He will be joining us in the food hall."

Yamme went ahead whilst Stirk took Scott and the girls on a guided tour of their massive space ship. They met several other members of the crew on the tour and got an insight into their way of life. Eventually the tour ended in the food hall, where John was waiting as they arrived. They all greeted him fondly.

"Have they treated you well?" Scott enquired.

John's smile suggested he was more than happy, "They have been very hospitable. I've seen images of Stoffia, there is a lot of work to be done but it's an amazing place," he seemed genuinely excited.

Emily asked, "What about your life on Earth and your wife?"

"We were about to separate and my career on the force has ended, so I have nothing left for me there. I'm not old, so this is a wonderful opportunity for me, a new start," John shrugged and smiled.

Joining Stirk and Yamme at the head table, Scott, Emily and Lucy were introduced to the crew, who all seemed welcoming and honourable people.

They enjoyed a typical Stoffian feast, which was beautifully presented and tasted wonderful. Their basic foods were similar in many ways to those on Earth, but each had its own unique taste, dependent on which region of Stoffia they had come from. Everything had a different name though, which was going to take them some getting used to.

After they'd eaten, Scott and the girls thanked them for their hospitality. Emily was hoping to persuade Stirk and Yamme to leave Jack and Laura on Earth. She passed her thoughts to Lucy who seemed to understand. Lucy studied Stirk and Yamme then looked back over at Emily and shrugged.

Emily decided to give it a shot anyway, "Is there any way you would allow Jack and Laura to stay?"

Stirk looked at Emily – a firm expression, "I'm sorry, our terms have been accepted. We will transfer them onto our vessel once the fifty thousand settlers have been successfully transported safely to our waiting ships!"

"I understand," Emily didn't push it any further in case of offending them.

Yamme explained, "We are honourable people, much like the Amish you speak of, we hope you are too."

Scott assured him that they were. He wondered how they were going to break it to Jack and Laura though.

Chapter 44

Wednesday 20th August 2008

Jack got a call from the hospital Wednesday morning to say Marion could come home. There were still some tests to be analysed, but they were confident with her new medication. No mention was made of the dreaded 'C' word that Laura was sure she'd heard, but until the tests came back, the hospital was unlikely to suggest it as a possibility.

Jack and Laura went straight there to collect her. When they arrived, Marion was already waiting in the ward reception. They got the impression she'd not been a model patient and were secretly glad to see her go. Half an hour later and back at Marion's, she was already sat in front of her computer with a bingo game on the go.

Jack called Leila to let her know he was running late, "You're not avoiding me, are you?" Leila said playfully.

He assured her he wasn't, aware that they'd been getting closer as the week progressed. Jack was grateful Laura had been with him for the most part, giving him an escape route most evenings.

Jack still wasn't sure if Leila had picked anything up from Laura, if she had, she wasn't sharing. Laura was certain Leila was angling for the two of them to get together. This worried Jack and he wondered how long they could avoid '*the conversation*' without upsetting Leila and the two of them falling out over it.

Marion was engrossed in her bingo game, having just won a line. Laura gave Jack that '*I'm bored*' look.

"Can I come to work with you please?"

"If that's alright with your Mom," he looked over at Marion for approval.

She nodded, not even looking up from the computer screen. He wasn't sure if he was doing the right thing leaving her alone and felt guilty about taking Laura, but for selfish reasons it suited him with the Leila situation ongoing. He wasn't sure how long he could hide behind Laura though.

It turned out to be a quiet afternoon at work and the atmosphere around the office was happy and relaxed as Mark was off again, much to Jack's surprise. He was normally such a workaholic. Leila was sticking to Jack like glue, which Laura found quite funny.

"Are you looking forward to coming to the games event press day on Monday, Laura," Leila said.

"Yeh! And we're going again Saturday with Emily and Lucy," she replied - excited, then covered her mouth and added, "Oops."

Jack felt himself cringe at her honesty and avoided eye contact with Leila.

"Are they your friends?" Leila looked a little perplexed.

Jack didn't know where to put his face. He guessed it was Laura's way of saying – '*Tell the girl the truth.*' She was right of course.

"Emily and Lucy are Sister's and friends of ours," He offered feebly.

"Friends as in what?" She eyed Jack suspiciously.

Laura replied for him, "Emily is Jack's girlfriend."

"You're a dark horse, so when were you going to tell me?"

She was still smiling, but knowing her as he did, Jack could see her dark eyes boring holes in him. He decided to come clean.

"We all met a few weeks ago when Laura and Lucy befriended each-other," looking over to Laura for support. None came. He continued anyway, "We've been seeing each-other since. Its early days but she is a lovely person. I wanted to tell you but then Roger walked out on you and, well - sorry."

"You should have told me instead of letting me make a fool of myself," she snapped.

Jack was a little angry at her outburst and Laura was looking uncomfortable, so he tried to defuse the situation. "I don't want this to affect our friendship or our working relationship Leila, and the only fool here is me for not saying. As I have already said, if I've offended you, I'm sorry."

"I've got some work to do in my office," she said, turning and walking away without another word.

Laura looked embarrassed, "Sorry, Jack, I didn't mean to upset her."

"It's not your fault, Laura, I should have told her."

Jack grabbed a coke from the fridge and handed it to her.

"Thanks. She really likes you, you know that, don't you?"

"I know, I think the world of her too, but I love Emily, even if things aren't perfect right now."

She gave him a one-armed hug. "I'm sure Emily has her reasons for keeping things from you, she'll tell you soon."

"Do you know?" He was suspicious that she knew more than she was letting on.

Laura smiled, "Well, not really. I'm not sure to be honest. I wanted to talk to you about it later. It's like I'm going crazy," she pointed at her head, twirling her finger.

"I'm sure you're not," he assured her as he made coffee for himself and Leila.

Taking Leila her coffee, Jack placed it on her desk. She muttered, "Thanks."

He was still a little angry, "You have no idea do you."

She looked at him strangely, "What do you mean?"

"Your friendship is very important to me, not to mention what a great team we make. I don't want to lose that. I'm sorry I didn't tell you about Emily, it's complicated."

She looked up from her desk and smiled, "You just surprised me, sorry, we're okay!"

"Who invented timing huh," he said, trying to lighten the mood, which seemed to work.

Later when Jack and Laura were on the way home, Jack asked, "Do you want to talk about the voices in your head?"

Laura pulled a face, "I think I'm going mad!"

He assured Laura she wasn't. In fact, he was certain of his prognosis, "The voices in your head are other people's thoughts or fore thoughts. Somehow you can read them."

"What does that mean?" Laura looked puzzled.

"It's what you think before you speak, well most of the time at least," he laughed.

"Can I try it on you?"

Jack turned his head away and in his mind, he thought - '*you can try.*'

Laura responded immediately, "Okay I will, think of something then?"

"I just did, you read it!"

Shock appeared on her face, "I don't understand," she said looking confused.

"It means you have telepathic abilities. Don't be afraid, I'll help you to understand, I promise."

"So how can I figure out who is saying what?"

"Practice, Laura, I'll help."

If Jack wasn't already in awe of Laura, he sure was then.

Chapter 45

Jack and Laura were up early Thursday morning and headed straight to the blue-room. Jack wanted to see Emily of course, but they both wanted to know what progress had been made in 2253.

When they arrived at their home, Scott, Emily and Lucy were seated around the kitchen table having breakfast. Knocking on the door, they walked in.

Laura shouted out, "Morning all."

Lucy was already up off her chair and hugging Laura, but Emily just looked up and smiled, then looked away again. Jack felt quite hurt but decided not to show it.

"So how did the meeting go with the Stoffian's?" He asked.

"It went well. Everything is going forward," Scott explained what had been discussed and their subsequent tour of the ship. Jack was happy to hear John was well as he'd been feeling rather bad about getting him involved.

Emily remained silent whilst Scott and Jack spoke, avoiding eye contact with him. Jack needed to talk to her and let her know how much he loved her. Not only that, he wanted to tell her about Laura and her telepathic ability.

Lucy, perceptive as she is, must have sensed this and suggested she take Laura to the stables. Scott quickly stood up and excused himself too.

Now they were alone, Jack said, "Heh, I've missed you."

He noticed a tear roll down her cheek, reaching out, pulling her close, "Is everything okay?"

"I'm alright, missed you too," she pulled away. "So how is your games event coming along?"

"All good! We were hoping that you and Lucy would come with us next Saturday!"

"That would be nice. I'm certain Lucy will want to go," still sounding flat.

Jack was sensing things weren't right between them with her being so distant, suggesting they take a walk. It didn't help though as Emily remained silent the entire time.

Arriving back at the stables, Laura and Lucy were just coming out.

"That time again," Jack said.

She nodded, "I know."

He turned to Emily and asked "Would you like to drop by later?"

"Do you want me to?"

He was a bit taken aback by her response, "I wouldn't have asked otherwise."

"Maybe tomorrow. Sorry, I have to go."

With that she turned and walked back to the house. Jack looked over at Lucy, she quickly looked away.

Laura grabbed Jack's arm, "Come on, let's go, you mustn't be late for work."

They said goodbye to Lucy and returned to the blue-room. Jack was still upset with Emily and the way she'd been with them, more in particular, him. Laura gave him a concerned look.

Jack shrugged, "What have I done?"

"All I could hear in Emily's head was - *'I can't tell him; I don't know how to.'* She said it repeatedly!"

"Did Lucy say anything?"

"Nothing said, but I got the feeling she knows what's up with Emily, but I can't always hear Lucy's thoughts, it's like she puts a wall up or something."

"Maybe Emily thinks she's made a mistake with me."

Laura shook her head, "I can't see that. I'm sure you're wrong."

"I hope so too," he sighed. "See if she shows tomorrow, if not, then I guess we will find out more Saturday."

They made their way out of the cave and up the path to the car. Jack asked Laura what she wanted to do for the day.

"Well, I could come to work with you."

"Why not call for Ayesha," he suggested. "I promise I'm not trying to get rid of you."

"I know, yes I will," she said smiling.

Jack dropped her off a few minutes later and he could see she was pleased to be with her friend. Heading off to work, he prepared himself to face Leila, who was waiting for Jack in reception when he arrived.

Leila grabbed Jack's arm and steered him towards the kitchen, "I need to apologise to you."

"No need," he assured her. "I'm sorry again I didn't tell you about Emily."

"You do know that if Roger hadn't have come along when he did, it would have been you," Leila said, running her hand down Jack's arm.

"I had no idea," he replied, those unwelcome feelings returning once again.

She leaned forward and kissed him. She smelt and tasted wonderful to Jack, but he still managed to pull away, a little embarrassed by her forwardness.

"Timing huh," he felt his cheeks burning red.

She smiled and poured them a coffee. Was he off the hook? Jack had no idea, promising himself he would get a copy of the manual about women as he couldn't figure them out sometimes.

The rest of the day ran smoothly, and with Mark still off, Jack got away at a sensible time. Pulling onto the driveway at five pm, he went straight into the house, hoping secretly to find Emily inside waiting for him.

It was empty though, so Jack got changed and had something to eat. He was tempted to go out, but instead chose to watch some TV as one of his favourite shows was on. He must have dozed off at some point, because when Jack awoke, he immediately felt something was different.

Then suddenly he heard a voice float into his woolly head, "Hello sleepy head," Emily said softly in his ear, "Are you pleased to see me?"

Reaching out, Jack pulled her towards him, "Of course I am, kissing her and holding her tight.

"I Love you," she said.

"I love you too," Jack scooped her up in his arms.

Seemed things were okay between them after all, but he still didn't know what she was keeping from her.

Chapter 46

Jack received a call from his boss, Mark, that Friday morning. He told Jack he was in London visiting his brother.

"I need you to do something for me," he asked.

"Sure. So long as you think I'm reliable enough."

Mark ignored his remark, "I've got a meeting booked with Kobel Electronics regarding their event in November. Can you take the meeting for me please?"

Jack agreed and scribbled down the details, grateful that he wouldn't have to go into the office and deal with the temptation of Leila. But at the same time, he couldn't help but be concerned for Mark. He'd heard an edge to his voice and felt something was wrong, so he didn't give him any more of a hard time than he usually did.

Calling Leila, Jack let her know what he was doing. She sounded disappointed, "I'll guess I'll see you Monday for the press event then."

"I'm looking forward to it, so is Laura. Well, have a good weekend," hanging up and cringed at his insensitive remark. He knew she was angling for an invite over, but he couldn't risk her walking into their precarious situation.

Jack told Emily about his meeting with Kobel, "Shall I stay and keep an eye out for Laura?"

"She'd like that, thanks," he said, texting Laura to let her know before setting off.

Jack considered his relationship with Emily as he drove to work. It was becoming clear that they were all but done, that's if she was off to Stoffia, as Laura had suggested – and he had no reason to doubt what Laura had heard in her head, he just didn't want to believe it. Feeling confused as thoughts of Leila crossed his mind, he considered how different Emily and Leila were. Leila was more of an open-book, but it was far too quick for her to be considering another relationship after her breakup with Roger.

Jack hoped that if Emily and Laura spent some time together that day, Laura would be able to read her some more. He didn't like relying on her for that, and deep down he knew she would probably only tell him what he wanted to hear, unless it concerned her too.

Emily stayed with Jack again Friday evening, so he didn't get a chance to quiz Laura. They'd all arranged to meet Scott in the blue-room at nine the following morning.

"I'm not sure I want to go with you tomorrow," Emily said.

"I can't imagine you would after what Jacob put your other self though," Jack said, reaching out and taking her hand.

"I'll watch from the blue-room. You don't mind, do you?"

"You do what feels right," Jack said, "Just know that I love you."

"I love you too," she said, putting on a DVD and sitting back down. Jack sat beside her and they snuggled up and relaxed to the sound of Celine Dion.

The following morning Laura was at Jack's door, dressed sharp for their meeting with Joseph. Jack had suited up too, out of respect for the man.

Scott was waiting for them when they arrived at the rock. Emily stayed in the blue-room to stand guard, just in case there were problems. Jack couldn't imagine there would be for one moment, but he'd been proved wrong before. On that occasion, it was Laura who'd saved them from the grips of Jacob and Joe.

They headed off to Joseph's house in Virginia. He was there waiting for them as they appeared in front of him. He still looked startled though.

"I understand why Jacob was so afraid of you, I'm not sure I could ever get used to that."

"I'm sorry. That's not our intention," Jack said.

Laura was standing by the kitchen larder door smiling. Joseph caught on quick, "Would you like a glass of lemonade, young lady?"

"Yes please," she smiled, a picture of innocence.

Joseph fetched the jug of lemonade and placed it on the table with some glasses. They all sat down to join him. His expression was very serious, stern almost. Jack wondered if they were about to be blown off. Looking over at Laura, she was still smiling though.

"I have spoken to the community; I've also contacted other community leaders. We have some concerns we would like to discuss with you please."

Jack remained quiet, studying his posture and expression, but to him, Joseph was giving nothing away. "We are happy to answer all of your questions," Jack said.

"As you know, we are an independent community and it is no secret that we despise society and what it represents. It is therefore of the utmost of importance that we retain our independence, and more importantly, to be part of a greater society with a similar outlook. What assurances can you give us that we will be left to govern ourselves?"

Jack was pleased with his response, glancing over at Laura, who probably had all the answers already. He felt sure with everything they'd been told about the Stoffian's, this did suggest the Amish shared a common interest.

Scott explained they would be able to build a larger society which would be more involved in future decisions regarding rebuilding the new world. But more importantly, they would be leaders of their own society.

When Scott had finished his speech, Joseph refilled their glasses and smiled, "Then it's agreed, I have already been authorised to accept your proposal on these terms."

They'd expected more questions, pleasantly surprised at his quick decision. Scott did have another piece of information which they decided not to pass on right away. The Amish didn't make it past the twenty first century, so this was an opportunity for them to ensure their people prospered into the future.

Jack asked, "What sort of numbers are we talking about, Joseph?"

"In the region on twenty thousand people including their families. We will require agreements in writing to support our independence and land ownership issues."

Scott explained that he had the authority, given to him by the Stoffian's, to agree to that.

Joseph spread his arms and smiled, "Then we must share a meal and celebrate our journey to the new world."

They were taken on a tour of the village, which had changed little in the past five years. There were a few more houses which had sprung up as the community naturally grew.

Joseph asked, "Will you be going to Stoffia, Jack?"

Scott answered quickly before Jack or Laura had a chance to respond, "We will all be part of the re-settlement programme with an option to go."

Laura gave Jack a concerned look, whilst he remained silent. She'd heard something different from Scott.

Joseph had no further questions and they returned to his house and enjoyed a meal with him and his family, who Jack and Laura had met five years earlier. All the girls were now married and had children of their own now.

Jack noticed during the meal that Laura had been watching Scott very closely, reading him, he was sure. After the meal, he caught her eye and smiled.

She wasn't smiling back.

Chapter 47

Returning to the blue-room after their meal with Joseph, Emily was waiting in the apartment beside the blue-room. She seemed distant again to Jack, but he figured it was because her dad was present and put it out of his mind.

After discussing their successful trip, Scott and Emily returned to 2253. Jack and Laura watched as they removed their travel-bands and left their blue-room.

Jack looked across at Laura - she was now close to tears, "I know what Emily's keeping from us," she blurted out.

"What is it, Laura?"

"They really are going to Stoffia," she was trying not to cry, "They're going to live there forever, I heard Scott say it in his head."

The tears exploded from her eyes and Jack reached out and pulled her close, tears welling up in his eyes too. They stood there for several minutes comforting each-other.

Jack had no reason to question what she'd heard and he fully understood why Emily and Lucy had been acting so strangely around them lately. He still wasn't sure how to tackle Emily about it, but after a good cry, they agreed to visit them Sunday and demand the truth.

Back at home, they checked in on Marion. She looked very pleased with herself, having just won two hundred and fifty pounds on the bingo. They spent the evening together to celebrate. Jack was pleased to see the two of them so close.

The following morning, Marion was in the kitchen making tea when Jack arrived, "Morning. Laura's just in the shower."

"No rush. So how are you today?"

"I'm okay. I've got to see the Doc tomorrow morning. Some test results are due in."

"It will be good to find out what exactly is wrong. Do you have any plans for today?" Jack asked.

"I'm a bit tired to be honest, are you and Laura going out?"

"We were going to meet Emily and Lucy," Jack said. Feeling guilty about leaving her alone, he added, "If that's okay?"

"Good, I'll get some rest then."

Laura appeared at the kitchen door moments later, "Ready when you are, Pop's."

Heading off to the cave, they found the traffic approaching the rock quite busy. Parking was a nightmare and the place was heaving with tourists. Peering down into the cove they could see a record number of fishermen on the rocks and several people milling around in the cove.

It was a beautiful day though, so it shouldn't have come as a surprise. Jack scratched his head, "So what do we do now?"

Laura smiled, "I have an idea?"

She grabbed his hand and led Jack down the path into the cove. Climbing up into the cave first, she shouted for him to join her. By the time Jack had reached the top, Laura had already run into the rear cavern and down into the blue-room. Jack heard the boulder drop back into place and moments later Laura appeared back by his side.

"Let's go," she handed him a travel-band. He caught on quick and followed her back down into the cove and back up the path. Continuing along the path past the green, they found a quiet spot then pressed the blue buttons on their travel-bands.

Jack complimented Laura as they arrived in the blue-room. He had to admire her quick thinking, "You're getting good at this huh?"

"I got a brain," she said cheekily.

Locating Emily and Lucy, they found them in their Kitchen. "I'm starving, hope they got some breakfast," Laura was rubbing her stomach, hungry as usual.

Appearing at the kitchen door, which was open, they walked inside, "Surprise," shouting together.

"What do we owe the pleasure," Emily asked, smiling this time.

"We wanted to see you, I hope that's alright?"

"Of course," she gave Jack a hug, "We were about to go into Newtown Village."

"Can we come?" Laura asked.

"I'll take you shopping with me, Laura, let the two love birds spend some time together," Lucy said laughing.

"So long as we're not intruding," Jack said.

Emily gave Jack 'the look', "Shut up," leaning forward and kissing him.

"I'm hungry," Laura reminded everyone.

"We'll get you some breakfast before you go shopping," Emily promised.

It was quiet in the village and it wasn't long before they were seated in the cafe they'd visited before on the ninety ninth floor of the main tower. Laura and Lucy woofed down their bacon rolls and headed off to the shops, leaving Jack and Emily alone. They took their drinks up to the viewing area on level 100.

Looking out over the wonderful view of Newtown village and the rolling hills surrounding them, Emily told Jack about her ideas concerning communities like the Amish, having been working relentlessly on them with Lucy.

Not being able to keep it to himself any longer, Jack spoke up, "Emily, I know you're keeping something from me."

She looked defensively at him, but said nothing. The expression on her face was that of sadness though, so Jack eased up a bit.

"You're going to Stoffia aren't you?"

"It's not that simple!" Emily said with a sigh.

"So tell me what's up. I don't want to lose you."

"We have to go," bowing her head. "It's part of the agreement with the Stoffian's."

Jack felt his heart had just been ripped out of his chest. "When?" A look of resignation on his face. Laura had been right on the money.

"As soon as we've completed the transfers!" Emily reached out for Jack, tears rolling down her cheeks, "I don't want to go, but we have no choice."

Jack didn't know what to say. They just stood there holding each-other, losing track of time.

Laura and Lucy appeared with several bags of shopping, all of them overflowing.

"Hungry work this shopping, can we get something to eat, Pop's?"

Jack and Emily weren't hungry though, but they followed the girls down to the cafe and had another drink whilst they tackled their burgers and fries.

Jack didn't want to go and was stressing inside about losing Emily, but he felt they should check in with Marion to ensure all was well. Back in the blue-room Jack repeated the conversation he'd had with Emily.

"You got more than me then, I couldn't read Lucy at all," Laura shrugged.

"I guess that's it then, no more team!"

She looked sad too, "You've still got me," a goofy smile.

"I'm grateful for that," he said squeezing her hand. "Let's go and check on your Mom."

"Can I stay at yours tonight? We're still going to the games event tomorrow, aren't we?"

"Yes of course, so long as your Mom's fine with that. I'm quite looking forward to the event, I wish they were all like this one."

Laura looked over at Jack with a serious expression, "I'm going to really miss Emily and Lucy."

Jack's face dropped, a sad expression, "I know, I will too!"

There was little else to say as they made their way back to the car, using the same method as before. They drove home in silence and went straight next door to see Marion. She was still in bed and sound asleep, so Laura left her a note asking her to join them for dinner a little later. Fetched her things ready for the morning, she returned to Jack's. Marion joined them an hour or so later.

After dinner, Marion left to go home. Laura looked tired, "I'm beat. See you in the morning," turning in for the evening.

Jack hi-fived her as she past, "Sleep tight."

Sitting back down, the phone rang ten minutes later. It was Leila. She seemed down and they chatted for a while until, finally, Jack got to bed.

It had been a strange day for him, on the one hand they had achieved half the goal for the resettlement programme, and on the other - he was losing a special friend, as was Laura.

He thought it'd been a pretty incredible summer though, the best in fact. He was just sad to see it end.

Chapter 48

Jack and Laura arrived at the games event well before everyone the following morning, except Leila of course. She was waiting for them by the drinks dispenser, as none of the outlets were open yet.

Pleased to see everything in place and looking very impressive, Jack said, "Reckon we nailed it huh."

"Must have been all the hard work Laura and I put in?" Leila pulled a face, hi-fiving a giggling Laura.

"Must have been, oh great ones," he said laughing.

Leila took Laura on a tour whilst Jack met with the rest of the team as they arrived. It wasn't long before the stands were up and running and their company representatives in place.

With everything sorted, Jack found Laura, just as the press were arriving and the event began. Laura was in her element and wanted to play every game console she could find. By lunchtime she'd set the highest scores on most of the games for all to beat.

They met Leila for lunch and Jack found himself being drawn to her once again. He wanted to fight it, but with Emily leaving them to go and live in Stoffia, he felt he'd already lost her.

He managed to tear himself away and watched as Laura filled two giant bags full to the brim with freebies - from play-station games to the latest board games. She also entered a competition to win an X-box with games. Later, when the results were announced, Laura had won that too.

To say she was happy that day would have been an understatement. This was Laura being a normal healthy ten-year-old having fun and she deserved to. Leila also seemed in good spirits and they went out to dinner a little later to celebrate a successful day.

Driving home, Laura was so exhausted she dropped straight off to sleep for the entire journey. As Jack pulled onto the driveway though, her eyes open a crack.

"Are we home?" she asked sleepily.

"Sure are, big day huh?"

"The best," she said smiling and yawning at the same time. "Can't wait to go again Saturday." Jack was certain she'd fill at least another two bags.

Laura was struggling to stay awake so he texted Marion to let her know she was staying over. She texted back saying it was fine.

"I'm beat. Thanks again for a great day," Laura said, wearily giving Jack a one-armed hug.

"I'm just glad you had fun."

"Oh by the way," Laura said as she got to the door, she had a wicked look on her face, "Leila is in love with you!"

"Oh," is all Jack could manage, not knowing what to do with that piece of information.

Half an hour later, Leila called and they talked about how well the event had gone that day. She couldn't stop talking about Laura and all the prizes she'd won. Jack agreed to meet her the following day, but a little later, as Laura was starting her new school.

In the morning, they went straight next door so Laura could get ready. Marion was in the kitchen sipping tea.

She looked a little better and colour was returning to her face, "Have you got any test results back yet?" Jack asked.

"I have to go back," pulling a face. "They want to run some additional tests."

"Don't they have any idea what the problem is yet?"

"They won't say until they've done more tests. I've got an appointment to go back tomorrow afternoon!"

Jack could see she was worried and didn't think she should go alone, "I'll get the afternoon off and take you."

Laura appeared at the door, all dressed ready in her new uniform and looking excited. She did enjoy school and had been looking forward to her new term.

"Did Jack tell you what I won yesterday?" Laura said.

"I was about to," he opened the bags and showed Marion what was inside, she looked quite shocked.

"You are a clever girl, well done. I'm proud of you."

"I'm going to win loads more on Saturday."

"Where will we put in all," Marion said laughing, giving Laura a hug, she wriggled away as usual. "I better get ready," Marion said.

She went to stand and almost fell, but managed to steady herself. Just in that short moment, all the colour had drained from her face again. Laura noticed too and looked over towards Jack with a sad expression on her face.

When Marion had disappeared upstairs, Laura whispered, "Mom does think she's got cancer, I heard her say it."

Jack had lost his own mother through cancer and hoped Laura was wrong. "It's too early to really know, let's just give her our support. I'm sure we will have all the answers soon."

But he wondered if they would find out in good time. By the time his mom had been properly diagnosed it was too late to treat her. He didn't want that to happen to Marion.

"Positive attitude," Jack said, just as Marion came back down the stairs.

Jack took them to Laura's new school and waited while Marion chatted to her new teachers. Eventually they left and he dropped her back home and went on to the event.

The rest of the week flew by for Jack. The event was a huge success with a record numbers of visitors. By Friday, Laura still held the highest scores on almost half of the games and looked likely to win more competitions.

Jack and Leila had got closer as the week progressed, but Jack kept his feelings to himself and remained faithful to Emily. When she didn't visit once during the week, he'd started to accept his loss.

Marion's additional tests were carried out and the results would not be ready for another week. Her medication was changed again, but her condition remained the same.

Laura was enjoying her new term and was quickly settling in and making new friends. She had been busy with homework and study and Jack had seen little of her during the week.

Friday came and Jack managed to get away from the event early. He drove straight to the cove and climbed into the cave without getting too wet. Quickly going to the apartment to clean up, he hoped Emily would be home as he knew Laura was looking forward to going to the games event with her and Lucy the following day.

In the blue-room, Jack dialled up Emily's home and found Lucy and Scott in the kitchen preparing dinner. There was no sign of Emily though. He tried the apartment and there she was, sitting at the desk, writing.

He slipped on a travel-band and sent himself outside the door, tapping on it.

"Go away, Lucy," she shouted.

"It's not Lucy," Jack said, opening the door.

"I didn't expect to see you," Emily got up and put her arms around him.

"Have you forgotten about the games event tomorrow? Laura is looking forward to seeing you both."

"If you still want us to come," Emily replied.

He could hear the sadness in her voice and pulled her close, kissing her gently, "You know we want you to come, and anyway, Laura wants to show you what she won on Monday."

They went back to Emily's home and joined Lucy and Scott in the kitchen, Emily announced, "One more for dinner."

Lucy looked at Jack oddly, "Where's Laura?" then smiled and nodded.

He answered anyway, "I came straight from the games event to take you both back with me."

As they sat and ate dinner, Jack noticed Scott wasn't his usual talkative self. He decided not to question it though, imagining he was still silently struggling to take everything in, as Jack was.

Lucy was looking forward to seeing Laura and quickly finished dinner and went to pack a bag. Jack helped Scott clear up while Emily joined Lucy.

"How do you feel about going to Stoffia, Scott?" Jack asked.

"Not something I planned for to be honest. I have a good life here, but we've made an agreement," he replied, avoiding eye contact.

Jack pushed on, "What's the reasoning behind their decision?"

Scott didn't answer immediately and Jack wished he'd had Laura with him to decipher that. Eventually he offered, "They would like us to be ambassadors for our people."

Jack didn't buy it. There were supposedly top notch doctors and scientists who could do that. He was about to delve a little deeper when the girls appeared with their bags.

"We're ready," they both shouted together.

Scott looked relieved and said goodbye to Emily and Lucy and they headed off to the cove. Whilst they made their way to the blue-room, Jack returned to 2008 and waited for them.

They were there minutes later and headed off to surprise Laura. Pulling onto the driveway she came hurrying out, smiling.

"I wondered where you'd got to, I was worried Emily and Lucy wouldn't come."

Going next door to see Marion, Laura was quick to produce her goody bags to show Lucy. Jack and Emily sat with Marion, who was still looking very pale. Jack was getting very concerned about her condition and frustrated with the amount of time the doctors were taking to identify her problem.

Marion decided to take the opportunity to lie down as Lucy was there to take care of Laura, so Jack and Emily went back to his place. When they were alone, Jack pulled her close and hugged her, not wanting to ever let go.

"I so wish you weren't going," he said.

"I have to, I'm sorry," she started to cry again.

"Is there anything I could do or say to change their mind?"

Emily shook her head. "Sorry, we have to go."

He didn't pursue it any further, happy she was there with him in then. But his heart was quietly breaking.

Chapter 49

The games event promised to be busy Saturday, and the car park was already quite full, and it was only ten thirty. The event started at eleven and the queues were already quite massive.

Taking the side entrance, Jack gave Laura, Emily and Lucy their passes. Laura was off at speed with Lucy in hot pursuit as she wanted to see how many high scores she had to beat. She was soon filling bags again, as was Lucy. The technology was quite dated to Lucy of course, but she didn't let on as Laura was having such a great time.

Jack and Emily followed them around and watched as they both attempted to beat every high score at the event. As lunchtime approached, they heard a voice shouting out trying to get their attention. It was Leila.

She came over and joined them and Jack introduced her to Emily and Lucy before they all went to eat. He noticed the amused expression on Laura's face while they were eating. She was obviously reading Emily and Leila.

Jack felt a bit uncomfortable with them both being there at the same time, but they seemed to get along well from what he could see. Lucy just sat there smiling – but poker faced. Jack reminded himself Emily still had something to tell him about her and he was sure he knew what it was now.

After lunch, Laura pulled Jack to one side, "You know what's going on there, don't you?"

"I can only imagine," he said laughing.

"I'll tell you later, one thing though. I still can't read Lucy."

This didn't surprise him. He had to admit, she didn't give much away in her facial expression or posture, which for a girl of her age was an achievement.

By the end of the day he'd noticed other things, probably because he was looking for them. Quite certain now, he decided he needed to talk to Emily about it later.

The event finally closed and Laura had collected her prizes for the many high scores she still held. The car's trunk was full of bags on their journey home once again.

Throughout the drive home, Jack kept an eye on Lucy - studying her body language closely. He noticed Lucy and Laura laugh when nothing had been said and wondered if Laura had given it any thought when hearing Lucy's voice, assuming she'd spoken out-loud. Either that or they were both keeping secrets.

Laura caught his eye in the rear-view mirror, shaking her head slightly. He smiled back and blew her a kiss.

No secrets.

Emily looked over at Jack and squeezed his hand. He felt the sadness overcome him again with thoughts of losing her.

Arriving home, Laura went straight next door with Lucy. Finally, Jack and Emily were alone. Seizing the moment, Jack decided to tackle her about Lucy before she had a chance to mess with his head, which wasn't that hard.

"I have a question concerning Lucy," Emily looked at him suspiciously. He wasn't sure quite how to ask, but went for the direct route, "Is Lucy a Telepath?"

Emily smiled, "Why do you ask?"

"Why are you avoiding the question?"

"Got me! Well, yes she is. How did you know?" She said.

"Initially it was Laura who gave me the idea."

Emily looked at him with a puzzled expression, "Why?"

"Why do you think?"

Jack saw the expression on her face change to that of surprise and possibly a little embarrassment. "You mean...?"

"Yes, Laura is a telepath too!"

"I guess we don't have any secrets from either of them," Emily said red faced.

"Tell me about it," Jack opened a bottle of Merlot. "Let's get drunk," he suggested, fetching two glasses.

"Let's," Emily agreed.

The following morning, they both had a sore head, but got no sympathy from either Laura or Lucy, who were in high spirits.

Laura said, "Let's do something crazy."

Lucy was smiling and Jack wondered what they'd been cooking up between them.

"What have you got in mind?" He asked.

"Let's go to Disneyland," they both said together.

Jack said, "Why not," as Emily nodded her approval.

They had after all saved the world, well, England and the Amish. Everything was going to plan, so they deserved it, right?

But things are not always as they seem, as they were completely unaware someone was watching them.

Chapter 50

2253. The Chilean Andres.

In 2011, sixty-six satellite dishes were installed on the largest Plateau in the world, The Liano De Chajnantor Plateau. It is situated on the western fringes of the Chilean Andres, forty kilometres east of San Pedro De Atacama, which is where their base facility was situated.

The Chajnantor observatory is 5080 metres above sea level and the size of at least two football pitches. This is where the scientists and technicians worked. The sole purpose of the operation was to examine data from outer-space and to find other life forms.

Over the years this had been scaled back as there had been no data to suggest there were any other life supporting planets in ours or our neighbouring universe.

By 2253 the observatory was run and operated by a small handful of scientists and technicians. They still lived in the base facilities in San Pedro De Atacama which was 2500 metres below the plateau and some forty kilometres away.

Professor Reggie Shrub, once a leading American scientist who specialised in Electronic Impulse Technology, was now in charge of the observatory. Reggie had worked for NASA 2, until the second space programme had been cancelled. He'd dreamed of finding life on other planets since he was a child and had been on three space missions during his time at NASA.

Now in his later years and semi-retired to the back and beyond, as he viewed it, his dreams were fading away. During his career, he'd consistently claimed he would prove his theories, but time had been running out and the respect he'd once had was lost, like his hopes.

However, there had been a surge of data some two years before which had renewed his hopes temporarily. Reggie had calculated the data was coming from a universe far and away from ours, but he was unable to locate the source.

Whilst the point of origin was impossible to establish, the data suggested a great deal of activity. This activity increased exponentially throughout the year. This was followed by a mass of confusing data, then silence.

Reggie was disappointed and had continued to monitor for similar data patterns. It was July in 2253 and he was due to take his annual sabbatical shortly. His mind was wondering as to where and what he would do when suddenly the data waves started again.

The automatic recording equipment clicked on immediately and his one-hundred-inch monitor filled with data.

Reggie watched for several minutes until the screens went blank once again and the automatic recording equipment clicked off. He remained staring at the screen for some hours waiting for the data stream to return and was about to leave for the base when the screens lit up once again.

The signal was strong, suggesting it was coming from a source closer to Earth. This could have been a neighbouring planet, but it was unlikely. More likely, he figured, they were coming from Earth and bouncing back into space.

Studying the data patterns, Reggie was sure he saw consistencies between these and the signals he'd started to receive two years previously. The difference was signal strength. The new data signals were much clearer, but the pattern was identical.

The data continued to arrive at irregular intervals during July and August and their strength remained consistent.

Reggie ran a comparable data analysis programme; one he had designed himself. Certain the data was identical, he set up the data array examiner. After many tests and calculations, he managed to confirm that the data signals were in fact coming from somewhere on the south-west coast of England.

With renewed excitement, Reggie booted up his super computer and initiated setup protocol connecting him to the now redundant NASA 2 spy-in-the-sky.

Entering the longitude and latitude readings he had, Reggie watched as the live image displayed a small cove by a formation of rocks in an area known as Torr Hills.

He decided this would be a great place to spend his vacation, picking up his phone and calling the airline to book a flight.

At last, Reggie thought. This was it, the moment he'd been waiting for all his life. This was definite proof of a link from Earth to another unknown universe far and beyond.

For the moment, though, Reggie decided to learn some more before sharing his findings and quickly collected all the data and recorded information and headed for the base facilities in San Pedro De Atacama. There, he had stored a range of portable data retrieval devices.

Packing his things, Reggie felt sure this was his ticket out of oblivion.

The Story Continues in...

Chasing Reality
STOFFIA

Turn the page for a sneak preview

Chapter 1
CEP Headquarters, Newtown Village. 2253

Dean Bent was seated at his desk in a back office of the CEP headquarters in Newtown Village. Bent was the new senior officer for the south-west of England and planned to make a name for himself.

Since his arrival two weeks earlier, he'd had his attention drawn to the Regional Government, as there had been reports of some strange goings on of late.

Further investigation led Bent to learn that the local regional government representative was a guy by the name of Scott C. VanDaley. He'd read up about the scandal involving Prescott Nuclear Fusions, where Prescott himself had gone missing without trace and their new Managing Director, Chris King, had allegedly planted his people on the committee VanDaley was chairing concerning the new plant to be built at Thatchers Rock.

It was reported that VanDaley had suspected this and with the help from two unknown accomplices and his daughters, he'd managed to stop the plant from getting approval. Chris King had denied any involvement of course, conveniently blaming his predecessor, Prescott.

They'd searched all the databases for information leading to the identity of the two unknown accomplices, nothing had been found though and the file had been closed.

Bent wanted it open again.

He'd been asking a great many questions about Scott VanDaley and was hearing some disturbing rumours. These involved his daughters, Emily and Lucy, who had both been seen with one of the unidentified accomplices. There had also been reports of a young girl of about nine or ten who'd been seen with them around the village. Emily, the eldest, was also employed by the government, but as what - Bent had no idea as there was no explanation.

He'd asked three of his most trusted colleagues to meet him that morning. A knock at the door indicated they'd arrived.

"Come right in," Bent shouted.

Phil Minder stepped in, followed by Rod Foster and Andy Gardiner. They had all transferred in at the same time as Bent, having worked together as a team for many years. They had a reputation on the force for using any method necessary to get results.

"Take a seat gentlemen," Bent addressed his colleagues. "I hope you've got something for me?"

Rod Foster passed Bent a file, "This is everything I could find in the way of surveillance. We have a clear picture of both of VanDaley's accomplices. We also have pictures of his daughters, Emily and Lucy with one of the accomplices, and a young girl."

"Can we put a name to these other guys?"

"One of them booked into the Tamworth Park Hotel under the name of John Short. You'll see that he's wearing the Government HQ uniform, but facial recognition gives us nothing. The other guy is a mystery, but his first name might be Jack. Again, no facial recognition."

"And the young girl?"

"Nothing!"

"There has to be a record of them somewhere, people don't just appear from nowhere, do they?" Bent said angrily.

Phil Minder shrugged, "All the agencies have been cross referenced."

"Okay, keep digging. Andy, what did you find out about Prescott Nuclear Fusions?"

"Nothing more has been said about the power plant," Andy Gardiner said, "but there is a rumour that the government have found an alternative power source, but no details."

"I would have thought something like that would have been publicised," Bent said. "Try digging around London HQ and see if anyone is talking. What about you Phil, anything useful?"

"I can tell you that the VanDaley's seem to spend a lot of time at Thatchers Rock. I've tried to follow them several times, keeping a distance, but each time they've given me the slip. I think we should put twenty-four-hour surveillance on them and see where that leads us."

"I agree," Bent said. "Get right on it. Keep this between us, I don't want the rest of the force involved, understood?"

They all agreed and stood to leave, "Do whatever it takes gentlemen," Bent said, "I want to know what's going on and why we're being kept in the dark."

Bent sat back down at his desk and looked at the surveillance pictures again. Who were these accomplices and where had they come from?

He was certain now that there was something strange going on. He'd get the answerers somehow, whatever it took.

Chapter 2

2253 - Somewhere on Dartmoor

Just before dawn one Saturday morning in September, 2253, a red and cream coach made its way towards Dartmoor. The coach was packed full of passengers, men, women and children. Everyone was cheerful and happy and laughter filled the coach, not unlike any group of people going on holiday. The coach trundled on down the bumpy road, rocking gently from side to side, which just added to the occasion. The coach driver dipped his headlights as he saw an Army land rover parked beside the road up ahead.

The driver of the land rover climbed out and held up his arm for the coach to come to a halt. Nobody panicked though. In fact, the excitement grew amongst the passengers in anticipation.

Slowing to a halt, the coach driver slid open his window and the soldier briskly walked over, "One hundred yards to the left you'll see another land rover. Turn left into the road immediately before the vehicle and follow the red lights."

Nodding, the coach driver pulled away and turned left as instructed. The red lights were torches being held by Army personnel and at even intervals along the road, pointing the way to their destination.

The occupants of the coach remained cheerful and happy as the coach continued up the bumpy road. After a while the red lights signalled the driver to turn right towards a small floodlit area one twenty metres away.

There were several army vehicles parked side-by-side and Soldiers were lined up either side of the giant marquee, which was large enough for the coach. The driver continued into the marquee without hesitation.

Pulling up at the end of the marquee by a set of large double doors, the driver switched his engine off and opened the coach door. The passengers made their way out and into the marquee, collecting their belongings. The driver closed the coach doors and pulled out of the marquee and back the way he'd come.

A larger set of double doors opened at this point, revealing a much bigger marquee, about the size of half a football pitch. It was very brightly floodlit inside. Both marquees were heavily camouflaged so as not to be seen from overhead by planes or helicopters, although at that time of the morning it was unlikely.

This was a special day, a landmark. The occupants of the coach were about to embark on an amazing journey, one which was going to take them to a brand-new life and a new era.

An Army captain marched up to the passengers, followed by two civilians, Scott VanDaley and his daughter, Emily. As the civil government's representatives, Scott and Emily were there to ensure these very important passengers began their journey safely.

The soldiers began loading boxes and suit cases onto a conveyor belt, which ran from the double doors to the rear of the marquee. Here, they were placed together beside an area cordoned off, which looked much like a flight departure lounge.

This flight was one way though.

The passengers consisted of doctors, scientists, chemists and engineers, along with their partners and siblings. Once they'd made their way to the cordoned off area, snacks and drinks were distributed amongst them.

The larger double doors closed just as another coach pulled into the outer marquee and the process of unloading began again.

Emily said, "I can't believe it's actually happening."

Scott put his arm around his eldest daughter, "It wouldn't be happening at all if it weren't for Jack and Laura."

Emily smiled at the mention of Jack's name and the past few months came flooding back to her. So much had happened in that short time and so much could have been lost forever was it not for Jack and Laura.

"I don't know what we would have done if we'd lost you, Dad," Emily said.

"You stopped Prescott, I'm proud of you for that."

"I wonder what he planned to do with the portal." Emily said, referring to Prescott, the evil power plant owner they'd disposed of when saving Scott. "And what If Jack and Laura hadn't have found me and Lucy?"

Jack and Laura had decided last minute to visit Thatchers Rock. On searching the caves above the cove, they had stumbled upon the secret entrance in the back cavern.

This had led them to the time-portal and an adventure ensued with many twists and turns. Emily and Lucy were rescued safely and events had been changed to stop Scott from being murdered by Prescott.

Together they attempted to save Thatchers Rock from destruction by the new greedy nuclear power plant boss who'd replaced Prescott, Chris King.

A solution to their problems arrived in the form of the Stoffian's, who had originally given the time-portal to Scott's ancestors back in 2003.

Their own planet had an abundance of a power-source they called crystallite. The Stoffian's had agreed to provide England with their crystallite technology in exchange for fifty thousand people to help repopulate Stoffia, after a war which had wiped out ninety per-cent of the population.

This had all led to today, as the coaches continued to arrive throughout the early morning. The frequency of the coaches slowed down until the last one arrived and its passengers disembarked.

It had to be done this way as it was a secret arrangement and they couldn't afford for anyone in the area to grow suspicious. The Army presence would appear to be nothing more than a regular exercise.

Scott and Emily made their way to the departure zone at the rear of the larger marquee. The cordoned off area was big enough for a hundred people.

Soldiers were checking off the last coach load of passengers as they made their way to the departure area and the marquee went silent. There were some concerned faces in anticipation of what was about to happen.

Scott and Emily had no such worries though. There were no beams of light or mysterious sounds and seconds later the last group of a hundred passengers simply disappeared.

They both remained silent until a large video screen behind the cordoned off area lit up and all one hundred passengers were waving, having successfully made their transfer to the waiting Stoffian transporter ships high up above the Earth.

There were ten transporter ships hovering above the Earth that morning, each held a thousand passengers. By the end of the weekend, ten thousand people would have left Earth to start a new life on the planet Stoffia.

Chapter 3

As dawn gave way to light, the army personnel quickly packed up their equipment inside of the giant marquees. They would, however, remain on the moor and carry out regular exercises to conceal the real reason for them being there.

Scott and Emily thanked the Army Captain and left to return home. They were due back that evening to prepare for another evacuation.

Whilst this had been happening, a quite magnificent looking space ship hovered above the transporter ships. The leaders of Stoffia, Stirk and Yamme, stood in their conference room looking out of their large panoramic window at the fleet below. Beside them were two large video screens. One of these displayed the passengers as they arrived on board the transporters and the other, the departure area back on Earth.

Scott and Emily waved as they were about to depart, "The start of a new era," Stirk said waving back, "Let's hope history can be re-written."

"I am certain the future will be good," Yamme replied.

"We will not make the same mistakes," Stirk said.

Yamme nodded, but remained silent. He knew only too well that a repeat of their recent war would most likely destroy the planet. Even with the re-settlement of fifty thousand people, it would still take many years to repair the damage caused by the war and even longer for the population to reach that of before.

While the transfers had been taking place, and not very far away, the first of the crystallite power stations was being prepared. The regenerating crystallite which was being provided for the power-station would be powerful enough to supply the whole of the south-west region. Only four crystallite power-stations were necessary to generate enough energy for the entire country. The crystallite energy would be directed into transfer stations and then into the electricity supply grid. It would be a single source supply. All other energy sources would be made redundant and sealed.

The old nuclear power stations would be taken off line and shut down forever as their product was no longer required. It would take years to clear up the mess made by the hazardous waste, but in the long term, pollution would be cut drastically.

This was the end of an era for Scott and his daughters, Emily and Lucy. They would soon be joining the others, Stoffia bound. Jack and Laura would be coming too, as ordered by Stirk and Yamme. One problem there, Jack and Laura still didn't have that piece of information. Instead they assumed they were saying goodbye to their new friends when the Stoffian's had completed the transfers.

Emily was in good spirits that day though, and more relaxed about the transfers now she'd seen it all go so well. Phase-one would be complete by the end of the following morning.

The first phase of ten thousand skilled people had been selected in secret by the civil government, but the next phases were down to the team. Twenty thousand people had already been located and had agreed to the Stoffian's proposal. These were the Amish people Jack and Laura had encountered when they were trying to find Lucy and Emily.

Had the beaches not been so busy that day back in 2008, Emily wondered if they would ever have found the cave. But they had and she was grateful for that.

"I can't wait to see Jack and Laura, they will be amazed when they see this," Emily held up the video camera she'd used to film the event.

"Not to mention seeing you," Scott said, referring to Jack.

Jack and Emily had fallen in love and Laura and Lucy were like sisters, sharing similar abilities. Together with Scott, they were a family now, but more than that, they were 'team-time,' as Laura had named them.

Emily was blushing at her dad's remark but quickly gained her composure and asked, "When are we going to tell Jack and Laura they have to come to Stoffia with us. I do hate keeping things from them?"

"I know, I understand that, but now is not the time, but soon. Let's see how our meeting goes with Stirk and Yamme tomorrow."

"They won't change their mind, Dad. They were quite adamant that everyone who knew about the portal would have to go to Stoffia."

"Maybe there is a way, give me a little more time please, Emily."

"I don't know how much longer I can keep lying to Jack. Not to mention the fact that Laura is a telepath, it's quite difficult to keep my thoughts away from her."

"I understand, we will resolve this I promise. In the meantime, Lucy can help you," Scott said, referring to her particular skill.

As well as being a telepath, like Laura, Lucy had other abilities she'd not openly shared. Emily and Scott knew of course, but nobody else.

Using her mind control ability, Lucy would be able to block Laura's intrusions into Emily's head temporarily. Whilst Laura would not be immediately aware of this, Lucy didn't like hiding things from her friend in this manner.

Lucy was at home sitting at the Kitchen table when Jack and Laura arrived outside of the kitchen door. She sprung from her chair and opened the door before they had a chance to knock. Laura immediately probed her mind, still getting to grips with her ability, but Lucy easily blocked her intrusions.

She knew Jack and Laura suspected they were still keeping secrets, which they were.

How would they react when they knew the truth?

A note from the Author

Thank you for reading Chasing Reality, POWER SOURCE. I hope you enjoyed the story and will be back to join us in Chasing Reality, STOFFIA. It will be a bumpy ride so you'll have to hang on, but you'll be glad you came.

Look out for more books in this series.

For those of you who prefer there fiction more traditional, how about a crime thriller. 1000 KILOS is a tale of murder, deceit and betrayal in modern day Malta. Would you steel off the Mafia? Yasmin did. Find out what happened.

For more information regarding my books and future projects, please visit my web-site.

Thank you again for joining us. Please leave a review.

Made in the USA
Columbia, SC
02 May 2017